The Future Can't Wait

ANGELENA BODEN

urbanepublications.com

First published in Great Britain in 2017
by Urbane Publications Ltd
Suite 3, Brown Europe House, 33/34 Gleaming Wood Drive,
Chatham, Kent ME5 8RZ
Copyright © Angelena Boden, 2017

A CIP catalogue record for this book is available
from the British Library.

ISBN 978-1-911583-14-1
MOBI 978-1-911583-16-5
EPUB 978-1-911583-15-8

Design and Typeset by Michelle Morgan

Cover by The Invisible Man

Printed and bound by 4edge Limited, UK

urbanepublications.com

In all chaos there is a cosmos,
in all disorder a secret order.
Carl Jung

For mothers and daughters everywhere.

THE FUTURE CAN'T WAIT

CHAPTER 1 ~◯

'*I*'d like to finish on a somewhat controversial note if I may. We've talked about the cognitive development of the brain not being complete until around the age of twenty-five, owing to the continued pruning down of the neurons and their synaptic connections. Not all neuroscientists agree with this I hasten to add.'

Kendra paused briefly and looked around the stuffy conference hall. Some of her audience were not hiding the fact that they were glued to their phones and tablets but most gave the impression they were interested in what she had to say. She felt hot needles stab at her throat as she reached for her pearl necklace.

The glare from her college principal took her mind off the hot flush and with a brief nod to him she pressed the button on her PowerPoint clicker, moving to the final slide on which was written in bold; Terrorism. My Brain Made Me Do It.

'We know the frontal lobes are the last part of the brain to mature in the mid-twenties. It means that young adults are vulnerable and open to suggestion. Think back to when you were that age. I bet you did some outrageous things that make you blush even today. I know I did.'

A giggle fluttered around the room. Kendra caught Sheila's eye as she took a deep breath to slow down her racing pulse. She knew she was taking a big risk with her theory.

'Look at the ages of the recruits to the so-called Islamic State. Most are falling into the age group we've been discussing. This is the age of bad decision making, impulsiveness and sensation seeking. Should we bring neuroscience into the explanation for the atrocities we are seeing on our screens today?'

Maurice, her Head of Department, was making cutting gestures across his throat, his eyes bulging, his veiny cheeks turning to puce.

'So Ladies and Gentleman, I will leave you with that thought. Thank you for your kind attention today. The handouts are available at the back.'

As the applause died down, Kendra Blackmore eased out her memory stick and slipped it in the pocket of her navy silk jacket. She stole a discreet look at her watch. It was the rose gold one her son Adam had bought for her fiftieth birthday.

Maurice scrambled up to her, tugging at his trousers which were belted below his belly. Kendra stepped back quickly away from the staleness of his breath and the overhang of cigarette smoke on his jacket.

'What were you doing?' He pulled out a cigarette from its packet then realising where he was, put it back. 'That wasn't in the plan. We'll be bombarded with complaints.' He ran a palm over the three strands of his comb-over.

A hand touched Kendra's shoulder.

'You were brilliant as always. You should have the seen their faces at the end when you came out with that gem about young terrorists.'

'Thanks, Sheila. Good to have some support,' she said, keeping her gaze fixed on her Head of Department.

'Well, I'm not saying your presentation wasn't outstanding as usual but I do think you should have warned me. This is

Birmingham and you know very well how sensitive things are. All educational establishments are expected to undergo the new training programme over the next few weeks to look out for signs of extremism whatever their nature. That's controversial in itself. If your ideas get out we could have kids saying, "Duh my brain made me do it".'

'You're over-reacting, Maurice,' she replied, fixing her ash-blonde hair back into its clip. 'As usual. I've got to go. I'm not in tomorrow in case you've forgotten.'

'But I think we need a meeting,' he called as her heels clicked down the aisle and out through the doors.

A gathering of Darwin Academy lecturers were hogging the bar as Kendra edged her way towards the exit.

'Drink?' called Sheila who was at the front of the queue.

'I've got to get home. I promised David. Call me later?'

Once she'd made her escape through the back entrance of the International Convention Centre, Kendra turned her flushed face towards the cool breeze and breathed deeply. The pale rays of the late afternoon sun shimmered on the canal, livening up the bright greens and reds of the narrow boats moored in Brindley Place. Kendra thought that if those outsiders, who were quick to condemn Birmingham as a grim city, rife with interracial violence, could bother to check their facts they might choke on their prejudice.

Much to her annoyance, her train back to Sutton Coldfield had been cancelled. The cross-city line being a fifteen-minute service meant that for most people it wasn't such an issue providing they could pack on to the next service. Kendra was thinking about her husband. She knew it was a mistake to give him any indication of times, knowing how he would constantly check the clock and be upset when she was late. She sent him a brief text, not confident that he would hear the house phone from his workshop.

'More train delays,' she called into the empty hallway, as she tugged her arms out of her jacket and kicked off her shoes. She paused to rub her blistered ankle. 'David?'

'Mum, stop shouting will you. I'm trying to study.'

Kendra looked up to see her daughter scowling behind her pink fringe.

'Sorry love. Dinner will be ready in about thirty minutes. Have you seen your Dad?'

'If you mean David then no. He'll be in his shed as usual.'

Frowning, Kendra pushed her aching feet into a pair of blue flats and padded into the spacious white kitchen. David was Rani's stepfather but she'd always called him Dad. She shook her head and turned her attention to what she was going to magic out of some chicken, a marrow and a load of overripe tomatoes. Opening the spice cupboard, she wondered if she could use something other than the mild paprika her husband insisted on.

'Not the curry powder. You know I have an intolerance to spices.'

Kendra jumped, clutching her chest.

'David, don't sneak up like that. We have an agreement, remember?'

A tall, thin man with hair like wire-wool, stood in the frame of the back-door, a circuit board in his hand. His mouth was in its usual downturned position. He fiddled with his glasses. Kendra noticed he'd repaired them again with a blob of glue. Sheila had once said he reminded her of Brains out of Thunderbirds.

'You said you'd make a banana cake tonight.'

'Did I? Ok, I will.' Biting down her annoyance she said, 'What have you been doing all day?'

David's gaze strayed over her shoulder then back to what he had in his hands.

'It would take me too long to explain,' he said in a tone that anyone but Kendra would have heard as patronising.

'I guess you're right. Has Rani been in all day?'

He gave her a blank look and disappeared back into the shed he'd partitioned to form two workshops, each one for a different purpose. He'd made a big fuss about not mixing things up. One was for telescopes and one was for electronics. He'd been talking about building a third but nothing had come of it.

Kendra chopped onions and placed the pieces of chicken, coated in paprika, into the pan. She had no idea what to do with the marrow. Gathering up her daughter's ironed clothes, she shooed away Vesta, their old cat who was trying to climb into the laundry basket, and took the pile upstairs. Sheila's voice stung her ear lobes. 'You're never doing her washing and ironing. She's an adult Kendra.'

'Rani?' She knocked gently on the door as she stared up at a spider dancing along the top of the frame. 'Ariana? I've got your washing here.' Kendra knocked a bit harder then tried the door handle.

'Leave it outside,' her daughter snapped, breaking off from her phone conversation.

'Dinner will be ready soon. I've got some white wine chilling.'

Kendra put her ear to the door which suddenly flew open with such force, it was in danger of being de-hinged.

'I don't want to drink wine. I'm trying to get a first because that's what you expect and you are getting in my way.' A young woman with clear olive skin and a swish of long black hair appeared waving papers in her hand. Her anger bounced around the walls.

'Hey, hey. What's going on? I know you're stressed but I'm doing my best to make things a bit easier for you. There's no need to be so aggressive.'

Rani groaned deeply and tried to slam her door.

'You nearly trapped the cat's tail. Calm down please.'

A squeal reverberated across the landing. Kendra bent down to pick up Vesta, wincing as her claws dug into her arm. 'Come on puss-cat. We know when we're not wanted.'

'And stop trying to force food down me.' Rani hurled the words one after the other down the stairs along with the clean clothes before disappearing back into her room. Kendra hovered on the staircase, stunned by another of her daughter's violent outbursts.

Later that evening, the three of them sat round the dining table in silence. David kept fiddling with a piece of wood and some wires while muttering something about the marrow being an overgrown courgette with no taste. Rani refused to eat the chicken, stabbing her fork into a jacket potato while checking her phone. Only Kendra sipped from her wine glass, guiltily putting it to one side as she caught Rani staring at it and shaking her head. Kendra was about to say that mobiles were not allowed at the table when Rani jumped to her feet, knocking a knife to the floor. David frowned at the noise.

'I've got to take this,' her daughter muttered, scraping her chair back from the table and heading for the stairs, her forefinger tapping on the screen. Kendra let out a puff of air. She'd wanted to share her day with her daughter, hoping they might have a giggle and some girly talk.

She'd given up trying to explain anything to David that was not clear and factual. It left them both frustrated and her upset. She cleared the kitchen whilst waiting for the kettle to boil. Her husband liked his tea five minutes after eating.

Some of her former friends saw him as controlling and advised Kendra not to keep giving into him. She'd given up trying to explain to them that David thought differently from other people and he couldn't help his need for routines. Her social group told her they felt uncomfortable around him but had promised to keep her involved in their various activities. After Kendra had accused them of being unfair and prejudiced she'd heard nothing more from them.

Mashing some overripe bananas into a bowl with honey, she cast her mind back to the time she first met him. A bitter divorce from her Iranian husband in the 1990s had left Kendra traumatised and in debt. She'd been arguing with the mechanic who'd fixed her car for the MOT about the cost when David had walked into the garage, demanded to see the itemised bill, got it reduced by twenty-five percent then offered to take her for coffee in The Bluebell pub next door.

She remembered how awkwardly he'd pulled out the chair for her yet watched her struggle out of her wet coat without offering to help. Although she thought he was odd, as they talked, Kendra warmed to his straight forward approach, focusing on facts not emotions. He seemed solid, reliable and calm. Within six months they'd got married, spent a couple of days walking in West Wales and settled in Kendra's home. It was the first time David had not lived by himself.

'That cake smells cooked,' he said, rubbing his palms in a circular motion. 'Is there any ice-cream left?'

Cutting off the burnt ends of the sponge, she heard the front door closing. Through the window, she saw Rani walking towards the park, head down, pausing to lean on a wall to talk into her phone. She was stabbing the air with a forefinger. For a moment she considered running after her but David calling out to tell her he couldn't find the sugar turned her attention away from her daughter's odd behaviour.

Gathering up the clothes that lay in crumpled heaps on the stairs, she took them back to Rani's room. She paused outside the partially open door feeling like a trespasser. Pushing it open with the tip of her finger she stepped inside and placing the clothes on the bed, she looked around as if expecting a rational explanation to emerge from the chaos.

The curtains had been dragged open across the window in such a way some of the hooks had slid off the track yet the creases in the duvet had been smoothed out and the white pillows arranged neatly on top. An untidy bed was one of her daughter's pet hates. An earless toy monkey, the only thing she had as a reminder of her father, was tucked inside. Kendra picked it up and tugging on its tail, felt her mouth go dry.

Papers and books were strewn across the desk and floor, covered in coloured Post-It notes. On the desk was a leaflet about a rally to be held in Victoria Square.

Kendra's eyes scanned the content. *Bloodiest month in Syrian Conflict. 6,000 dead.* Images of slaughtered children were scattered around together with brochures on how to help the humanitarian effort in the Middle East. Kendra picked up one from Islamic Aid. *Donated £50.00* was scrawled across it in her daughter's handwriting. Kendra was about to leave when her eye caught the edge of another leaflet sticking out from the lid of the laptop. Kendra felt a blast of ice across the back of her neck. *Marriages Arranged.* Rani had scribbled something indecipherable on it and circled the phone number.

She heard David's tuneless whistling coming from the foot of the stairs.

'Kendra, Are you up there?'

'Just a minute,' she called, slipping the papers back in a way she hoped Rani wouldn't suspect anything.

She needed to talk to somebody about what she was feeling but it couldn't be her husband. He didn't understand emotional thinking. As if on cue, the phone rang and Sheila broke into a rant about her younger son Jo.

'That little toe-rag's overstepped the mark this time,' she said close to tears. 'He's not been home for two nights and he's not answering his bloody phone again. I could swing for him sometimes.' Sheila's Brummie accent became more distinct when she was angry. Night became noight. 'He could have been stabbed and thrown in the canal.'

Kendra suppressed a smile.

'He's seventeen, gorgeous looking. He's got girls slobbering at the sight of him. Where do you think he is?'

Sheila blew her nose loudly, prompting Kendra to move her ear from the phone. 'But he always calls me. He knows how I worry. He's got AS levels starting soon. He's going to fail if he doesn't buck his ideas up.'

'Try his friends but you know what will happen. He'll wander in looking for food. Try the Bisto challenge if you want him sniffing his way back.'

'You're no help,' sniffed Sheila. 'This city isn't as safe as it used to be. Muggings, knifings, gang warfare….'

'What? It's Birmingham not Chicago. You're over-thinking it. Remember the lecture I gave. Bad decision making, insensitivity. He's just being a teenager.'

'Hang on a minute. Jo? Is that you Jo? Where the hell have you been?' A crash in the kitchen told Kendra it was time to sign off.

'Stay calm. That's my advice. You're the parent remember.'

So much for the chat. Kendra went in search of her husband. The shed was dusty and had a charred smell about it.

'What are these?' She placed some tiny pieces on her outstretched palm.

'Resistors, these are capacitors, diodes and inductors. Please put them down. I've sorted them all into separate sections.'

'I wish I hadn't asked.' She peered down at them. 'I hope I don't find one of these in the dinner. We'll both end up at the dentist.'

David placed his hands carefully on the bench and breathed out slowly before speaking.

'You will never find these in the dinner. I store them away carefully. You mustn't touch anything in here. I get…. concerned if I can't find what I need.'

Kendra slipped her arms around his neck, feeling him tense up. 'I know you do. I'm sorry. Can I get you anything?'

He slapped his palms together twice and shook his head. 'You go and rest. You've had a long day.'

Kendra raised her left eyebrow. *Was this David showing some empathy?*

CHAPTER 2

The route from Sutton Coldfield, or the Royal Borough as some locals insisted on calling it, to the east side of Birmingham had become so clogged with high-sided lorries that Kendra found it less daunting to take the train to work. That was her excuse. The real reason was that her stomach muscles went into spasm whenever she got behind the wheel of her new car. Sheila had said something about the menopause causing loss of confidence but Kendra had turned her nose up at the suggestion of hormone replacement therapy.

The loudspeaker crackled above her head to announce the delay of the 7.20 due to a signal failure in the Lichfield area. Again. A couple of regular commuters sidled up to her on the platform to say hello and moan about the appalling service. Kendra smiled and flipped open the cover of her Kindle, hungry for the next chapter of The Adolescent Brain Book. By the time the train arrived, the platform was crammed with commuters talking loudly on their phones or taking up too much space on the double seats. Kendra's mood darkened.

As they pulled into the newly redeveloped New Street station, she drained the last of her coffee from her travelling mug, screwed the lid back and waited in the crush for the automatic doors to open. Striding out the short distance to the Victorian Moor Street station from where she took her second train to the Academy, she paused to drop some money into the paper cup of a homeless young girl. It wasn't something she would normally do, believing that food or a hot drink was more useful, but the sight of her torn clothes and bitten down nails made her feel uneasy. She had to shake off the irrational idea that it could have been Ariana sitting on a piece of grubby cardboard, a euro and a button rattling about in a paper cup. *But then her daughter wouldn't just run away. She'd talk things through and they'd sort out the problem together.*

By the time she'd picked her way through the grim estate leading to the college, broken toys littering front gardens, barking dogs and harassed mothers pushing their young children towards the primary school, Kendra felt defeated before she'd set foot in the place.

A passionate believer in the route out of poverty being through education, she'd spent ten years working hard to ensure her students got their ticket out of hell, a version of which greeted her in the form of Year Ten girls screaming fuck off at each other.

'Get to your classrooms, now,' she yelled. 'I'll deal with you later.' She bent down to retrieve the remains of a maths text book and handed it to George Downer. 'One of yours?'

'Little shits,' he grumbled, as Tanesha Norris knocked his elbow, sending the book spinning back to the floor.

'Sorry sir.'

Sheila was in the staffroom, making ouching noises as she plucked a tea bag out of her mug. 'This is the bit of teacher training I must have missed. How to retrieve a tea bag from boiling water without a spoon.'

'Use the end of a pen,' Kendra said, hanging up her coat. 'I got a distinction for that bit of initiative.'

'Time for a chat?'

Kendra pointed to the clock and shook her head. She had three classes to teach and a growing mound of paperwork to get through. The Darwin Academy was proud of its excellent record in the Social Sciences and Humanities which put Kendra under pressure. Her new role as Curriculum Manager for psychology had grown exponentially but the staffing levels had not.

Maurice mumbled on about budgets and resource management whenever she tried to raise the issue of recruiting a part time teacher for the GSCE classes. Kendra felt her neck muscles gradually unknot themselves as her group waited patiently while she assembled her papers.

'What are we doing today Mrs. Blackmore?'

'Finishing the module on "Understanding People" by looking at the role of non-verbal communication,' she replied, scrolling through her iPad to find the slide presentation. Turning back to the twelve students who were ready to tap out notes on their tablets, she posed the question, 'So, what do we mean by Body Language? And let's be mature about it as I know you can be.'

'Signs and signals we give out.'

'Ok. Janine, can you give me an example?'

'Err... smiling?'

'Excellent. A smile is the best thing we can offer someone if we want to send out a positive signal. It shows we're friendly, open, and approachable. Many businesses train their staff in how to smile at customers.'

'That's stupid,' grunted Jaz, a deep furrow settling between her over-plucked eyebrows.

'I'd like you to draw up two columns. Positive and negative and think of examples of gestures and facial expressions for each category. Smile goes in the positive and frown goes in the negative.'

Kendra drew the chart on the whiteboard.

The session passed quickly and peacefully. Kendra knew she was lucky to have students who were fascinated by psychology even if they harboured a hidden agenda of *"How to Impress a Boyfriend"*, or *"How to Lie to Parents and Get Away With It"*.

As she watched them complete the assessment sheets, her thoughts drifted back to Rani and the pressure she must be feeling to get a first. Adam had scooped every exam jackpot since GCSE and David had a starred first from Oxford as well as a PhD and a string of fellowships.

Her students' intense discussions lifted her mood. When she was teaching, she felt the girls were part of her family. She idly wondered where they would be in a few years' time. Before the school got Academy status, too many of them ended up either on the long term unemployment register or as teenage mothers on benefits. Now it was all about exams and grades and never mind the stress levels. The Principal was ex-military and unyielding discipline was the backbone of his management style. Some said he was still having treatment for post-traumatic stress since his final tour of Iraq.

'Leave your sheets on my desk please and go quietly to your next lesson.' Kendra waited till they'd gone before texting her daughter to suggest a shopping trip and maybe somewhere in the fancy new Grand Central for dinner. She felt an urge to give Rani a big hug and reassure her that everything would work out fine. They'd both been snappy and it was time to put things right.

'Why is it that kids never answer their phones these days?' Kendra grumbled to a half-empty staff room.

'They're all the same. When they're not texting or Facebooking they get withdrawal symptoms. The art of communication is in serious decline. Look at the grammar in this essay. Could *of*. I ask you. And they want to be running the country. I wouldn't let them run a bath.'

The handful of staff taking their break exchanged glances. The Head of Communications was off on his daily rant. Kendra half nodded in agreement as she marked some papers. It was an issue her A level group had been working on. *The impact of modern technology on the developing brain.*

'Give it a rest Geoff,' said Sheila, rolling her eyes. 'I'll be in the Art room if anyone needs me.' With a fresh squirt of perfume on her wrists, she vanished into the maze of bottle-green corridors.

Despite sending a second message to her daughter, Kendra got no reply. *OK missy. Your loss.* She drummed her nails on her desk and stared glassily at some papers she needed to take home. In her hurry to get into town, she ran for the train, turning her ankle as she squeezed through the closing doors. As she filled her basket in Anil's mini market, Rani's distinctive ringtone filled her pocket. Kendra leapt on it like a woman dying of thirst.

'What do you mean you're not coming home tonight? Where are you staying?'

'Does it matter? I'm an adult Mum. I don't have to tell you anything.'

'Legally no. You're right. But you live with us so, out of courtesy…'

'It's my business.'

'This means you've got a boyfriend doesn't it? I'm not a fool Ariana. We agreed not until finals are over.'

'We agreed nothing and stuff finals. Don't tell me how to run my life. I don't want to do astro bloody physics anymore so I don't care what degree I get. Back off Mum.' Rani's voice grew more forceful. 'You got pregnant with Adam in your last year so you can't talk.'

Kendra felt she'd been stung by a vengeful wasp. It took a few seconds to recover. Lowering her voice she said, 'Let's not argue. Come home later. In a taxi if you like. Just get this next month... over.' Kendra found herself talking to a dead line. She called back but was greeted with a voicemail message. Customers were pretending not to listen. A young assistant was unpacking potatoes. Shaken, Kendra put down her basket and left the shop. When she arrived home, David was holding the empty milk carton in his hand and looking at her with a raised eyebrow.

'I'm sorry. I forgot. Can you pop down to the garage and I'll get the dinner. I'm shattered.'

'Me? Ok.'

Kendra stabbed two potatoes with a fork and tossed them into the microwave. She checked the tins of tuna for what David called brain destroying additives and made sure the poor fish had been humanely killed. His insistence on checking labels drove her to distraction sometimes. *Why couldn't he prepare dinner sometimes? Even sausages on sticks would do.*

She chopped tomatoes, shredded lettuce and sipped from a small glass of white wine. While she waited for David to return, she went out into the garden where the bold, blue delphiniums stood proud amongst multi-coloured gladioli. Thick clumps of African marigolds bordered the figure of eight lawn mingling with patches of wilting English bluebells. David regularly pulled up the Spanish ones saying they didn't belong in an English garden. The old push-mower was lying on its side minus the cutting blades. No matter how many times she argued for an electric one, David set his mouth, refusing to make eye contact with her. He could be so stubborn.

With both hands, Kendra pushed back her hair from her face and scrunched it into a band. She closed her eyes and sighed deeply and wished it was bedtime.

In the early hours of the morning, after a fitful sleep, she went downstairs to get a glass of water. A light snaked underneath the door of Rani's room. Kendra gently pushed open the door to find the bed untouched. The light from the laptop caught her attention. A number of Skype messages were waiting to be read. Kendra felt a gritty dryness in her mouth. The temptation to read them was too great even though she knew her daughter would explode if she found out. She clicked on the blue icon.

The first message was written in Arabic script. Kendra frowned. Looking more closely she recognised a couple of words. It was Farsi. A completely different language to Arabic with fewer markings over the letters. She copied and pasted them into a translator. *Are you on for tonight?*

Rani didn't speak Farsi anymore. She'd switched off that part of her brain when she was five years old. Hassan had walked out on them without a word and returned to his family in Shiraz. He'd been an engineering student in Leeds and they'd met in a night club just after the Iranian Revolution. He was so drunk she'd had to bully him into not getting into his car to drive her home. Forced to stay in England or risk persecution in Iran as a non-Muslim, he'd persuaded Kendra to marry him after only a few months. It was years later when she realised it was for a permanent residence and home student fees.

Kendra tugged at her lower lip and looked at the translated words again. *Did that mean last night or tonight? On for what?* She was positioning the cursor to open the second message when David appeared in full yawn.

'What are you doing? Where's Ariana?'

'Stopping with a friend. I saw the computer on. It's wasting electricity.'

'Hmm. Yes.' He scratched his chest. 'I'm going into the workshop.

I've got an idea I want to work on.'

He turned to go, yelping as he stubbed his toe on something sticking out from under the bed. Bending down, he pulled out an old CD box set. 'Farsi for Foreigners.' It was stamped, University of Birmingham library and well overdue. Kendra couldn't dispel the feeling of alarm as she pushed it back into place.

Unable to go back to sleep, she sat in the living room and turned on the TV. More ISIS crisis, more economic misery, more Katie Hopkins controversy. Kendra stared dully at the screen as the headlines flashed up on repeat and thought about the generational crisis David Cameron was talking about. The entitled, tech-savvy Millennials.

She'd not seen much evidence of it in her classes, although other teachers despaired about vacuous minds and an outrageous focus on self-interest. *Didn't all generations come in for their unique criticisms?* Sipping her tea, she remembered her father's fury whenever Mick Jagger and Elvis strutted their stuff on a Friday night. "Disgusting", he would say, switching it off and ushering her out to "do something useful".

Light poured into the living room, promising a warm day. A whole weekend stretched before her with nothing much to do. Resentful of the time David spent engrossed in his own world, Kendra wished she had the nerve to pack a bag and go off for the weekend for a bit of "me-time". But where? She had no family to visit anymore. Adam was in Boston. The thought of going alone filled her with dismay. Sheila would tell her to book a city break, eat delicious food and flirt shamelessly. She was deep into her lesson planning when Rani appeared in the dining room.

'Hi,' she said, staring at a point on the wall above her mother's head. 'Can we go shopping like you said?'

'Mm. Why not? There's an exhibition at the Ikon gallery I'd quite like to see it if you've got time. It's an Italian thing. Contemporary.'

'You don't have to sell it to me Mum. I'll come with you. I need some black trousers and loose tunics. Can we go over to Ladypool Road to get them? I'll drive if you don't want to.'

'Why over there? Don't you want something more …western looking?'

Rani folded her arms, the corner of her eyes narrowing.

'What's that supposed to mean? Frumpy department store stuff so I look middle-class and respectable? Forget it. I can buy online from Dubai.'

'I didn't mean anything by it. Let's see what there is in town first. The car's in for a service so we'll have to go by train.'

Kendra felt the crunching of the eggshells with every word she uttered. The bang of the bathroom door told her that all efforts to broker peace had come to nothing. Rani was showing all signs of stress but that wasn't like her. She was very much like David, calm, unruffled, logical. Towel drying her hair, Rani stood at the top of the landing and glared down the stairs. 'Have you been in my room?'

Kendra breathed slowly in through her nose and slowly out. If her daughter was looking for a fight, she'd be disappointed.

'Only to turn off the lights and close the window. You know what Vesta's like.'

'Some of my stuff has been moved.'

'Kendra?' David was holding a hammer in his hand and the cordless phone in the other. 'For you.'

'Tell them I'm out,' she hissed, waving him away.

'But you're here.'

Kendra glared at him and shook her head. She grabbed the phone from him and disconnected the call. 'Rani. Don't shout at me like that.'

'It's you doing the shouting, mother.'

Shopping trips with her daughter had always been full of gossip and warmth. In Rani she saw something of her father from the early days. He was relaxed and fun until he became fixated on the number of his fellow Iranians being slaughtered in the Iran-Iraq war. He'd became moody and difficult, spending more time on protests in London than focusing on his work.

Hassan had ranted for hours about how being a pretend Muslim was a denial of his Persian heritage and that too many people were ignorant of their oldest religion. He was angry with the Ayatollahs for calling Zoroastrians sinful animals and had raged at the burning down of their fire temples in systematic persecution. His own confusion and identity crisis had led to their children not being brought up in any faith. Rani was adamant that science was the only truth.

'This shop will do.' Rani pointed to a place down an alleyway by the old C&A department store. She pushed open the door, its black paint flaking from neglect, and began checking the racks. With an armful of shapeless tops in browns and greys, some loose unflattering trousers, she slipped behind a curtain to try them on. Kendra looked around, bemused by the different styles of Islamic coats, scarves and coverings on display.

'I don't understand,' she said to Rani as they made their way to a coffee shop by the canal. 'Why are you buying this stuff?'

'It's comfortable to wear. Don't make any assumptions. I've put weight on round the middle and it looks terrible. I'll go on a diet after exams,' she added, biting into an almond croissant. 'Stress eating.' She chewed on a mouthful, dusting the crumbs from her front. 'Let's go. I've got more revision to do on dark matter.'

CHAPTER 3

The jangling of the front door bell made Kendra jump. A teaspoon fell from her hand and clattered on the wooden flooring. Glancing in the hall mirror, she pushed her hair behind her ears before opening the door.

'If it's lunch you're looking for you're out of luck. I can probably find a crust or two.'

'Well that's a fine welcome I must say,' said Sheila, putting down her capacious handbag and following Kendra into the kitchen. 'I've cut out all wheat and gluten to see if I can lose some weight. Look at this.' She patted her midriff, screwing her face up in disgust. 'I'll be wearing caftans next.'

'Not you as well. Rani's complaining about her weight.'

Sheila settled herself on a stool at the breakfast bar and rested her elbows on the grey speckled granite. She looked around and sighed.

'I do love this place. If Tony hadn't invested in that damn computer company we'd have held onto Virginia House.'

'That huge pile in Four Oaks with room for a swimming pool?' Kendra set down two mugs of coffee. 'Too much cleaning. Who wants six bedrooms these days?'

'We were nearly bankrupt you know. Tony was so stubborn.

He wouldn't see the writing on the wall. I don't know how our marriage survived.'

'It did and that's all that matters. The past can be dangerous territory.' Kendra reached into the fridge for more milk.

'Do you ever hear from your ex? You don't talk about him.'

Kendra shook her head.

'Not much to say. His family called him home after his father died and I suppose he shut us out of his mind. We don't exist.'

'Can people do that?'

She nodded. 'If something is too painful to deal with we can block it off. Repressed memories are usually the result of trauma. It's called disassociation. Splitting off one part of your inner life from the others. Post-traumatic stress is an example of it. Most people think it's only war vets that suffer from it but anyone can. Memories that have been repressed come flooding back when the defences are down. Sorry. You didn't ask for a lecture.'

'It's interesting stuff. I think Tony went out to the States to work so he could block it all out. Men and their pride. I know he feels guilty about what happened.'

'Mm.' Kendra was hunting through the pantry for the gluten free biscuits she'd bought for Rani who'd refused with the curl of a lip on account of them being made with pig fat.

'Anyway, the reason I've come round is to tell you I'm giving in my notice.' Kendra opened her mouth then quickly shut it.

'The kids, sorry, students, are really getting me down and Jo's behaviour isn't helping. I feel frazzled all the time and it's upsetting my stomach and my sleep. The bureaucracy at Darwin is getting ridiculous and now we have to check on who might be at risk of online radicalisation. The world has gone mad. Only a few girls wear the hijab and they're too innocent to get mixed up in some terrorist group.'

David appeared in the kitchen and began whistling between his teeth when he saw Sheila.

'Extremism includes far right tendencies as well. The counter balance. It's not all about religion.' Kendra reminded her as she poured them some more coffee. 'And anything else considered off the spectrum.'

'I don't understand what's driving all this. We've always lived in reasonable harmony here in Brum. Ok, so we've have a few riots before but nothing like this. I'm scared to open my mouth these days and have you heard that Jade Smithies? Saying we should bring back fascism as if it's a fashion item like hot pants. She can't even spell the bloody word. That's her dad pumping her with all this garbage.'

'We have to go shopping,' David said, pointedly looking at his watch then at Sheila.

'It's ok. I'll go as soon as I've finished this.'

They both watched him retreat back to his workshop.

'Sorry about that. You know he how is with his routines. Carry on.'

'I'm going to set up a sewing school from home. There's that big room at the back that never gets used. So many people have no clue about how to sew on a button or fix a hem. Basic common sense stuff our grannies taught us.'

'It's a great idea. You can have a monthly membership or something. I would join. The amount of money I waste replacing stuff when I could repair it at a fraction of the cost. In fact, Rani needs a couple of zips replacing and I've got no idea how to do them.'

'Pass them over in return for a testimonial.'

'Are you talking about me?'

Both women turned to look at the scowling young woman with

spots of crimson burning her cheeks. A nerve twitched below her eye. Kendra noticed she'd lost the pink streaks in her hair. She relayed their conversation to her daughter.

'She's saying I'm fat.' Rani's eyes sparked as she chomped angrily on her gum. She turns to fix them on Kendra.

'Not at all. You're gorgeous,' Sheila jumped in quickly. 'How is it all going?'

Rani ignored her.

'Mum. I don't want you in my room for the next few weeks. Ok? OK? I've got all my notes exactly where I need them. Just put clean bedding and clothes outside my door. You said you wanted to help. This is how you do it. Get it?'

The two women exchanged glances. A dark flush rose from Kendra's throat. With great effort she said, 'Yes. Of course.'

Sheila fiddled with her mug, turning it round on its coaster.

'Woah. That's harsh. Jo's acting out as well if it's any consolation. He doesn't want to study. He keeps threatening to drop out and join his dad in Florida. Even Rich has stopped talking to him because of his attitude and vile language. Every other word seems to begin with f...'

Kendra turned her face away to look out of the window, afraid that Sheila would pick up on her growing concern. The Japanese cherry tree had lost most of its pinky-white blossom. It was Adam's favourite tree. She missed him.

'Rani's attitude has changed. The stress is getting to her but exams will soon be over.'

They chatted for a while longer until they were interrupted by David making a show of putting on his jacket.

'I'm off to my hair appointment. Time to chop this off and become a silver foxette,' she said running her hand through long chestnut waves. 'I can't keep up with the roots.'

'I think you mean vixen,' they giggled in unison as Kendra followed her into the hall to whisper something in her ear.

'Kendra Blackmore, really!'

By the time they returned from the supermarket, David was cracking his knuckles, one after the other and doing a funny blowing thing as if he was struggling to expel air from his lungs.

'Go back to your work and I will bring you some lunch,' she told him, patting his arm. 'Try and relax. I've got some work to do.'

She threw herself onto the sofa to read a recent article on drug addiction and young people. She toyed with the idea that her daughter might be taking some stimulants to help stay awake. Her pupils were enlarged at times and she'd noticed the jerking of her hands.

David was still unsettled when she called in him for lunch. She sat next to him on the garden bench. 'What's wrong? Has something happened?'

He didn't reply but continued to slap his thighs. 'Maybe you should have a lie down for a bit. Give your brain a rest.' She gave him the option to join her for a walk around Sutton Park but he wasn't interested.

Slipping into her walking shoes, she made her way towards the Town Gate entrance, mulling over what might be troubling her husband. He found it difficult to articulate feelings but somatised them into some vague physical discomfort. Hungry, she called in at Jim's Plaice for a small tray of chips. It felt like an act of defiance.

Kendra sat by the lake and peeled open the white paper, seeping with vinegar. Scooping up a chip with a wooden fork, she thought about her daughter. Maybe it was her behaviour that was upsetting David. Changes in routine upset his system and whatever was bothering Rani was not solely due to astrophysics.

Kendra was aware that she was overprotective but it was difficult to ignore the sudden flashes of temper and acting out. Mothers being friends with their daughters was something she advised against but Rani was fun and adventurous, always encouraging Kendra to try new things. Together they'd braved a hot air balloon ride, Kendra screaming as the basket swung from side to side, gone pot-holing in the Brecon Beacons and even tried out a new club on the Hagley Road. She hadn't actively encouraged Rani to study locally but she'd not argued against it even though Adam had expressed strong views against it.

'You've got to let her go to live her own life,' he told her. 'She'll resent you otherwise and maybe rebel against these restrictions you put on her. You don't want to lose her altogether do you?'

Her mind was free-wheeling as she stuffed the remains of her dinner into the overflowing bin, tutting at the discarded paper cups and plastic bottles on the floor. She shivered but ignoring the drizzle, strode out to spot some of the wild Exmoor ponies that roamed Sutton Park. Joggers breezed alongside her, armed with monitoring gadgets and disk sized headphones. A cyclist swerved, turning his head to shoot out a string of expletives.

By the time she got home, David was asleep in the chair and Rani was on her way out, wearing the new shapeless clothes and a black scarf hanging loosely around her neck.

'Have you eaten something?'

'I'm going to Maryam's for Fesenjan.'

'But you don't like Persian food! You said you hated pomegranate sauce. Who's Maryam?'

'Yeah, well people change. Back late or I might stop over.'

'Rani, come back a minute. We need to talk.'

'No we don't,' her daughter shouted from the bottom of the drive. 'I'm moving out soon so you'd better get used to it.'

With trembling hands, Kendra grabbed the phone and dialled her son's number in Boston. *Dr. Adam Najafi is not available. Please leave a message.* 'Adam, please Skype me tomorrow. It's important.'

After another disturbed night, during which she'd dropped in and out of sleep listening out for Rani's key in the door, her neck and shoulders ached. Yawning loudly, she rescued two slices of burning toast as the phone rang.

'Ma? You're not answering Skype.'

'I didn't hear it ring. Thanks for calling me.'

'What's up?'

Kendra walked into the garden and sat on the low wall by the pond. The sunlight shimmered on David's goldfish.

'I don't know exactly. Rani's acting strangely. She's become aggressive which isn't like her. I can't say anything without her picking a fight.'

'Finals, Ma.'

'Yes I know that. There's something else. She's become very secretive and acting out of character.' Kendra told him about the shopping trip.

'It means nothing on its own. What are you thinking? That she's preparing to go off to fight with the Peshmerga or get married and disappear to Iran? I don't think so.'

A laugh grumbled in his belly.

'Adam. We did a course on spotting signs in young people getting caught up in fanatical movements. It's a huge issue here at the moment. A girl did go missing and they found her in Turkey. She'd been radicalised on line. I think…'

'Whoa. Stop there. Rani's not religious or into politics, so that does not apply to her. If she said she wanted looser clothes for comfort, then accept that. You're sounding paranoid.'

'I found a load of stuff in her room about Syria. Some horrible pictures of beheadings. She's been donating to Islamic Aid.'

'So what? I've sent money for medicines. Ma. Calm down. When the pressure's off, she will return to her old self. The only cause Rani would support is Save the Teddies.'

'Adam!'

'You've spoiled her, letting her live at home. I did say it was a bad idea. She needs to grow up. That's all that's wrong with her. Let her loose.'

Kendra heard her son clear his throat. It's what he did when he was lost for something to say.

'Promise me Ma that you'll push all these crazy ideas out of your head. I agree there seems to be something going on in the minds of this generation. Entitlement. Attachment. Selfishness. You don't need the lecture but we've got to be careful we don't lump them all together or make it sound that they are all mad. Think back to your late teens and twenties. Rock and Roll. Flowers in your hair. LSD. Every generation has its own quirks. It's called finding your identity.'

'I suppose so.'

Kendra ripped off the nail of her little finger. She winced.

'I've got to go. Alison wants to go up to New Hampshire to see her friend who's had a baby. Talk next week. Love you Ma.'

Adam tugged on his attempt at growing a beard as he looked over Harvard Square. His sister hadn't been very friendly towards him of late and he'd been disturbed by her diatribes against the Syrian government. World tensions were rising. Subtle racist comments had been fired at him from a couple of his fellow American doctors but Adam had made himself Teflon coated over the years. His only concern was treating the mentally unwell.

David was tipping the toaster upside down to release the bits of trapped bread. A spray of crumbs hit the floor. Kendra reached for the broom.

'I'll clear it up,' he said with a hint of a smile. She was relieved he was back to his old self.

'Do you want to go for a drive somewhere?' He'd spread out a map showing some of the attractions in the area. 'What about Aston Hall? It's practically on our doorstep but we've never been. Grade 1 listed Jacobean mansion house with magnificent gardens,' he read out.

'Good idea. I'll pack a flask and there's some cold chicken and salad we can take. Saves wasting money in a café.' She knew the irony was lost on him but she couldn't help herself. 'But we can afford an ice-cream,' she added, kissing her finger and pressing it to his lips.

He beamed. 'Goodo.'

CHAPTER 4

When Kendra got home from work, she was relieved to release the dull weight of her bag, the strap of which had left a deep red welt on her shoulder. The thought of having to mark so many assessments that night made her head spin. The end of term couldn't come soon enough.

Rani was seated at the dining table, poring over a complexity of equations as she wound and rewound bits of her straggly fringe around her forefinger. Piles of papers and books were stacked around her leaving little room for Kendra to put her glass.

'Tamina's coming for dinner so I need to get some chicken,' she said without looking up.

'There's plenty in the freezer.' Kendra went to rifle through the stuffed drawers, making a mental note to do a sort out.

'Here, lots of it.'

'It's not halal. I need to buy halal,' she repeated.

Kendra eased herself off her knees, muttering under her breath as the joints creaked.

'I don't know where to get it from in Sutton. Couldn't we do something vegetarian? There's some tofu left.'

'We'll have to go over to Sparkhill or Handsworth.' Rani carried on filling a page with what looked like squiggles, unaware of the look of disbelief on her mother's face.

'I'm sorry Rani but I'm not going anywhere tonight. I've got a load of marking to do and I've no idea how to get to either of those places. You'll have to put her off or order in a pizza.'

'She doesn't eat pizza. I promised I'd cook chicken with apricots. It's her favourite.'

'We don't have any apricots either. Sorry Rani but I'm not going out.'

'Fine. Just fine.' Rani pushed back her chair as blood rushed to her cheeks. She was breathing heavily as she pushed her face into Kendra's. 'Tam's mother would do anything for her. She wouldn't spout pathetic excuses about marking stupid papers. You're not a proper mother,' she snarled, elbowing Kendra out of the way. Angry footsteps banged up then down the stairs. 'Forget it, I'll go to hers.'

'What's going on?' David stood in the kitchen looking perplexed. He scratched his cheek with the end of a screwdriver.

'Nothing. What do you want for dinner?' Kendra plunged her hands in to the washing-up bowl to stop them trembling. Her life seemed to revolve around food, moods and badly written test papers.

David was rubbing the corner of his eye with a dirty index finger. She was about to remind him about the germs but something in his manner told her to keep quiet. His face was unusually pale and he seemed tired.

'Not very hungry. A can of Big Soup. The first one on the shelf. They're all in date order. I'll scrub this paint off my hands first. Maybe have a shower.' His voice trailed away.

'Bring those dirty clothes down with you. I can't imagine what you've been up to all day.' She pressed her teeth down on her lip to bite down another sarcastic comment. David took everything so literally.

Kendra punched out a text to Rani saying she was sorry but stopped herself. *I'm not taking responsibility for her behaviour.* She felt she had nothing to apologise for.

Fearing she might be right about drug abuse, she was determined to make Rani tell her the truth. Adam suggested she might be a bit depressed and anxious and advised his mother to tread carefully.

'What's all this mess? Where do we eat?' David pointed to the table, impatience etched around his mouth.

'Go in the garden. I'll bring you a beer.'

'It's chilly.'

'Well… wear a jumper.'

By the time Kendra carried a tray out to the gazebo, her favourite part of the garden, David had nodded off, a pair of secateurs in his hand. As she eased them out of his hand, he woke up with a start.

'I hope that syringa vulgaris is going to bloom better this year than last. I think I over-pruned it.'

Kendra bit into some crusty bread, wincing as something sharp caught on a back tooth. She arched an eyebrow in question.

'Lilac.' David waved his spoon in the direction of the bush. 'We've been cultivating them in this country since the sixteenth century.' He went on to explain its history. ' I'm thinking of getting a white one if I can find one at a good price.'

'Well you seem a bit brighter. You spend far too much time in those sheds.'

'Any ice-cream?'

'Mint or pistachio?'

David dabbed at his mouth with his cotton handkerchief while he thought about it.

'Mint. It's a mint day.'

Kendra was scooping some into a dish when she heard her

phone ping. It was Sheila. 'Jo's refusing to go back to school. Can you talk to him?'

Kendra sighed. She was tired of fledgling adults flexing their muscles. David peered into his bowl, a look of ecstasy in his eyes. He dipped the tip of his spoon into the melting ice and rested it on his tongue. As he closed his eyes and groaned, Kendra imagined that it was David's replacement for the intimacy they'd lost.

'OK. I'll come round.' Kendra felt like a piece of elastic that was about to snap. By the time she'd walked the mile to Sheila's mock Tudor house, she'd got rid of the headache brought on from wading through some of the poorest essays she'd ever marked. Geoff was right. Standards of grammar and punctuation were poor, with some students committing the ultimate sin of slipping into text speak. Teachers did their best but they fought a daily battle against the negative side of technology.

No sooner had she pressed the bell when Sheila flung open the door and pulled her inside. Kendra noticed her reddened eyes.

'He's locked himself in his room. I've tried to get hold of his dad but as usual he's not answering and Rich was just… well rude when I called him. I'm at my wit's end. He says I can't make him do his AS levels but if he quits now what's going to become of him?' Sheila voice was spiralling into a wail. 'I don't know what I can do. He won't listen to me. But you know about these frontal lobe thingies. Can't you … I don't know… psychologically manipulate them.'

Kendra grinned.

'It doesn't work like that. If it did, I would have sorted out Rani's mood swings.'

Sheila grabbed her hand.

'Please try.'

'Coffee first or even a brandy. Let's see if he emerges first.'

They took their drinks into the conservatory crowded with plants and orange trees which released a pleasant tangy scent. Kendra slipped out of her fleece and leaned back into the squashy cushions.

'Has something upset Jo?' she asked, reflecting on her daughter's recent bursts of unprovoked anger.

'He's pretty laid back as a rule.'

'Girlfriend?'

'Nobody special. I don't think it's that. He seems unable to cope with the workload. I know he's very confused about his future and university. His brother sailed through and knew from a very early age that he wanted to do law. I wonder if we push our kids too hard these days partly out of fear for them and embarrassment for ourselves.'

'It's a middle class disease. Then we wonder why they have a career crisis at thirty, but then we are changing and evolving all the time. Even if Jo does take time out it doesn't mean he's doomed for ever. We grow at different rates and in our own unique way. If he thinks you are anxious for him, he will soak that up and become anxious himself. Support him but let him be captain of his own ship.'

Sheila pulled open a drawer to retrieve a packet of cigarettes.

'I thought you'd given up?'

'I have,' she said, stuffing it back. 'He's driving me to it.'

Kendra held back from reminding Sheila that she couldn't blame her son for her choices.

'I know how you feel.'

Sheila traced a pattern on the table with her finger.

'How's Rani getting on with her finals? I saw her the other day with some girls wearing the hijab. She was wearing a scarf thing on her head. She caught my eye then looked away.'

'Was she? Kendra tried to sound unperturbed. On its own,

covering her hair amounted to nothing. In her mother's day, it was de rigeur to wear a flowery triangle on her head to go shopping or after a shampoo and set at the hairdressers.

'Don't you worry about what she might be getting into? Birmingham's become a bit of a breeding ground for fanatics. You don't know who's setting foot on university campuses these days.'

'Don't broadcast those views to the outside world. Things are sensitive enough as it is. I don't think Birmingham is any different from other multicultural cities and besides, the religious leaders are working hard to educate their communities. It's this sort of melodrama that's fuelling the paranoia.'

'What I meant was...'

Kendra folded her arms and gave Sheila a long hard look.

'Rani's not interested in religion. She's a scientist. She's got an enquiring mind and tries to understand things from the inside. I'm not concerned at all.' After the briefest of pauses she added, 'I trust her.'

The door opened and a young man with messy brown hair and fidgety hands stood in the frame.

'Hi Jo. How's it going?'

He tugged at the raffia of the chair until Sheila had to tell him to stop.

'I've told Mum. I'm quitting. Pink Banana are recruiting. I've just submitted an application.' He scowled at his mother.

Sheila looked as if she was about swoon.

'Ok. What do you think that will give you?'

'Money. Freedom. Sleep.'

Kendra tossed out a few casual questions and waited to see what he decided to pick up.

'It's not so much the money,' he conceded, tugging at the leaves of a lemon tree.

'Jo, will you stop doing that. Mrs. Blackmore's talking to you.'
Kendra shot her a warning look.

'So you've got four weeks before exams start. I doubt any Banana will take you on before that.' Jo grinned.

'They'll want to see if there are other candidates with AS or even A levels. Quite a few degree holders are applying for these jobs while they decide on their next course of action.'

Jo looked up, his eyes wide with shock.

'But it's a crap job. I mean for qualified people.'

'Lots of competition for basic jobs. What you could do of course, is just have a go at the exams and see what happens. No pressure.'

Kendra could tell Sheila was holding her breath.

'Suppose,' he said.

'Don't bother revising. Read through your notes, go out with your mates and just have a go. Nothing to lose.'

Kendra was on her feet.

'OK. Thanks Mrs. Blackmore. Just tell Mum to get off my back. She's the real problem.'

Sheila was about to protest when Kendra led her to the door. She put her finger against her friend's lips. 'Reverse psychology. They always do the opposite of what you want them to do.'

THE FUTURE CAN'T WAIT

CHAPTER 5

*D*avid, can we talk? It's important.'

Her husband carefully laid down his telescope on the paint spattered work bench and jiggled his fingers in a way which made the knuckle joints crack. Kendra pulled a face.

'Please don't do that. You know it sets my teeth on edge.'

He stopped, then began whistling, *Home, Home on the Range.*

'David!'

Kendra could feel the tension in her jaw as she gritted her teeth. She perched on the edge of a stool and waited for him to look up.

'Could we have some tea first?' he asked. 'And some of those biscuits with the pink icing?'

'Afterwards. Please listen and keep still.' She gently rested her hands on his drumming fingers.

'Rani's going to take up a three month internship in London for the summer. It's a research project of some sort. She's not very forthcoming at the moment but I'm sure she'll tell me more in her own time. The thing is, it's unpaid like most of them are these days so I'm giving her some of the money from my Dad's estate.'

'How much?'

'About five thousand. She's got a friend in Tooting she can stay with for a small rent. It's what she wants to do.'

David carried on soldering.

'Then what? She has to get a job doesn't she? We can't support her forever.'

Kendra pressed her lips together.

'She knows that. Give her some breathing space. She's confused about what she wants to do. I don't know what the career path of an astro-physicist entails but I'm sure she'll sort it out.'

'Teach or join a space programme.'

'Right. I can see you're not going to be supportive.' She turned to go back into the house then paused. 'By the way, I'm going out to Boston to see Adam for a couple of weeks.'

'OK.'

Kendra stared at the back of his head. 'You could show some interest.'

Rani led the way up to her front door, her two friends following closely behind. They were still shaking from the verbal insults from a group of teenagers in the shopping centre. *Rag heads, fucking terrorist scum.*

'Let me fix your scarf, Rani. It's showing your fringe. Your hair has to be completely covered.'

'Does your Mum know about you wearing this?' Royah shifted from one foot to another. 'In fact does she know about… you know…'

'No. It's not her business.'

Kendra opened the door to take out the paper and bottles to the recycling bin, taken aback as the three women in their long black coats and coloured scarves giggled on her doorstep.

'Mum. Stop gawping,' she hissed. 'This is Tam and Royah. Can we come in please?'

Kendra opened her mouth then clamped it shut. Her cheeks

filled with colour as the green box slipped from her hands. The girls bent down to help her gather up the mess.

'Please go inside. I've just taken some ginger biscuits out of the oven. Oh, but they're not halal. Sorry.'

Kendra dived into the cupboards to look for something else she could offer the girls.

'Crisps? Apples? Bananas?'

'Calm down Mum. You've got food on the brain. I'll make some tea. We've eaten at Tam's house.' Turning to her friends she said, *'Chai irani nadaram. Bebakshid.'*

Royah fiddled with her scarf, bringing it forward to make it more secure, then pushed it back again, exposing some of her coppery hair.

'English tea is fine. A big mug please.' She hoicked her Chanel bag onto her knee and pulled out a plastic box. 'My mum made these for you. Shirini keshmeshi.'

'Oh sultana biscuits with rosewater. I used to love those. Thank you so much.'

Kendra held off from giving the shy, softly spoken girl a hug. They sat around the table, exchanging glances as Kendra launched into her questions.

'So where did you all meet?'

'Uni. Persian society,' said Tam, unbuttoning her long coat and slipping off her matching scarf. Chestnut waves with blonde highlights flowed over her shoulders.

'What happens at Persian society?' Kendra was aware she sounded like a primary school teacher.

'We talk about fashion, food, latest Iranian artists. Just stuff really.'

Kendra swivelled her eyes to where Rani was picking at a loose thread in the table cloth.

'Sounds fun. Do you have guest speakers and things like that?'

'Sometimes. We talk about politics. What's happening in Iran. My parents escaped after the Revolution but they would like to go back now they are getting older.'

'They must miss it. I used to love visiting Shiraz and Tehran.' She turned to her daughter and patted her hand. 'Sweetheart, look after your guests while I go and find something.'

'Does your mum mind us being here? She seems nervous.' Tam flicked open a compact mirror to check her make-up.

'She's fine. Probably a bit shocked about you guys. I don't tell her much about my life. She'd end up giving me a psychological analysis of my every thought. My mother can't just be Mum.

Kendra returned, out of breath, a pile of photograph albums in her arms. Rani groaned loudly.

'Oh No. Mum. NO.'

'I thought your friends might like to see some pictures of our time in Shiraz.' Kendra was unaware of three frozen expressions as she opened up the biggest of the albums.

'This is my wedding to Rani's father. It lasted three days and I wore three different dresses. Look at the styles! 1970s.' Kendra gasped as she looked at the modest white frock which covered every part of her body. 'Some of the Persian women who got married at the same time were more daring than me despite the fact we were in the middle of the revolution.'

'Very pretty,' they mumbled, catching Rani's eye as Kendra turned over the pages of yellowing plastic, lost in her memories.

'And this is one of me tying the grass on *Noh Ruz*. You're supposed to make a wish on New Year's Day and I wished for a daughter. After Adam I had two miscarriages...'

'Mum, that's enough. We've got stuff to do.' Rani inched back her chair, indicating their departure for her room just as David strolled through the kitchen and into the garage. Royah quickly retied her scarf and said hello to Rani's stepfather who stared at her, a confused look on his face.

Kendra was back in time, poring over the picture of her in a similar kind of long loose coat, Adam happily playing with his cousins, Rani sitting on her knee and Hassan sporting a drooping moustache which gave him a grumpy look.

She recalled how he'd changed during that last visit to Shiraz. He'd disappear to some relative for a couple of days, expecting his sister to take care of his wife and family. Kendra would ask Sara what was wrong with him but she'd shrug and carry on cleaning the rice or wiping off the thick dust from the furniture. '*Delesh tang e*. He's homesick,' she'd sigh, pausing to place a sugar cube between her teeth and slurp amber tea from a glass. 'It'll be OK. Insha'Allah.'

The Iranian reliance on fate and the will of Allah annoyed Kendra to the extent she wanted to shout, there is no God but she'd had to learn to blend her behaviour and attitude to fit. One wrong word or look could have put them in serious danger. It was a time when the religious police were watching foreigners closely. Especially women.

It was late when a Mercedes with blacked out windows pulled up at the house, the driver tooting twice. Rani followed her friends out, hugging each of them for a long time. Kendra watched the scene from her study window. She was surprised to see Royah wiping away tears as she climbed into the car. When her daughter returned to the house, she was deep in thought. So many questions churned around in Kendra's mind but knowing the current mercurial nature of her daughter's moods chose not to risk another onslaught.

Late June 2015

The night before Rani was due to leave for London, the air was balmy giving it a Mediterranean feel. Kendra's restlessness meant she was inclined to be over-talkative.

'David, shall we have a barbecue tonight and celebrate Rani's first? Well done my lovely girl. I knew you would do it. It must feel great.' Kendra pulled her daughter into her arms for a hug but feeling her stiffen, she let go. She watched David arrange charcoal in a pyramid and set light to the carefully arranged cardboard. The flames leapt up in a thick smoke which she worried might annoy the miserable neighbours at the back.

'That's a lovely style Rani but I do miss your long hair.'

Rani smiled and kept busy in the kitchen. She wanted the evening to be memorable for them all.

'It's grown up hair,' she said, piling sliced tomatoes onto a plate. 'David? Can we do some star-gazing tonight.'

Her step-father's face lit up. He clapped his hands together like an excited school boy.

'I'll set up the telescopes. It's a clear night so we might be able to see Jupiter.'

As the sky turned to inky black, Rani pointed out the constellations and talked animatedly about their origins and some of the mythology behind their names. They took turns in looking through one of David's most powerful telescopes, marvelling at how bright and bold the gas giant appeared in the sky.

'1,300 times bigger than earth,' said Rani. 'Some stupid people believe planets and constellations affect us here on earth. In this day and age.'

'You mean astrology? It was a big part of Iranian culture at one time. Shiraz was full of people getting their charts cast or whatever they do.'

'Yeah but it's not consistent with science is it David? How can planets affect us when they are millions of miles away? It's superstitious nonsense from medieval times.'

'Carl Jung didn't think so,' Kendra cut in, taking a sip from her wine glass. 'He developed the theory of synchronicity. A sort of "as above, so below" idea.'

'Well he was wrong. Mum, don't fall into the trap of those gullible people who believe in fairies, crystals, faith healing and candles in your ears. Astrology belongs with all that and those crooks are making a fortune about of people who can't cope with uncertainty or want to predict the future. It's rubbish.'

'Thomas Kuhn argued that the concepts of astrology are non-empirical. It answers that question I think,' said David. 'Any more sausages?

CHAPTER 6

'*I* can get a taxi to New Street. You'll never get parked on a Saturday.'

'But we want to see you off properly.' Kendra tried hard to keep her voice even. Rani had been so secretive about her plans, changing the subject or vanishing whenever questions were asked, that alarm bells were ringing.

David gave the tyres a kick, muttering about the air pressure.

'She's right. Taxis can go right in front of the station.' He wiped his hands on some rag unaware of the tension between the two women.

'I'll come back for a weekend.' Rani tapped out the numbers of the black cab company that her mother had always insisted she used. 'It'll be here in two minutes.' She leapt upstairs to bring down her luggage, extracting a twenty pound note from her purse.

'Can you manage all that across London?'

'Stop fussing.'

'And you're stopping with Freya in Tooting? Can I have the address?'

'Taxi's here,' called David, before Rani had a chance to reply. The driver got out and helped load the bags.

'Just email or text.' Rani reached out to her mother and kissed her cheek.

'Cheer up Mum. I'm not going on a Mars mission.' Turning to David, she said, 'Look after her.' Then she was gone.

Closing the front door, Kendra looked into the hall mirror. She fingered the fine lines around her eyes horrified that they had deepened into crevices. Folds of loose skin, the colour of pumice stone were beginning to form around her jaw piling on the years. The stress was taking its toll.

The house was deathly quiet apart from the annoying tick of the tiny cuckoo clock Adam had brought home from a ski trip to Zurich. She'd not had the heart to take it down. David had gone to the garage down the road to sort out the car. The postman waved as he passed by the window. Everything looked normal but felt so wrong.

Kendra sat on the edge of David's wing-backed chair holding her feelings in her hands as if they were a broken wings of a sparrow. She didn't know what to do with herself. Time had taken on a new dimension with each minute feeling like a month. Adam's Skype call made her jump.

'Have you booked your flight Ma?'

'Hmm? What flight?'

'Boston Logan. Were you asleep or something?'

'No. Rani's just left for London.'

'Ah. I see. Empty nest blues. I've put some money into her account so she can celebrate her results. She did well winning the Charles Pimford medal. It'll be the Nobel next.'

'Have you spoken to her lately?'

'She never replies so I gave up. I did email to say I'd dropped her a thousand bucks. Come on Ma. Get that flight sorted. Birmingham, Dublin, Boston. Clear immigration in Dublin. It takes the hassle out of it at my end. Ally's looking forward to seeing you and the weather is perfect now.'

A week later

Kendra woke up to a grinding in her stomach and a reminder from the glare of the digital clock that it was 5.10 am. The flight to Boston from Dublin had been made bearable by a pleasant conversation with a young woman going home after twenty years in Ireland to care for her mother.

Kendra stretched out in the king sized bed, luxuriating in the Egyptian cotton linen and the memory foam pillows. A sour taste had settled on her lips so she crept into the kitchen to pour iced water from the dispenser in the fridge. She was desperate for a cup of tea but the gadgetry in the huge kitchen was beyond her technological competence. She longed for a simple kettle, a tea bag and a big mug.

A batch of cinnamon muffins, the size of bandstands, sat invitingly on the counter top. Sitting down at the end of the glass table, Kendra pulled chunks off one and chewed on them slowly.

'I thought I heard you get up. It takes a day or two to adjust.'

'Sorry if I woke you Adam. Show me how to work that monstrosity.'

'It's a coffee station with a hot water option. Tea bags are kept in this box. It's easy. Look and learn, Mother.'

Despite being an overworked doctor, her son retained a mischievous look in his brown eyes and a tease in his voice. His supple limbs were a testament to his running regime. She was reminded of when he used to play basketball in the Alexander Stadium, or was it football? Her mind wobbled around like a jelly. She put it down to the jet lag.

'I'm on duty at six. Here's a set of keys for the apartment and for the front door although the concierge is there 24/7. The lift key is this one, first security lock, second one. Ma are you listening and watching? You don't want to lock yourself out.'

'Sorry love. Yes, I've got it.'

'If you walk a few blocks to the right, you'll find Harvard Square. There's a train that goes into Boston from there. Just ask someone. They're a friendly lot. Mainly students. I hope it won't be too noisy for you after sleepy Sutton Coldfield.'

'Help yourself to anything you like. I'll try to get home early,' called Alison, hair and legs flying out of the door and down the two flights of stairs. 'Sorry I've got so much to do.'

'I'm off now Ma. Have a good day.' Adam grabbed his bag and jacket and dropped a kiss on his mother's head.

The streets were alive with commuters clutching large paper cups of coffee as they strode, head down, towards the station. From the apartment, Kendra hugged her second mug of tea and watched a couple strolling along the pavement – she couldn't think of it as a sidewalk – hand in hand with nothing but a glowing future to dream about. The girl's long auburn hair blew about her face as she paused to yield to the kiss of her boyfriend. Kendra looked away.

One day that would be Ariana. She would leave home for good, maybe pursue her career in Boston or Washington. She'd talked about it enough times. Kendra felt a pricking behind her eyes. She moved her gaze to the other side of the street in an attempt to push away what she recognised as a mounting panic.

She needed a plan for the day. It was clear Adam and Alison wouldn't have much time to entertain her. She looked around to see what jobs she could do in their pristine apartment but apart from preparing dinner there was nothing to do. She padded bare foot into the huge guest bathroom and turned on the power shower, wondering if she'd done the right thing to come to America on her own.

Once Kendra had begun to feel more confident in her new environment, she took a trip into Boston on the Redline to energise her spirits. By the time she reached the Cheers bar for an early lunch she felt buoyant. The nagging doubts about Rani's recent behaviour was turning into something more rational. *I must have been mad to think she was mixed up in some sort of extremist movement.* She put a hand to her mouth to suppress a laugh.

A chatty bar tender persuaded her to try one of the beers which he delivered to a discreet table in the corner. Kendra liked nothing more than to observe people and that was the ideal vantage point. A balding man turned to give her the eye, waving his bottle in her direction. Kendra smiled back without being encouraging. She'd planned to spend the day in the city on her own so to reinforce her message she buried her head in her guide book.

By the time she got back to the apartment she was exhausted. Blisters throbbed on one of her heels as she pulled off her trainers. The thought of cooking in the humongous kitchen with an oven resembling a space ship was overwhelming. *Maybe I could take them out somewhere. Isn't that what Americans do?*

When Adam pushed open the front door, Alison trailing in his wake with bags of shopping, he saw his mother fast asleep, mouth open, on the sofa.

'You start the dinner. I'll have a quick shower. Pour me a glass of something. I'm desperate.' He leaned over to shake his mother's shoulder. 'Ma? Wake up or you won't sleep tonight.'

Kendra stirred from a dream that involved a shouting match with her daughter on the phone. Rani had called her from the Turkish border before slipping into Syria. It took Kendra some time to get to grips with the fact it was just a dream. She rubbed her eyes and pulled herself into a sitting position.

'Sorry I just conked out. I must have walked miles.'

'That's the good thing about Boston. It's a walkable city unlike others in the States. Did you get down to Faneuil place and the waterfront?'

'Not yet. I spent most of the time in the centre just walking. It reminds me so much of a European city and of course I went to Cheers.'

'Sounds like you had fun,' called Alison, handing Adam a knife and a red bell pepper. 'I hope you like Korean food.'

'I don't think I've had it before. Can I help with anything?'

'No. It doesn't take long. Just chill.'

Kendra rested her head against the squishy cushions and closed her eyes. She was missing home already and felt an urge to call David. He wasn't on Skype so she asked Adam if she could make a quick call.

'Use the phone in your room.'

David picked up the extension in his workshop on her third attempt.

'I was concentrating,' he said irritably. 'Are you alright?'

'Yes. Just missing home and wondering what you're doing.'

With a burst of enthusiasm, David began to explain the intricacies of something technical.

'So you're not missing me then,' she laughed.

'No. I can get on in peace. Oh dear. I've said the wrong thing haven't I? When are you back?'

'Five days' time. I must go. Adam and Alison have prepared dinner.'

'I'm having a jacket potato, beans and strawberry ice-cream.'

'Not all together I hope.'

'Of course not.'

Kendra heard the receiver click into place. It would be impossible to explain David to anybody. An enigma, her mother had called him. 'Sure there's nothing I can do?'

'Nearly ready,' called Alison. Adam appeared with plates, chopsticks and cutlery as Kendra uploaded some of her selfies to send on to Rani. She'd not expected to hear from her daughter for a few weeks but now she was feeling anxious that there'd been no contact.

'Adam, stand next to me. Selfie time. We can send this to your sister.' They grinned into the camera on Kendra's phone. 'This technology is amazing.'

'Has she been in touch?' Alison asked as she served a heap of noodles onto Kendra's plate.

'No. Not yet. She forgot to give me her friend's address so I'm relying on email and texts. It's a strange new world we live in.'

All evening Kendra kept lifting the cover of her phone to see if a reply email had arrived from her daughter. By the time she went to bed the tension across her shoulders had become so unbearable she took two painkillers and a shot of brandy. Alison yawned and excused herself.

'Have a soak in the tub. That usually helps me,' she said, fluffing up Adam's hair as she went.

'I think I'll lie down and read for a bit. Night both.'

Concentration eluded Kendra as she scanned the page of her Kindle for a third time, the words crawling about as if looking for an escape. She tuned the radio on her phone to the world service. As she closed her eyes and drifted into sleep, the last thing to hit her ears was news of a massacre on a beach in Tunisia with many Britons dead. ISIS had claimed responsibility. Kendra shuddered with revulsion along with the rest of the British population. *What on earth is going on with these people?*

CHAPTER 7

*V*isitors, students and locals fought for space in Harvard Square, jostling Kendra as she attempted to create some elbow room so she could take a batch of photographs for David. Not being a traveller himself, he enjoyed examining the micro detail and technical skill of other people's compositions. The sun beat down on her uncovered head forcing a retreat into Crème de la Crème café where she managed to squeeze onto a corner of somebody's table.

'The ham and spinach quiche is beyond delicious,' said the woman opposite in a drawly kind of voice. She picked out a green fleck from between her front teeth.

Kendra gave her a zipped smile and studied the menu, not wanting to get into conversation. Amongst the crowds of visitors and students she felt an acute loneliness. Boston was a friendly city but Kendra didn't feel like engaging with anyone. Her head was full of her daughter. The minute her coffee was served, a ping from her phone announced a new e-mail. Hoping it was from her daughter, she opened it to find it was a return to sender. An intense burning filled her chest as if a hot stick was being poked about in it.

'You ok, honey? You've gone awfully pale.'

Kendra threw down a note and hurried over to a quiet spot in the square where she sat to recover her balance. Shielding the screen from the sun, she checked the message again. The address was correct. It had been imported from her address book. Maybe there was a problem with the server or the cloud thing. Kendra had visions of data stacking up on fluffy cumulus which got lost when it rained. She sent the message again. Immediately it was returned with a failure to deliver notification. She tried to call Adam but his voicemail reminded her he was running his clinic all day. A sudden urge to go home on the evening flight took hold.

Returning to the apartment, she logged onto the Aer Lingus website and booked one of the remaining six seats available in economy to Dublin and on to Birmingham. It meant she'd lost money but it was *her* money and there was no reason to tell David. Throwing stuff into her bags, she tried some yoga breathing… in, hold, out… in, hold, out, to calm her nerves. The trilling of the phone in her room felt like an electric shock.

'Hello?' she said tentatively.

'Ma? Have you been trying to get hold of me? What's up?'

'Adam. I'm going back tonight. Something's come up I need to sort out.'

'Couldn't it wait? Ally and I had planned to take you to New York this weekend.'

'Sorry love. Rani's emails are being returned and I need to find out what's going on.'

Adam blew a raspberry. 'My crazy sister again. It's probably a technical glitch, that's all. You're worrying too much. You know Ma, you've got all antsy these days. Menopause probably.'

'I'm just worried Adam. I'm sorry love.'

'I'll let Ally know. She'll be disappointed. Get a taxi from the square. Let me know you've got home safely. Sorry I can't drive you to the airport. I'm full on.'

'Thank you both for a lovely time. Bye.'

☙ THE FUTURE CAN'T WAIT

They didn't call it the red-eye for nothing. Kendra rubbed at the imaginary grit under her eye-lids and drank water to get rid of the hollow feeling in her stomach as she waited for the bags to appear through the plastic curtain strips. She needed the bathroom but didn't want to miss the cranking up of the belt. By some miracle, her bag was one of the first to arrive. Striding through customs, she headed for the taxi rank. She could have easily caught the train from Birmingham International to New Street but her energy was sapped and she needed to get home.

As they inched their way through the heavy traffic, Sutton Coldfield seemed further away than Boston. The driver's Punjabi monologue into his Bluetooth headset was punctuated by the occasional curse in a strong Brummie accent. Pushing some notes into his hand, she fumbled for her keys and dragged her bags up to the front door.

'David? David? I'm back,' she called, pulling off her coat and hanging it over the newel post. Some moments later, her husband appeared, in dirty blue overalls, his thick eyebrows pulled together in a downward pointing arrow. He was wiping a brush with a rag.

'There's no need to shout.'

'I've come home early.'

'Oh. I was about to make some tea.'

Kendra stood in the middle of the kitchen staring at him. Is that all he had to say? His life revolved round his hourly tea routines. One of his university colleagues used to call him Mr. Spock. She could see why. There was no point sharing her fears about Rani's email situation. Even to her own ears, now she was back amongst the familiar, it seemed lame. She sensed that he was put out by her early return.

As she went upstairs to change, she noticed Rani's door was wide open as was the side window. Hearing the gentle flapping of the curtains, she poked her head round. Something about the room seemed off. Opening the wardrobe door, she found dresses and spaghetti strapped tops folded into piles on the shelves. Shoes with heels were marshalled in neat rows along with handbags and jewellery in the pull out tray. Kendra fingered through the necklaces and rings gasping as she realised all the Persian gold Rani had been given over the years had gone. Gold was a serious bartering currency in Iran. She calculated quickly. It must have been over five thousand pounds' worth. Hassan's family had been very generous to them all at one time.

Her eye strayed to the grubby outlines and empty nails on the walls. Rani hadn't taken down the photographs to take with her. *Had she?* Kendra pulled open the drawers in the desk unit, emptying them onto the bed. A half-completed application for an Iranian passport fell out along with a crumpled letter from the bank asking Rani to contact them about an unauthorised overdraft. A sudden thought slapped her between the eyes. Where was Rani's British passport? With the determination of a detective, she turned the room over, her heart thumping. She shouted for her husband.

'What's going on? You've got to tidy all that up now.'

'Have you been in this room David?'

He gave her a blank look as if he didn't understand the question.

'Things are missing from here. Has Ariana been back?'

'No. Calm down.'

'Have you been out at all? Maybe she came back when you were in your shed.'

'It's a workshop Kendra. I didn't hear anything.'

He paused then tapped his hand against his cheek in a Morse code like rhythm.

'I did go to the supermarket and Tool Box. I had to wait for forty minutes to be served.'

'So long enough for someone with a key to come into the house.'

'Well, I suppose so. I left at 11.05 and was back by 12.30.'

Kendra saw the distress in his eyes. She patted his arm.

'I'm not mad with you.' His face relaxed. 'Rani's passport isn't there.'

'She'll have taken it for ID purposes. Isn't that what most people do?'

Kendra sat on the edge of the bed and tried to think.

'I don't know. Something's going on.' She told him about the email.

'Technology problems that's all. I couldn't get the car to start.'

'I'm probably over-reacting due to lack of sleep. I'll try and nap for a bit.'

Warm sunshine flooded into the living room where she stretched out on the sofa but Kendra felt a chill bury itself deep in her bones. She tucked her hands under the fleecy warmth of the blanket. Needing to share her fears with someone who would understand, she called Sheila.

'How was Boston? Get down Shap. This bloody dog is getting on my nerves. Always wanting attention. It's like having another kid.'

'It was fine. Good to see Adam so well and happy with Alison. The wedding's later this year in Devon.'

'Ooo and it won't be long before a little someone's calling you Granny,' Sheila teased. 'I'm going to have to take this creature out for his walk. Do you fancy coming?'

'Ok. I was trying to sleep off the jet lag but it will make me feel worse tonight. Give me twenty minutes and I'll meet you at our usual place.'

Sheila had taken off her tracksuit top and was tying it around her waist when Kendra strolled up to her, hands deep in her pockets, a scarf wound round her neck.

'Don't tell me you're cold? I'm roasting. You've not got this bug that's going around have you?'

Kendra pushed back bits of hair that felt dry and brittle in her fingers.

'Just a bit chilled. Let's walk. Hello Shap.' She bent down to fondle the Border collie's ears.

The two women walked arm in arm through the wooded part of the park, pausing to check the dog wasn't getting into mischief.

'What's up,' asked Sheila. 'I always know with you. It's written on your face. Is it Adam?'

'No, no. He's never been any trouble. It's Ariana.' Kendra told her the story.

Sheila grimaced.

'I think she's deactivated her email address so we can't get hold of her.'

'Jo's done that with his phone. Blocked me on several occasions when he's been in a strop. He changed his mind thought when he needed a lift. Shap... leave that puppy alone.' She mouthed sorry to the owner as she tugged on Shap's collar.

Kendra carried on walking, eyes to the ground, chin sunk into her scarf.

'I think there's something wrong. I mean, I feel there's something wrong. She's taken some jewellery, stuff she never wears but was bought as in investment by her Iranian relatives and her passport's missing.'

'Kendy, you're not going to like this.' Sheila stopped and faced her friend. 'You're sounding like a control freak and a bit obsessive. If you're really worried, then call her workplace. She'll hate you for it but at least you'll have some peace of mind.'

'Hmm. The thing is….'

'Don't tell me you don't know where she's working. What are you like?'

'She's barely spoken to me except to pick a fight. It was like she was doing it deliberately.'

'That's bloody selfish. Supposing something happened to you or David. Who could get hold of her except the police?'

Sheila snapped a piece of dark chocolate from a bar, pressing it into Kendra's hand.

'I thought the worst of child rearing was over at eighteen. That's such a myth. It seems the problems are just beginning. Jo behaves as if he's had a personality transplant. The way he speaks to his father on the phone is unforgiveable. I think that's why he took this sabbatical. To get away. Rani's different though. I've never heard a bad word come out of that girl's mouth. I'm sure there's nothing sinister going on. She wouldn't put you through that knowing what you've suffered already with the divorce, and the death of your parents and then your sister's cancer. Look, I think you're exhausted. That college is becoming a hotbed of stress. Thank heavens I've working my notice now. Maybe it's time for you to move on too.'

Kendra felt the ginger in the chocolate sting the back of her throat. 'Maybe.'

'Try again.. Rani's too close to you to just leave things hanging. If you hear nothing after a couple of weeks, then maybe you need to get some advice. You must have colleagues in your field that could help.'

'Yeah, I belong to a professional group that meets in the city every month. We raise issues of concern for open discussion but I've not been for months. I could ring the Samaritans I suppose.' Sheila missed the touch of irony in her friend's voice.

'But you're not suicidal. Are you?' Sheila studied Kendra's face. 'Are you?'

'No. Just upset and a bit anxious.'

'Yoga Saturday morning. That's not a suggestion. It's an order.'

'I suppose I could contact the police.'

Shap came bounding back and jumped up, muddying Kendra's cream jogging bottoms.

'You bad boy. I'm so sorry Kendy.'

'They'll wash. Don't shout at the dog.'

'I can't see the police taking it seriously. Rani's an adult and she's gone to London. They won't list her as a missing person. If she chooses to cut contact for a while, then it's not a crime. I can hear them saying it with a smirk on their faces. I lost trust in the police when Rich reported a drug dealer at Exeter Uni. They believed he was involved. Remember?'

'I do. What a mess that was.'

'Bloody coppers have got baked beans for brains.'

'You've got a way with words. I'd better be getting back.'

'There's that bloke you fancy with the itsy- bitsy terrier.'

'Ha Ha. Projection. More like you have.'

As they prepared to leave each other to take their separate routes, Sheila said, 'Post on Facebook. I can't see anyone under eighty weaning themselves off it yet. She might see it and respond. Then see if she's got a twitter handle. There's loads of social media I've never heard of but the kids are bedded in to it. Jo will help you. Street angel, house devil is Jo.'

CHAPTER 8

AUGUST 2015

The summer days held no promise for either blue skies or news of Rani. Kendra had to drag herself out of bed to go to English Best, a language school in the city centre, where she'd signed up to teach intensive courses of academic English. She hadn't wanted to work during the holidays but David had pressed her to do something with her time other than mope around.

'It's not helping you or anybody else,' he'd said. 'You can't change what's happened. Time will sort it out so you need to be patient.'

Her students, high spirited Italians, were pleasant but hard work. The lessons she'd thrown together seemed tedious even to her. The revolt which she was half expecting came a couple of weeks before the end of her contract.

'This is boring,' said Alfredo, standing up and slamming books back into his leather satchel. 'My father, he pays good money for these classes. I apply to Oxford to study the chemistry but I will fail because of you.' He pointed at the board then at Kendra. 'This is for the babies.'

The class fell silent as they watched the drama play out.

'I'm gonna complain to the proprietario.'

Kendra's eyes twitched as he slammed out of the room. *Don't react. That's what he wants.*

'Does anyone else feel the same? I don't want to teach people who don't want to be here so please feel free to leave.'

Her voice wobbled as she choked back a mix of anger and hurt. The rest of the small class began to pack up and sidled out with apologetic shrugs as they scrolled through their phones. Kendra pressed her forehead against the cool surface of the whiteboard. She'd tried to distract herself as David had suggested but all she really wanted to do is block out the light and crawl under the duvet.

'Are you alright Mrs. Blackmore?'

The Head of Academic English looked up as she pushed open his door. As she explained what had happened, he fiddled with some papers on his desk.

'I'm sorry but I need to finish my contract today. I'm not feeling well,' Kendra finished, putting her hand to her cheek.

'Alfredo caused a lot of trouble for a teacher last year. Here's the report. I don't know why I agreed to take him back. He's got a big ego and a bigger mouth. I'll give you a class of lovely Japanese ladies. So respectful and hard working. Please would you stay? I've had some glowing reports about your classes.'

Kendra shook her head and slipped away. Bunches of students hung around the coffee machine, breaking the rule of "English Only". The murky sky was growing darker, blocking out any hope of the promised sunshine. Kendra held out a hand to test for rain.

At New Street station she got confused. She couldn't see the Lichfield train listed on the board. Her knees were trembling as she looked around for a member of staff.

'You alright bab?'

A plump woman in a blue jacket emblazoned with a Network Rail logo approached her.

'Which train's going to Sutton?'

'Platform 8a in ten minutes. You need to take the far set of escalators. Go through these barriers then back in through the other side. It's marked.'

Kendra felt glued to the ground. She ran her fingers through her hair.

'Why can't I go down this escalator? Why has it all been changed? Made so complicated? It's ridiculous.'

'It's been like this for quite a while. You a tourist?'

Kendra shook her head as she processed the information. The busy concourse was making her feel panicky. She looked to where the woman was pointing.

'Come on. Follow me. It takes some getting used to.'

Like a robot, Kendra walked alongside the woman, noticing that the straining waistband of her skirt hadn't been fastened properly. With horror, she found herself wanting to say something. As she stepped onto the escalator, the ground swirled below. Kendra thought she was going to fall.

'I thought you were at work.' David was hoeing the front garden when his wife appeared on the drive.

'I've quit.'

He carried on, his mouth set in a line.

'But the money was good.'

'For God's sake David. Why is it always about the money? Can't you see I'm barely capable of getting dressed in the morning? Minimum wage, train fares, no free coffee. No it wasn't good. I'm going to lie down.'

She pulled back the curtains in her study and curled up on the day bed. The swaying of the lime trees in the garden next door had a mesmerising effect that made Kendra feel sleepy but she couldn't settle. Her nerves felt like shards of ice pushing through her skin. She ran a bath then felt agitated in the heat of the water. The cat was scratching at the door. Every sound grated.

'For fuck's sake,' she yelled, throwing a sponge at the mirror.

David was sat at the table carving the crusts off a sandwich and picking at some half-cooked chips, his mouth settled in its default scowl. He was so engrossed in the Sudoku puzzle in the local paper he took him several minutes to acknowledge her presence.

'There's some post for you,' he said, dipping the last chip into some brown sauce. He pointed to a pile of junk mail, a couple of brown envelopes and a stiff white one. She was aware of him watching her as she ran her finger over what looked to be Rani's handwriting. It appeared bigger and looser than before but the fancy B in Blackmore was definitely hers. Her heart stopped for a second.

'I told you she'd be in touch,' he said, spooning ice-cream into a bowl. 'There's no chocolate sauce left.'

Kendra went into the pantry and brought out some caramel. 'Try this.' Affection mixed with relief flooded through her veins as she wrapped her arms around his neck. 'I do love you and I'm sorry I've been such a pain.'

'Are you going to open it?'

'In a minute. Let's sit in the living room.' Kendra held the envelope to her chest, wanting to savour the moment. David was right as usual.

'I can't believe it's the end of August and the nights are closing in again. It's so chilly.' She pulled a rug around her shoulders, eyes drawn back to the promise of relief that balanced on her knees. She wanted to rip the letter open and dance around the room but something held her back. For that moment, it represented the end of a nightmare but questions began to crowd in her head. *Why a letter? What happened to her email?*

The postmark said London so there was nothing to indicate that Rani had been coerced into going to Syria. *What a stupid idea that was.*

She carefully slit open the envelope, her senses on guard as she pulled out a sheet of paper torn from a spiral notebook. Kendra scanned the few sentences. She shook her head as if trying to clear a fog from her eyes. Her mouth worked quickly as she read out the words but her brain was seconds behind as it tried to compute their meaning.

Dear Mum, I know this is going to be a huge shock and I'm sorry. I'm not coming home again and I won't be in touch. It's important you don't call the police as I'm not missing and I haven't been coerced in doing anything against my will. Everything I'm doing is my own choice and decision. Love you always. Ariana. x

Kendra's hands shook violently as she passed it to her husband. Fat tears plopped onto and smudged the word Mum. David adjusted his glasses as if he was trying to decipher a strange code.

'I don't understand,' he said quietly. 'You don't do this to people. It's cruel. Especially your own mother.'

Kendra felt her limbs fold up like a marionette being put back in its box. The body blow left her doubled in physical pain as she collapsed across David's knee, sobbing. Digging her nails into her palm she tried to scream out but it was as if a hangman's noose had been tied around her neck. Her violent shaking made David realise he had to do something. He dialled their GP's emergency number. By the time a locum arrived, Kendra was almost catatonic while David slapped his thighs and paced with such anxious repetition that the doctor ordered him to sit down and calmly tell her the story.

'Your wife is in deep shock. I'm going to give her a mild sedative. Get an emergency appointment with your own doctor tomorrow. Mention my visit. I'm Dr. Norris. If she seems suicidal then go to A and E. She needs to be kept warm, quiet and calm. No phone calls. Sleep is the best thing at this stage. I can see myself out. Stay close to your wife Mr. Blackmore. She needs you.'

Kendra slept for twenty-four hours without waking. She found herself tucked up on the sofa and David asleep on the chair next to her. As she struggled to sit up, her head felt as if it had been covered in ready mixed concrete. A large jug of water was on the side table. She poured some into a glass and drank deeply which helped to peel her swollen tongue away from the roof of her mouth. Her mind was a blank.

'David? What happened? Did I get drunk? I feel drunk.'

'Adam wants to speak to you. I've told him about the letter. He's on Skype now.'

'What letter?' Kendra struggled to her feet but fell back against the cushions.

'Ma? How are you feeling? Those sedatives are heavyweight.'

'Sedatives? Will someone please tell me what's going on?'

'Listen to me. You've had a traumatic experience which has led to a severe form of shock. Do you remember any of it? A letter? From Rani?' Adam watched his mother's eyes shift from right to left, up and down as she struggled to recall a memory.

'Oh God. Yes. She's never coming home again Adam. She's cut us off. She hates me. I don't know what I've done. Adam? Adam are you there?'

Kendra buried her face in her hands, swallowing a glob of vomit that had shot into her throat.

'She's a little shit doing this to her family. I'm affected as well but I have to stay objective. In my practice I've got other devoted parents broken down by their kid disappearing for no apparent reason but I know that doesn't help you right now.'

'Maybe she's had a breakdown?'

Kendra tore at another tissue as she stemmed the unrelenting flow of tears.

'No she's not. It would be easier to understand. The only way to deal with this is to wait until she comes to her senses and wakes up. You have to find a way through by focusing on your own life. Talk to your colleagues about this because you need a lot of support. You need to see your doctor so he or she knows what's going on. This is a form of grief but with no conclusion so it's easy to get stuck in the depression phase. Understand me Ma?'

Kendra nodded, gripping David's arm.

'But supposing she's joined some extremist group. She was becoming political and had all these Iranian friends. She started covering up.' Kendra's voice faded out.

'No. Iranians hate ISIS like the rest of the world. Look what they've being doing to the Shia. Most Muslims condemn these groups. She'd need Arabic not Farsi to survive and the idea of Rani in the hell-hole of Raqqa with no organic shampoos and hot chocolate, being passed around like candy … well it's laughable. Rani is not a Muslim even if she has been playacting. She's an atheist and a scientist like me. You need to keep a grip on reality or I will have to drop everything and fly over. Pass David over. I need to talk to him.'

'Supposing she's gone to Iran to get married and didn't want to tell us? Maybe these girls she brought home are in on the plot.'

'Supposing Ma, she's being a selfish, irresponsible brat.'

CHAPTER 9

*Y*ou sure you don't want me to come to the surgery with you? I've got plenty of time on my hands now I've gone part-time. I knew I'd get talked into doing two days a week. Mind you, there's not much take- up on the sewing school yet.'

Kendra stared at a frog that was contemplating a jump from a rock back into the pond. The crackling of a crisp packet in Sheila's hand hurt her ears.

'This weather's amazing for autumn,' said Sheila, lifting her face to the sun. 'You need to eat something. Maybe Adam's right. A short course of tablets would help with the appetite and the sleep problem. You're fading to nothing.'

Kendra picked at a loose thread in her cardigan. She was aware she hadn't changed her clothes or showered for three days. All the fight had left her. Sheila leaned over the table and squeezed her arm.

'I can't bring Rani home but I can support you if you tell me how. Maybe some counselling would help or a support group. I found Parent Online when I was having problems with Jo. It's staffed by parents who've had similar issues with their kids. I'll email you the link.'

Kendra folded her arms and counted the cracks in the patio slabs. A shifting pattern of thoughts tumbled through her head.

'There's this guy in Melbourne,' Sheila continued, tapping her forehead as she recalled the name. 'Dr. Attily. He's written a book on parent-child estrangement. I've been doing a bit of research. At least have a look at it. He does say though that parents have to look hard at themselves to see if they've contributed to it in any way.'

Kendra shielded her eyes from the sun with her hand and turned to face Sheila.

'Is that what you think I've done? Pushed my daughter away? It's always the mothers that get the blame.' Kendra snapped a hairgrip between her fingers.

'I'm not saying that at all but it's like divorce. Both parties have some responsibility in the breakdown. Maybe she felt, oh I don't know, suffocated and this is the only way she could break away. It's heartless and over the top but it's a phase, like Adam said. It won't last but I know it must be bloody hurtful.'

Kendra went back into the house and stared out of the kitchen window.

'I'm sorry if I've upset you. Me and my big mouth. If you want me to come to the doc's for some moral support, then let me know.'

'No. I don't.'

Kendra sat in the recently refurbished waiting room, twitching every time the digital strip above the reception desk flashed the name of the next patient. She picked up a magazine and thumbed noisily through the glossy sheets. A man opposite looked up from his Reader's Digest, flashing her a disapproving look.

She scanned an article, *Are You Too Fat for Your Man?* wondering what her students would make of it. A stab of guilt caught her unawares. She'd not returned to work after the summer holiday and Maurice hadn't been happy having to pay for a substitute teacher. She turned to the back page looking for the agony column but instead stared at a picture of Astro-Martin. Like many people she couldn't resist seeing what nonsense was forecast for her sign of Libra.

Your world is being turned upside down. Sudden changes in personal relationships will leave you upset and confused. People are no longer what they seem. Who's been secretive in your life? Fasten your seatbelts, Libra. You're in for a roller coaster ride. Call Martin for more.

Kendra caught her name flashing up and without thinking, stuffed the magazine into her bag. Ten minutes later she was out with a sick-note and a prescription for some new type of anti-depressant that was, allegedly, side-effect free. In her baggy jacket and over-washed jeans, she'd felt invisible and unheard. Another sad woman who couldn't face the empty nest. The doctor didn't need to say it. It was written across his forehead.

Adjusting her bag on her shoulder, she crossed the road and over to the park. It was the school run and the noise from the children emerging from classrooms was deafening. Kendra was forced to step back off the pavement as they ran towards cars parked on double yellow lines.

'Someone should report these drivers to the council,' grumbled an elderly man as he navigated his walking frame with difficulty. 'Ridiculous having tanks for cars. It's not Kensington.'

With a brief apology, Kendra eased her way round him and made for an empty bench. Pulling out the magazine, which she vowed to return the next day, she turned to the back page and ran her finger down the horoscope signs looking for Rani's.

Cancer. Your home-loving nature is about to get a radical shake up. Break away from routine and do things your way. Don't let family hold you back. It's your time now.

Rubbish, she thought, stuffing it back in her bag. It meant that a twelfth of the world's population were getting ready to dump their families and become self-seeking bastards. Kendra felt a surge of anger. David was right. Astrology had never been tested scientifically. How could you test nonsense? It was well-known but she found herself drawn back to the page. Four signs mentioned the planet Uranus. It was a planet Rani had been particularly interested in because of its rings rotating up and over as opposed to round the middle like Saturn. She remembered her drawing it as a child, tongue sticking out, as she traced the outline, colouring it in with green and blue crayons.

Kendra walked home quickly, skirting the edge of the park to avoid the late afternoon dog walkers. Astro-Martin was on her mind when she went in search of her husband.

'Could we have a look at Uranus tonight through that new telescope of yours?'

David gave her a strange look. 'You mean *Uranus?* When William Herschel discovered it on March 13th 1881 he wanted to call it George after the king. It's a pity he didn't. It would have stopped people making these puerile jokes all the time.'

Kendra let him carry on as she cleaned the mess he'd made in the sink.

'You can't see it with the naked eye. At its closest, it's 1.6 billion miles away but the solar system is in constant motion so it changes daily. It can be as far away as 1.9 billion miles.' David was in full flow. He took off his glasses to give them a quick wipe on his sleeve.

'So... not with your telescope?'

'You need one with at least two hundred times magnification. Then you would only see a pin-prick of bluey-green. Why are you so interested?'

She couldn't really explain.

'It's supposed to be a very cold planet. I remember Rani saying.'

'Minus 224.2. Degrees C.'

David hovered about whistling some random notes as he waited for his wife to give him some instructions. She'd talked about setting up the telescope but she hadn't said when.

'The moon's waxing gibbous tonight.'

'And you, my love, are waxing lyrical as usual.' She reached up to kiss him.

'It will be a wonderful sight,' he added helpfully. 'That means the moon is more than half-illuminated by the sun and waxing means...'

'Growing. That's all I understand. I've got some things to do now but maybe you could light the chiminea and we can sit outside. Enjoy the last of this Indian summer.'

Kendra closed her study door quietly and switched on her laptop. She found Astro-Martin's website and clicked on the tab marked general forecast for 2015. Stuff about Mercury spinning backwards and the effect on communications was like gobbledegook to her rational mind but she remembered the time the school's computer system crashed. It fitted one of these periods. When she asked David, he snorted. 'Planets don't go backwards. It's an optical illusion.'

The bath had become a place of refuge and a return to the safety of the womb. As Kendra let the hot water flow over her body, she caught a quick glance in the mirror at her skinny legs and arms. Sheila was right about the weight loss. Most of the muscle tone in her thighs from swimming and yoga had gone, leaving silvery stretch marks like snail trails. Wood smoke, with a faint aroma of apple, drifted through the window. She hurried into some warm clothes and joined her husband for a drink and some star gazing.

The fire crackled in the darkness, the wood spitting out sparks into the cooling air. Kendra studied David's profile, noting the hollow cheeks and a tightness around his eyes. *He doesn't look well.*

'Why does the moon look so close as if it's about to gobble us up?'

'It's at the closest point to the earth.'

Kendra sipped her brandy.

'Do you think it has any effect on us? Moods? Behaviour?'

David frowned and stroked the stubble on his chin.

'It affects the tides. I read somewhere that we've adapted how we behave to the different lunar phases. The moon was the only light we had.'

'There are some stats that show on a full moon, more people are admitted into psychiatric units. Even the police have recorded an increase in arrests.'

'Coincidence. Look up there to your left. Orion's belt.'

Kendra followed his gaze but her mind shifted back to her daughter. *Was she safe? Had someone made sure she'd had a good birthday? What the hell was going on?*

CHAPTER 10

Getting out of bed in a morning was becoming an effort. As she swung her feet onto the carpet, now covered in fluff and bits of crisps because she couldn't be bothered to run the cleaner over it, Kendra felt as if someone had strapped weights to her thighs during the night. An autumn chill clawed its way through the house but David was reluctant to turn on the central heating until mid-October.

'For God's sake, I'm freezing. Don't you care? Is saving money more important than how I feel?'

A muscle in his cheek twitched as he continued to scrape butter over his toast.

'Go back to work Kendra. It's because you sit around all day doing nothing.'

'Oh? How would you know? You're never in the house. I notice you've taken the one and only convector heater into your shed.'

Kendra pulled on a worn- out pair of fleecy boots and a thick cardigan with a ripped pocket. David tutted as he stirred his coffee.

'You look a mess. Get your hair cut,' he said, backing off as a dark cloud crossed her face.

'Right. The cure for all ills. That and a cup of tea of course. Do you really think I want to sit in the hairdressers listening to the inane chatter about holidays and being asked if I've started my Christmas shopping?' She yanked her head up to glare at him. 'Well? Do you?'

He pulled his face into a scowl. A gust of wind was tossing the ruddy brown leaves that were falling from the sycamore tree. He thought about clearing the paths but his shoulder felt too sore for vigorous broom pushing. He turned back to face his wife.

'If you went back to work, and it's not about the money, you'd be amongst people you can talk to. You'd have the support that I don't think I can give you. I can do the garden and a bit of clearing up if you give me instructions but...' He looked into her eyes, puffy with exhaustion...' I don't think that's enough, is it?'

Kendra pressed the heel of her hand against her temple.

'I'm sorry David. I know I'm not easy to live with at the moment.' Kendra stuffed her hand into the biscuit tin and pushed a digestive into her mouth.

'Eating junk isn't going to help either. You've barely eaten a proper meal in weeks.'

'Your nagging isn't helping either.' Turning her back she walked into the living room and shut the door.

David was right. Staying at home behind closed curtains wasn't helping her. She could see her husband was under some strain. Trying to cope with change and upset to his routine could push him into a long melt-down and Kendra didn't think she had the energy to help him through it.

She flicked through the local paper to find the daily horoscope page but it was vague as usual. Astro-Martin was her early morning fix, picking out a word or line that resonated with her situation. Sometimes she woke in the early hours to see if he'd posted something new. *A family member close to you is giving you a hard time and for Librans, the sign of harmonious relationships, this is causing you great distress.*

The evenings were the worst. Kendra's low mood took on a different dimension. Unable to stay awake beyond the nine o'clock news, she went to bed early so she could crawl into her cocoon of nothingness and shut her mind down, yet even in sleep, the psychedelic dreams were so real and frightening that she woke up clutching her chest and crying out for David.

'You need to turn off the radio before you sleep, Kendy,' he told her not unkindly. 'It's too suggestive. Ariana's name isn't going to be announced. Do you want some hot chocolate?'

He climbed back into bed and pulled her awkwardly towards his chest, stroking her hair as he struggled to find something that would inject some rationality into her thinking. He'd fallen for Kendra because he felt she was a kindred spirit. Not given to over-reacting or displays of high emotion. She was turning into someone he didn't know or understand.

'Breathe slowly. It will calm your nervous system. You've had a panic attack. I read about them in a magazine at the dentist's. Do you need a paper bag?'

'I'm ok. It was a bad dream. I'll go round to see Sheila tomorrow. There's usually some drama in her house that will get my mind off things.'

'Good. I'm going to down to watch the snooker. Is that... ok? I'll be quiet.'

Sheila was in the middle of a shouting match with Jo when Kendra rang the bell. She could hear the volley of threats and blame from both sides.

'And don't you dare use that language with me again Joseph!'

The two women exchanged glances as a crash was heard at the back of the house.

'That boy will be the death of me. I'm hoarse from screaming at him.'

'Then don't scream. It gives him the reason to carry on acting out like a five-year-old. You need to provide the adult role model here. It's easy for me to say. My parenting skills are nothing to be proud of.'

'Kendy, stop blaming yourself for what's happened. You did everything you could for that girl and more. Drink?'

'Brandy if you've got any. Dash of soda.' She pulled out a chair and sat facing the window which had a good view of the railway station. Every time a petite girl with dark hair and clumpy black boots stepped onto the platform she thought it was her daughter.

'David thinks I should go back to the Academy.'

'Me too, to be honest. Cheese sarnie? I'm always starving after a row.'

Kendra shook her head. 'But I'll have some of those crisps.' She pointed to a pile of multi-coloured packets on the work-top.

Sheila tossed her a packet of ready-salted, startled at how quickly she wolfed them down.

'I've been thinking. You could contact the Missing People helpline. Just for a chat. They'll have a lot of experience to draw on.'

'But she's not missing. She's chosen, voluntarily, to cut herself off from us. It's not the same thing.'

'I know but maybe they could help *you*. Talk things through. Share positive results of when people have eventually come home. Give you a bit of hope. I've looked at their website. There's a section on what they call ambiguous loss. I can't remember the details but please, at least check it out.'

Kendra twiddled the stem of the glass between her fingers.

'Ok. I'll have a look.'

Jo sidled into the kitchen, unable to make eye contact with the two women.

'I'm sorry Mum. I shouldn't have said those things. Is it alright if I go out tonight with Kim and Joel?'

'Oh I see. Let me guess, the next question is… and can I have some money? What about your Saturday job at Pink Banana? Have you spent your wages already or do they pay you in ripped jeans like those you've got on? More holes than denim.'

'Nooo. I wasn't going to ask for money. But… could I borrow the car.'

'Not a chance Jo.'

'But Mum.'

Sheila picked up the warning glance from Kendra.

'Sorry love but I'll give you money for a taxi home. We'll talk about car usage at the weekend.' Jo rolled his eyes and sulked back to his room.

' Shee… do you believe in psychics and stuff?'

'Nope. Con artists the lot of them. Oh no. You're not thinking of having your palm read or have Mystic Rose do a crystal ball reading?'

'The police have used them to locate missing bodies so there's got to be something in it.'

'Kendra. You are a psychologist. You know all about cold reading, mentalism and mind trickery.'

Kendra ploughed on.

'I've been looking at this website. *Psychic Dawn*. She's reads for people all over the world.'

'People with more money than sense.' Sheila bit into her third sandwich, letting out a sigh of pleasure. 'What do you want them to do? Tell you where Rani is so you can drag her home by her hair?'

The empty glass sat between them. Kendra shook her head at the offer of a top-up.

'I want to know why she's done this. The note. It's cruel. It isn't the work of my daughter. Somebody's been brainwashing her or... or she's on drugs.'

Sheila sighed and dusted crumbs off her black T-shirt.

'Like Adam says, all she wants is some space to grow up. I know it's a drastic way of going about it but I am sure she'll come to her senses at some point. You keep telling me young adults do the craziest of things as their brains are rewiring. Take your own advice but please don't put your faith in some voodoo.'

'I think the term is woo-woo,' replied Kendra, turning up the corners of her mouth into a semblance of smile.

'You do need to go back to work and get busy again. Time's hanging too heavily. It's dragging you down. It's so easy to get caught up in some bad habit or obsession. The devil makes work for idle hands so my Dad used to say. Bless him.'

'I guess you're right. Kendra picked up her bag and made moves to leave. The conversation was making her feel dizzy. It wasn't enough to say her daughter was going through a phase and she should let her get on with it. Deep down Kendra felt there was something more sinister going on and she needed to know.

David's car was not on the drive when she got home a couple of hours later. She noticed that some late flowering dahlias had been broken off at the stem and scattered over the front lawn. He sometimes lost his cool when over stimulated but he wouldn't destroy his own work. She ran up the side of the house checking windows and the side entrance before retracing her steps to the front door.

'Someone's trying to intimidate us. It could be connected to Rani. Some kind of warning.'

'Ariana's got nothing to do with the flowers. How do you make that link? It will be hooligans coming from that school on Lox Lane. You're beginning to sound paranoid. I did find the interconnecting door from the garage to the kitchen open though. One of us forgot to lock it.'

'Don't look at me. You're the one with the memory problems.'

David pursed his lips and strode down the path to clear up the front lawns.

'I've got a call to make about work, she called. 'It will be a bit awkward so please don't disturb me.' Kendra watched him for a few moments wishing she could be more open with him.

She logged onto Psychic Dawn as she dialled the main number, relieved when the operator told she could pay by credit card rather than through her phone line.

'Putting you through to one of our psychics now.'

A prickle of excitement ran down her spine.

'Hello. This is Amber. How can I help you today?'

'I was hoping to speak to Dawn.'

'Dawn is not available today. How can I help?'

Kendra felt as if she was ringing a catalogue order line.

'I … um … My daughter is missing. Well not missing exactly. She went to London and wrote to say she was never coming home. I want to know where she is and what's going on.'

'You obviously care very deeply for your daughter. Describe her to me.'

Kendra was in full flow when all of a sudden she realised she'd walked straight into the woman's trap of hot reading. Drowning

THE FUTURE CAN'T WAIT

in the woman's mesmerising ramble, Kendra found she couldn't hang up, as if she needed to hear every last word, no matter how ridiculous. Ten minutes later, three beeps indicated the end of the call. She was fifty pounds poorer.

The notes she'd scribbled down made no sense. Anyone could have made the same vague statements. There was nothing psychic about it. Sheila was right. Desperation had driven her into the hands of a big con-artist.

CHAPTER 11

*K*endra looked through the streaks of bird muck splattered across the high window of her classroom, and watched Jim, the maintenance man, emerge from the boiler room, to have a quick puff on his e-cigarette. The sky was bloated with a promise of snow. Kendra glanced at the classroom clock. Her Personal and Social Development group were already six minutes late. Her fingers clutched a Visa bill, the numbers swimming in front of her eyes like tadpoles. Psychic Dawn £90.00, Astro-Martin £105.00, Hot Psychics £120.00 and two items she couldn't recall.

'You've gone all pale Miss. Are you alright?'

Kendra busied herself at her desk and she ushered the girls to their places, reminding them about the importance of punctuality.

'I'm fine, thank you.' She'd been half hearted about returning to work but now she was amongst lively young minds she felt a bit more grounded.

'Look, it's snowing,' said Martha. 'Can we go home early?'

'No you can't! Not unless the Principal says so.' Eyeing her student she said, 'Can you pull your skirt down a bit further and that applies to the rest of you. You know the school rules. It's a uniform and that means…'

'Yeah, yeah, we all have to look like frumps. Kim Kardashian wouldn't be seen dead in this horrible thing.' Martha reluctantly unfolded the waistband of the dark grey skirt and pulled down her bottle-green jumper with sleeves that seemed to be unravelling at the cuffs.

'Mustn't get the male teachers excited,' scoffed Leanne, throwing her books onto the desk. 'It's their problem if they can't control themselves.'

'Women have a responsibility to choose appropriate behaviour too. I bet your parents don't know you roll your skirts up as soon as you leave the house but it's nothing new. In the sixties we did the same. It was like a two fingers up to the establishment. We live in different times now but ladies, rules are rules and you are expected to comply.'

'But Miss…'

Kendra stuffed the credit card bill into her handbag before raising her hand to say discussion closed.

'For this last lesson of term, I'm going to pose a question. Fast forward to the future and imagine you are a mother.' Kendra flashed up a slide.

Suppressed giggles rippled round the room. All eyes turned to Sasha who was pregnant.

'Your child has gone missing.'

'You mean like Madeleine McCann.'

'No, I mean an older child, let's say between eighteen and twenty-five. Someone who leaves home and it's been six months since you last heard from them.'

'That's not a child. That's a grown up. You can do what you like then. I can't wait to leave home. My mum's an evil bitch.'

'Jody. That's enough.' Kendra threw her a warning look before continuing. 'Legally you can make your own choices but I'd like you to think about the work you've done on the changing brain and think of the moral implications of behaviour and its impact on other people. How would you feel if this happened to you?'

'It wouldn't happen Miss. You can't go missing these days if you've got a smart phone. It tracks you all the time.'

'Yeah Miss. You couldn't even commit murder and get away with it.'

'Stop shouting out. You know the rule.'

'Social media can find you anywhere. I tried to make my Facebook private but some geek hacked in and sent me disgusting pictures of his...'

'Stop right there or I will ask you to leave the class.' Kendra paused to clear her throat. 'If you can't be mature about this then I'll give you some exam questions.'

Silence bounced off the walls.

'Right. Thank you. Let's say all communication devices had been de-activated. Try to get into the mind of this young adult. Happy home life. No apparent problems. What would drive someone to do this? Cut off from family. I'll give you ten minutes to discuss in groups of four and make notes under these headings.' Kendra flicked to the next slide.

Low murmurings punctuated with outbursts of giggling made Kendra feel positive about moving away from the tightly controlled curriculum. She would argue that it was applying knowledge to real life problems if questioned. Through the corner of her eye she saw Maurice lurking outside the open door trying to catch her attention.

'We're closing the school at lunchtime,' he told her. 'The school bus service rang. The snow's piling up in some of the Warwickshire villages. Yours is the last class, so let them go when they've finished.' Kendra backed away from the smell of alcohol on his breath.

His eyes strayed over to the screen then back to Kendra.

'Interesting,' he said before shuffling out of the room.

'Finished?'

She turned to the whiteboard, a marker pen at the ready.

'Drugs, boyfriend, joined a cult, can't hack it anymore, suicide, murder, spontaneous combustion...'

'Fugue?' suggested Martha, twiddling her pen.

'Creep,' hissed a girl behind her.

'Fugue? Interesting idea. It's too rare though. It happens following a trauma when the brain shuts everything out and you forget your previous life.'

'It's like your memory gets wiped Miss. I watched a film about it.'

'Anymore ideas?'

'You get fed up with your life with everyone on your case about uni or jobs so you run away. People do it all the time. My friend's dad did it. They've never heard from him since.'

'Tosser.'

'Ladies. What have we said about use of bad language in this room? Do you want detention Sarina?'

'No Miss. It's the Christmas holidays.'

'So apologise to the class and to me.'

Sarina pursed her lips and looked defiantly around her.

'Your choice Sarina.'

'I've not said anything Miss.'

'Silence is a choice.'

'OK. Sorry for being rude.'

'Would any of you vanish into the mist and cut off from your family and friends?'

The girls looked at each other.

'You don't know until you get to that point. I don't think it's planned. You pack and then poof... you're gone. I might go for a bit but I couldn't hurt my Mum. She's got enough problems with our Emily.'

Kendra pushed them on their thoughts and ideas for a bit longer until she realised they were giving her curious looks. She looked at the clock and hearing the din coming from other classrooms, ended the lesson.

'Have a good Christmas, Miss,' they shouted above the noisy exodus.

As soon as the board was wiped clean and the used papers discarded into the recycle box, Kendra closed the door and sniffed hard. The thought of Christmas with David locked away with some new gadget, expecting a full roast dinner, stuck in her throat like a snapped wishbone. She was dreading it without Rani.

The staffroom was empty apart from Harry Clarke, retired head of chemistry who'd come back to part-time teaching after the death of his wife. He looked up from his steam railway magazine.

'Kettle's just boiled.' His lower denture clicked when he spoke. 'I don't see you in here much these days.' Kendra dunked a camomile tea bag into a mug of hot water, yelping as boiling water splashed against her wrist.

'Run it under cold water. My Moira always used to say that.'

Kendra did as he suggested, blowing on the burning skin.

'I heard about your daughter from one of the staff. I'm really sorry.'

'Let me guess. That'll be Sheila.' Kendra gave him a wry smile as she took a seat next to him.

'If it's any help, we went through something similar with our Jack. He said he was going to Thailand after his finals and we didn't hear another word for five years. He turned up on the doorstep one day as if nothing had happened. Talk about the prodigal son.'

Kendra sipped at the tasteless liquid before pouring it down the sink.

'His mother was demented with worry. I'm convinced it was the grief that took her before her time. I can't quite forgive Jack even though he's got two wonderful children and a lovely wife who spoil me rotten.'

'That was very selfish of him.'

'We don't talk about it. I can see it causes him pain but…'

Harry shook his head and swallowed hard. 'I don't know what my Moira would make of it all now, I really don't.'

An unsteady flow of air whooshed from Kendra's lungs. *Five years*.

'I'm sorry if I've been intrusive. I wanted to say, get on with your life as best you can. My wife was consumed by grief and it made her ill. She didn't want to fight the cancer if Jack wasn't coming home.'

The staff room was filling up with teachers, rubbing their hands at the thought of a long break. Maurice followed them in.

'Can I have your attention please? Geoff? Lottie?'

'I don't want to put a damper on the holidays before they've started, but there's something I need to say. On the doors of the woodwork sheds there's some very offensive graffiti. Shirin Patel's father came to see me about it. He's one of our governors. It's been photographed and the police have been informed. Jim will be cleaning it off today and an additional CCTV camera will be connected.'

Maurice paused to dab his temple with a crumpled handkerchief. Kendra thought he might be about to have a stroke.

'I can't stress how serious this is. We need to look out for all forms of political and religious extremism and nip it in the proverbial bud. So… Happy Christmas everyone.'

'Shouldn't that be Happy Holidays, Maurice?'

'Some of us have to come in next week,' muttered Geoff, waving his hand over his overflowing desk.

'You coming for a drink at the Nag?' Sheila poked her head round the door.

'Where've you sprung from? You escaped Maurice's lecture.'

'No, I heard him. His fat butt was blocking the doorway so I waited outside. He's got a point though. I'd not given it much thought.'

'Gone are the days when we could teach and not worry about politics. Internal or International. Sorry Sheila but I'm going home. I'm drained.'

'Come on. I'll drive you back. Just a drink and natter.'

Kendra shook her head as she pulled on her woollen gloves. 'Come round for lunch sometime,' she said before striding out to fill her lungs with crisp December air. An inch of crisp snow had settled on the grass verges with a promise of more to come. By the time she got home, Kendra felt her head spinning and sparking like a Catherine wheel. Turning on the radio, she caught the end of a programme talking about the police having some success using remote viewing to find people whether alive or dead. She turned up the volume.

'That's a bit loud isn't it?' Her husband reached out to turn it down.

'Shush David. I was listening to that.'

'Oh.' Her husband stood in the middle of the kitchen scratching his chin. 'You're addicted to the news. Ariana isn't going to be mentioned. I told you that the other night. Why not put some music on?'

'I'm not addicted,' she muttered, lifting an empty milk carton from the fridge.

'Why do you keep doing this?' She shook the carton at him.

'There's a drop in there.'

Kendra glared at him before tipping it up onto the floor. Specks of milk spattered across the tiles. 'Yeah. Right. Two drops actually.' Kendra wrenched open the cupboard doors rifling through the tins and packets until she found a box of out of date herbal teas.

'Why are you angry?' David took off his glasses and began to wipe them in slow circular movements. An awkward silence wedged itself between them. David tried again. 'Do you want to go out somewhere? I've got an hour to spare.'

'No,' she called from half way up the stairs. She didn't want to be in the same room with him. His lack of sensitivity to her feelings was triggering a waterfall of negative thoughts about him even though he was just being his usual self.

Sitting at her desk, Kendra flexed her fingers over the keyboard to tap out remote viewing into the search engine. The Wikipedia entry was clear about it being a pseudoscience and no evidence had been provided to show it worked but part of Kendra's mind dismissed that as she searched for the names of practitioners who were experienced in finding missing people. Many of them were located in the States and offered professionally filmed videos of their work on You Tube.

As the hours ticked by, she pored over the profiles of people who boasted their track record in finding lost keys, bodies in rivers, ideal homes to buy and those who were plain crazy, saying they could locate aliens and fairies in the back garden.

Kendra lifted her arms above her head to release the tension and looked out across the road. She conjured up a memory of her daughter hanging around at the bus stop with friends on a Saturday afternoon to go on a shopping spree or to the cinema. She would look up and wave before boarding the bus giving Kendra the peace of mind to potter in the garden or curl up with a book knowing she'd be back eager to share stories and lark around as they made dinner together.

About to log out, Kendra's eye swept across the site to a pop-up. *All Seeing Sally. International Visionary.* She fought the urge to click on the link by moving away from her iPad to tidy up her study but her gaze strayed over to the invitation to check out the website. As if tangled up in a spider's web, Kendra finally succumbed. *All Seeing Sally* would only take payment via the phone line at £1.50 a minute. The woman on the end of the line told Kendra not to give her any information but to hold something of the missing person in her hand so she could pick up the vibration.

'*Mm. I see a young woman wearing a ring with a pale blue stone.*' Kendra immediately thought turquoise. She heard the scratching of a pencil on paper and assumed the woman was sketching. In her impatience, Kendra pushed the psychic to tell her the location but the woman rambled on telling her to be calm and patient in a syrupy voice.

'For fuck's sake, where is my daughter?'

The line went dead. With a finger paused over the redial button, Kendra swayed in her chair as she realised what she was doing. The urge to call somebody else to ask the same question was like the alcoholic fighting with a bottle of whisky.

Dragging herself away to splash her face with cold water took huge mental effort. It was the deep, slow breathing she'd learned at yoga that helped take the edge off her urge to get another fix. That and the fact she could hear David calling up the stairs.

CHAPTER 12

'Who do you keep calling? It's daytime rates.'

'I'm thinking about doing another degree so I'm doing some research. You're right about me needing to find a new focus.' Kendra was aware of how tetchy she sounded. She snapped down the lid of her laptop and shoving her feet back into her slippers ushered her husband out of the door.

'I thought I might re-decorate this room since you spend so much time up here. It's the sunniest in the house.' David ran his hand down some flaking paint on the windowsill.

Kendra looked round at ivory cream walls, her eye drawn to the odd scuff mark by the desk and a blue crayon mark. She ran the tip of her tongue over dry lips. She'd caught Rani drawing circles on the wall in different colours and had pulled the crayon from her hand. She'd screamed and thrown herself on the floor, holding her breath. *Maybe I was too strict with her. Maybe this is my fault.*

'Kendy? What do you think?'

'Mm?'

The box room, with its sloping ceiling, had become her sanctuary, especially now she'd installed a foldable daybed.

'It's fine as it is. Those seventies curtains need to go. Psychedelic is out. I know they were your mother's but I don't think she'd mind, do you?'

'My mother has been dead for fifteen years,' he replied with no hint of humour.

David followed her down the stairs, his woodwork apron clanking with tools.

'Why do you need another degree at your age? Will you get funding? University fees are astronomical.'

'No idea about funding but I'm interested in parapsychology and what drives people to it.'

'You mean the supernatural? Because they're stupid. They don't understand science.'

'Interesting hypothesis.'

'Anyway it's all be done before hasn't it?'

Kendra stood on the wooden floor of the dining room and bent forward into a relaxing yoga pose to ease the compressed feeling in her back. She counted her inhalations and exhalations before slowly bringing her arms up towards the ceiling.

'Now I've got acid,' she groaned, filling a glass with iced water. 'I don't know what research field hasn't been covered which is why I am looking into it.'

He gave her a quizzical look.

'Seems a bit pointless.'

'Thanks for the boost of confidence.'

David slapped his hands together and gazed into the distance.

'Adam called. He wanted to know why you've been avoiding him.'

Kendra pulled out a bunch of carrots from the salad box and began grating them into a bowl.

'I haven't been avoiding him. I'll call him this week. Damn.' Kendra ran her cut knuckle under the tap.

'Are we putting up a Christmas tree?' David took the shrivelled carrot from her hand and said, 'See, if you do it this way you won't scrape your skin off.'

'If you want to. Do you think Rani will come home? She loves Christmas.' Kendra made a big thing of wrapping a plaster round her finger.

'I don't know. Adam says don't get your hopes up.'

'You mean she's not going to jump out of a cracker and say, Hello Mum, Joke.' Kendra rested her hands on the worktop as a wave of anxiety whooshed up through her body and settled in her chest. She closed her eyes, waiting for it to pass.

'What are these carrots for? I want beans on toast tonight.'

'Fine. I'll finish the coleslaw and you can have it tomorrow. I'm not that hungry.'

Kendra freed up his hands and pulled them around her waist. She needed to be held, to have her hair stroked and be told her nightmare would end but it was like interacting with a robot. David had never tuned into her emotional needs, seeing the world, as he did, in pure logical terms. She clutched his shirt trying hard not to cry. 'David, she will come home won't she? I can't bear this.' He patted her hand as he mentally calculated how long it would take to get a mission to Saturn. He was interrupted by the phone.

'David Blackmore. Hello? Hello? I can't hear you.'

'Do 1471. See who called.'

'Number withheld. Why do people do that?'

'One of those call centres probably.'

Kendra noticed a shadow cross his face. 'David? What's up?'

'I can smell burning.'

Kendra was glad it was the last day of term for the staff. Maurice had gone to China to speak at some conference and now that the students had finished, she'd managed to get all her marking up to date and paperwork completed. With a sigh of relief, she dived into one of the high backed armchairs in the staff room which the Head of Resources had got free from a house clearance and rustled open her copy of the Guardian. A piece about Saudi women being given the vote and running for election in local councils caught her attention. It seemed incongruous in the light of jihadi terrorists either treating women as sex slaves or stoning them for adultery.

Other staff slowly filtered in, complaining about the upcoming Ofsted inspection which put everyone in a mood and had them fantasising about their escape plans. Celine, the French teacher, had smugly announced she was leaving to go back to her family villa in Provence. It had the effect of winding everybody up. Especially Sheila.

'I could wipe that grin from her perfectly made-up face,' she snarled. 'Oh by the way. Jo's got some news for you. Said something about a Farah Jamieson he's tracked down on Facebook. One of Rani's old friends.'

'I've not heard of her.' Kendra folded the newspaper and stuffed it in her bag.

'Might be worth 'friending' her and asking if she knows anything. You could say you've lost her phone number or something.'

'I don't really use Facebook. Rani set up an account for me ages ago but it's not my thing.'

'Just an idea.' Sheila drained her coffee mug. 'I've got so much to do. Rich is coming home for the holidays.' Her hand flew to her mouth. 'I'm sorry. That was bloody insensitive of me.'

'It's ok. I hope you have a good time with everyone together. Tony's back as well isn't he?' Kendra worked at keeping her voice light.

Sheila nodded. 'Come round Boxing Day. You don't have to be on your own.'

'I'm not on my own. There's David.'

'I know but… well you know what I mean.'

Kendra pointed to the magazine Sheila was rolling around in her hand.

'Can I have a quick look?'

'You thinking of doing some interior design? Great idea. I can help.'

Kendra thumbed her way to the back pages pausing at the monthly horoscope. Sheila craned her neck to look.

'Oh Kendy. I can't believe you are still falling for this claptrap. It's damned irresponsible of people writing this rubbish. It gets vulnerable people hooked. Look at this. Aries. That's me. *Venus and Mars come together in the house of relationships. Jo will continue to be a pain in the ass. Expects some ups and downs. Yeah. Tony's home. A time to get more intimate. Not a chance.'*

'You're such a cynic.'

'So what does yours say?'

Librans love harmony and what better time than to bring family and friends together this Christmas.

'See, it's so general,' she cut in. 'They get paid for writing this drivel. I really, really hope Rani gets in touch even if it's just with a few lines on a card. Hell fire. Look at the time. I'm meeting Jo to buy his present. I don't even know what it's supposed to be.'

Kendra switched on her iPad and flicking through her diary to find her password, logged onto Facebook. Several Farah Jamiesons around the world popped up but it was easy to see the one she needed to speak to. She had the distinctive Persian nose.

Birmingham City Centre was rammed with shoppers, not caring what injuries they might inflict with their giant carrier bags.

Kendra rubbed her right knee when a woman, in a bright orange coat and red hair pushed her out of the way on the escalators in the Bull Ring centre. The smell of perspiring bodies and a hint of weed was enough to turn Kendra's stomach. Fighting a light headed feeling, she pushed through the crowd towards the nearest exit, oblivious to the hurl of verbal insults.

Once outside, she sat on a low wall, dropped her head to her knees and tried to slow her rapid heartbeat. Blurred images of shoes passed in front of her eyes: clumpy trainers, colourful sandals, smart wedges, polished brogues, lime green laces, kitten heels, stomping, clomping and tapping their way over the once gleaming flagstones. Kendra hauled herself up and brushing down her trousers headed for the train station, her overloaded senses unable to cope with the noise and smells. She stuffed half a granola bar into her mouth in the hope it might settle her stomach.

A security alarm had been sounded earlier so she found herself joining the hordes of evacuated passengers on the concourse. She tried calling David to ask him to collect her from Sutton station but he didn't answer. A young woman with a pushchair gave her a mouthful for pushing in through the barrier, her words stinging in Kendra's ears as she ran down to the platform.

She needed the safety of her study and the relief she got from dialling one of the psychic hotlines even if it was only for a couple of minutes. Without pausing to take off her coat, Kendra bolted up the stairs and shut the door. Her laptop leapt into action reminding her to make a mental note to erase her browsing history. She doubted David would be checking up on her. It wasn't in his nature but she had to be sure her frequent search for the perfect clairvoyant couldn't be traced. This time she tried somebody calling himself a psychic detective. His website boasted his successes including helping to solve some high profile cases to do with children.

'I believe you can finding missing people?'

'That is what I do but I work with the police, not individuals.'

'If it's a question of money.'

'What's the problem?'

Kendra told him in a rush of words which sounded ridiculous to her ears.

'Your daughter isn't missing. She's chosen to cut off all contact with you and she's an adult.'

'But maybe she's been kidnapped. Or dead.' The dam of tears burst open as Kendra whispered her deepest fear.

'I'm sorry I can't help you.'

Kendra felt her breath leave her body. 'Please. I just want to know where she is and if she's safe. I'm her mother. This isn't like her. She may have joined a cult or got involved with some extremist group.'

'Look. I've been contacted by a Pakistani family in Wales whose daughter disappeared. They had evidence that she'd gone to Turkey to cross the Syrian border but there was nothing I or anybody else could do. Maybe you should talk to the police or get a private detective. You sound in a lot of pain. You know sometimes people just reappear. Can I give you some advice?'

Kendra felt her stomach walls contract.

'OK.'

'Don't get hooked on calling psychics who do readings. They will tell you anything you want to hear and use a pile of tricks to get information out of you. I must go. Good luck.'

A ping announced a new email. Farah Jamieson had accepted her friend request. Noticing she was available to chat she typed in a message. Within seconds she received a reply she didn't want.

How's Rani? I haven't heard from her in ages. I think she's closed her Facebook account. Can you nudge her to get in touch with me?' Then she was gone.

CHAPTER 13

$\mathcal{D}$espite it being the most hellish time of the year to travel, Kendra waited on the cold platform at Moor Street for the Marylebone train. It was fast, clean, comfortable and normally not overcrowded. Commuters preferred the faster route to Euston. Kendra only ever went to London on business trips but a psychic called Rose was so convincing that her "viewing" of Rani in a French patisserie near St. Paul's was accurate that Kendra felt compelled to find out for herself.

Hunched into a window seat, she pulled out a book on cold reading and mentalism which she hid in a magazine away from prying eyes. As she scanned the account of a woman who'd become addicted to calling the hotlines she felt a wave of heat rush through her body. Not wanting to read anymore, she stuffed it back in her bag and she stared out of the window for the rest of the journey.

As the train pulled into Leamington Spa, an overexcited group of students from the University of Warwick piled into her carriage. They seemed to consume all the oxygen in the carriage. Paralysed with fear at the volume of people pouring down the escalator for the Tube she frantically looked around for the taxi rank. The terror alert was high and images of being trapped underground loomed large in her mind.

The driver weaved his way in and out of the bumper to bumper to traffic suggesting Kendra walked the last few hundred yards to the cathedral to save some money. Checking her paper map, she hurried along the pavement until she came to Patisserie Du Cite. It was a cliché of old leather armchairs arranged around tables decorated with small bunches of holly and mistletoe in a glass vase. Kendra was disappointed to find they were plastic. She put in her order before dropping her bags by an armchair near the window. Silver and gold lanterns hung from the ceiling, swaying as the door opened to let in more customers, none of them resembling her daughter. As the adrenaline cooled in her veins, Kendra realised she was on a fool's mission.

An hour later, as the lunch queue snaked outside the door and down the length of the window, she felt pressed to vacate her seat. On impulse, she pulled out a picture of her Rani and showed it to the waitress who was already clearing her table. The girl said no. The manager came down the stairs to check on the seating and shook his head apologetically.

Kendra tramped the streets behind clusters of tourists, her radar honed to spot anyone who looked like her daughter. Red-eyed and defeated, she headed back to Birmingham and to a trail of dirt on the kitchen floor and a pile of unwashed dishes in the sink. Her rage burst from its chains as David came into the kitchen. She picked up a mug to smash against the wall, protesting loudly when he calmly took it from her hand and placed it in the dishwasher.

'I was going to do it,' he said. 'Then suggest we go to the pub for dinner and you can tell me all about London. You look exhausted.'

Christmas Day 2015

Despite making a promise to God about going to church and doing more for others in return for ending her torment, Kendra wasn't surprised there was no reciprocity. David couldn't see the point of the religious festival, although he enjoyed the food, telling anyone that would listen, that gods of any flavour were a product of an overactive imagination and fear. It was why she'd stopped accepting invitations from friends.

'It's egotistical to think that we don't die like the rest of the natural world but get admitted to some fairy tale land,' he'd told the head of religious education at the one and only staff party he'd attended.

Lunch was a solemn affair. Kendra could hear David's jaw rhythmically chomp on some undercooked carrots. A piece of dry turkey stuck in her throat, eased only by a third glass of wine. The Brussel sprouts she hated so much looked soggy and unappetising but that didn't deter her husband as he spooned seconds onto his plate.

She tuned out his monologue on his latest telescopic modifications, brooding on what her daughter might be doing. *Is she thinking about me? Does she regret what she's done? Maybe she thinks she's got herself into a corner and can't back down.* No matter how hard she tried to stop her thoughts from circling like vultures in her head, Rani's eyes stared into hers. Memories popped up like targets in a shooting range. The more Kendra tried to knock them down, the more they laughed in her face. She pushed away her plate.

'Is there any pudding?'

'There's a small rum thing to go in the microwave.' She looked at David wondering how he could be constantly eating yet his clothes hung loosely on him.

'Any ice-cream?' He rubbed his stomach and winced. 'Maybe later. Should we walk this off?'

She wanted to disappear into the park by herself but she couldn't walk out on him since he was making an effort for her.

'Don't you have stuff you want to do?' she asked hopefully. 'I don't mind.'

'Not today. I want to spend it with you. What time will Adam be calling? Maybe we could go after that.'

Kendra looked at the clock as she cleared the table. The phone rang. 'That's him now. Can you answer it?'

'I'll clean up. You go and speak to him.'

Kendra wiped her hands down her trousers and sat down on the sofa in the living room. Jigsaw pieces lay over the floor and there was a fresh stain on the corner of the rug. She frowned.

'Adam?'

'Happy Christmas Ma. Have you pulled the crackers yet?' He laughed when she said she'd forgotten to buy any.

'Alison's feeling a bit queasy this morning so we might be holding off on the traditional. All she wants is yoghurt and garlic. She's still conked from last night. We went to some friends in downtown Boston. So what have you got planned for the rest of the day.'

'We're going for a walk somewhere.'

'You sound really down. It must be tough for you this year.'

'Mm. You haven't......?'

'Not a dicky bird. I've been following up a few leads but nothing. It's snowing here. You should have come over.'

They chatted about nothing in particular until Kendra could hear Alison calling out in the background.

'I'll let you go. Bye love.'

Kendra unplugged the phone from its socket. She didn't want him calling back. Talking to Adam had unsettled her.

'Ready?'

David appeared in his parka which he'd zipped up to his chin.

'Where shall we go?' He tied and retied his scarf until it was angled over his coat to his satisfaction.

Kendra looked out of the window. It was a gloomy day but not cold and the sky had a strange pink glow behind the clouds.

'Cannock Chase? It's not too far is it?'

'Fourteen and a quarter miles. Shall we take a flask and some cake? You did make one didn't you?'

'No I didn't,' she sighed. 'I bought some iced slices. Don't look so hard done by.'

As they sat in the car, waiting for the engine to warm up, Kendra looked over at the fat, overdressed pine trees in the bay windows of the houses opposite. She wondered what was going on behind those wreathed doors. Was it all happy families or were dark secrets of anger and blame being acted out under the influence of too much drink?

The roads were quiet the way David liked them to be. He seemed to be more relaxed as he whistled Christmas tunes along with the radio. With a final burst of God Rest Ye Merry Gentlemen,' he turned into the car park and clapped his hands.

'Nobody around. Goodo.' He checked the map and retrieved a whistle and compass from the glove compartment. Kendra's phone rang out. David frowned and told her to leave it.

'Hello, hello?' Nothing but a crackling sound. She felt a cold trickle of sweat down the back of her neck.

'Rani? Is that you? Blast,' she muttered staring at the screen.

'Check the call log,' her husband suggested, carefully pulling on his woollen gloves.

'No number shown. It's Rani. I'm sure of it. Didn't you take a dead call yesterday? It has to be her. She wouldn't not call me on Christmas day.'

'If it is, she'll try again. Come on let's walk. The temperature has dropped two degrees already.'

David strode on ahead through the frost covered trees, slapping his hands together. A dog barking in the distance disturbed the stillness of the woods. As they got deeper amongst the Corsican and Scots pine, Kendra checked her phone to find she had no reception.

'We need to go back to the car. She might be trying to get through.'

'I want to finish this circuit first.'

Kendra grabbed his arm, waving her phone in front of his face. Her chest felt tight as she struggled to speak.

'No reception. Look. You finish your walk, I'm going back.'

The muscles around David's mouth tightened. She sensed he was going to have his equivalent of a temper tantrum. He bent down to pick up a twig and snapped it into pieces. His mouth was set in a stubborn line.

'Fine, well I'm going back. You please yourself.'

He stomped along the trail behind her, but when she tripped over a tree root he left her to pick herself up. Kendra wanted to shout at him to stop being a selfish pig. She limped towards the car, waving her phone in the air. *Ring damn you.* She understood the reality "of being beside oneself"'- outside looking in on this strange, demented woman with damp hair clinging to her face and shouting at an oblong bit of metal.

'It'll be one of those computerised call centres again. They work all year,' he told her, putting the car into reverse. 'Don't get so worked up.'

'How dare you talk to me like that? After everything I've gone through. No, correction, going through. Let's go home eh?'

It was getting late. A necklace of hail trimmed the grass verges. She felt chilled, empty and alone as if her heart was dangling over a bottomless chasm. Nobody understood how she was feeling. Nobody really cared despite their pretty words.

ᕔ THE FUTURE CAN'T WAIT

They travelled back home in silence punctuated only by sudden traffic announcements of an accident on the M6. The sky was tar-black, a perfect backdrop for the huge moon. She pointed it out to her husband.

'It's the first full moon on Christmas Day since 1977. We won't have another until 2034. It's only full for the moment that it is 180 degrees opposite the sun in ecliptic longitude. It's the last one of the year so it's called the Full Cold Moon.'

'Pretty isn't it?'

David frowned as if he couldn't relate the word to the science.

'You can see the twin stars of Castor and Pollux. Look, over there.'

By the time they arrived back, Kendra was almost asleep. David had talked nonstop about Metonic cycles throwing in some complex equations to keep it interesting. He piled a plate with left overs and disappeared into his shed without a word. Like an obsessed teenager, Kendra kept checking her phone, willing it ring. *Please Rani. Please.*

She lit some tea lights in her study and turned on the side lamp which threw out a pink glow. The local radio station was playing some golden oldies from the eighties which brought back memories of Hassan and the flat they'd shared in a rough part of the inner city. Christmas had meant nothing to him so he'd spent the day working on his master's dissertation. She'd cooked some Persian food and they'd watched a documentary about the Shah.

Kendra spotted a book she'd ordered online - 'Easy Tarot for Beginners'. She sat on the floor and spread out the pack of cards that came with it, checking them against the explanations in the book. Confused, she logged onto a YouTube video and watched a woman with big Celtic rings on her fingers draw some cards for her astrology sign.

Lost in the magic, Kendra heard the church clock chime ten. She rubbed her eyes, sore from watching a dozen different tarot readers from all round the world in the hope that something might resonate. A jumble of words and promises that the universe would deliver meant nothing in Kendra's rational mind but it didn't stop her from believing that there was something meaningful in the messages. She decided she wasn't skilled enough to interpret them. Yet.

Pangs of hunger cut into her concentration. A picture of bananas and custard flashed into her mind. Nursery food.

'What you are looking for?' David was seated at the dining table, spooning cold Christmas pudding into his mouth.

'Custard.'

'You don't like custard.'

'Well I do now.' She moved tins around on the shelf.

'I had the last tin. With two mince pies.'

'All of it? The whole tin?'

Kendra's jaw dropped. Her eyes narrowed as she glared at him. David's face was blank.

'You told me to finish it up as you hate custard. Said it reminded you of school dinners.'

'Right I see. You know David. All our conversations these days are about food. Shopping for it, preparing it, cooking and eating it. We don't talk about important things. You bombard me with scientific facts, knowing full well I don't understand, but you don't talk about … us. Have you got nothing to say at all about your step-daughter? Me? Can't you see what's happening to us all?'

David stared at her for a moment. 'No,' he said. 'Don't think so.'

Kendra grabbed his space magazine with two hands and ripped it in half.

'That's what's happening to us.'

CHAPTER 14

*Y*ou are coming, aren't you? New Year's Day lunch is a ritual in this house. It wouldn't be the same without you after all these years.'

Kendra rubbed at a throbbing pain under her eyebrows. The last thing she wanted to do was face a barrage of questions from Sheila's intense and self-absorbed friends who talked about nothing other than house prices and their baby Einstein and Mozart reincarnations.

'I'm not very good company Sheila. David won't come anyway. You know what he's like.'

'Just for an hour or so. You can go when you've had enough. Please.'

Greg, her new tarot reader had told her to take back her power and learn to say no.

'OK just for an hour.'

She hung up, annoyed that she'd given in to Sheila's pushing.

As Kendra busied herself stripping the tree of its lights, her eye caught sight of a figure in a dark jacket with an upturned collar staring into her window from across the road. She carefully detached the silver baubles from the tree, yelping as yet another pine needle stabbed her finger, whilst letting him know he'd been seen.

'Vesta, get off.' She moved the cat out of the pile of tinsel, an uneasy feeling pooling in the pit of her stomach. Opening the front door to take out the rubbish, she walked to the end of the drive and peered down the road. There was nobody around other than a man running after a little boy freewheeling downhill on his bike.

The books Adam had sent her for Christmas lay on the hall table. She ran her hand over the dark red cover of one of them, keen to read about Carl Jung's ideas on synchronicity. She was fascinated by his idea that things didn't happen by chance but as a result of meaningful coincidences in time. Adam had warned her not to take Jung's interest in astrology too seriously.

'I'll cut the tree up and take it to the recycling tip. David dragged it to the front and began attacking it with the secateurs. 'Why are you dressed up?'

'I'm going to Sheila's do. I take it you don't want to come along?'

'Me?' His eyebrows shot up in surprise. 'No thank you. Will you be long?'

'I don't know David. Stop trying to monitor everything I do.' Kendra gave an extra punch to the cushions as she tidied the living room. 'Clear the paths if you're looking for jobs. There's a dangerous patch of ice by the garage and the boiler needs some adjustment. The water's lukewarm.'

'Saved by the bell,' said Sheila, pulling Kendra into the overheated hall. Angry voices could be heard from the kitchen.

'Jo and Tony are driving me to commit crime. They're like a couple of kangaroos squaring up to each other.'

Kendra balanced on one foot then the other as she took off her boots and slipped her feet into a pair of blue satin shoes with silver sparkles. Taking outdoor shoes off before entering a house was a habit left over from what she called her Iranian days.

THE FUTURE CAN'T WAIT

'Love that dress. Blue is so you.' Sheila fingered the soft material of the skirt. 'You're too skinny,' she said with a frown. She reached out to grab Jo's sleeve. 'What's in that glass?'

'Coke.'

'And what else?'

'Ice,' he grinned. 'Hey, Willow. There's some of that non-alcoholic red in the kitchen. You can't party on water for fuck's sake.'

'Jo, what have I told you about your language. Stop showing off like a five-year-old. Come on through Kendra and get a drink.'

A text buzzed in on Sheila's phone.

'Bloody typical. You remember Hilary and Hamish Tucker? Lived at Lilac House, round the corner from you? They're not coming. Some family issue. They do this every time. We've all got bloody family issues,' muttered Sheila, shouting out as her wrist caught the hot oven door. She placed a tray on the work surface and licked her scorched skin.

'It so easy to bail out on people these days. Quick text to say, "Marriage over."'

'Ha. One day they'll be a device which can send a message from the grave. 'Hi all, in case you hadn't heard, I'm dead.'

'With the way technology's going...'

Sheila studied her friend's expression.

'Nothing from Rani?'

Kendra shook her head and told her about the aborted phone calls.

'I'm really sorry. But hey, it's a new year and new possibilities.'

'Is the food ready love? I think everyone's a bit peckish. Hello Kendra. Long time, no see.' Sheila's husband was six foot four with arms like nutcrackers. He embraced Kendra so tightly she had to fight for breath.

'I'm nipping down to Bargain Booze to get some more beer.'
Tony jangled his keys in his hand.

'Well avoid talking to some man about some dog will you? I
need you here.'

'Still doesn't trust me,' Tony winked at Kendra and whistled his
way through the front door.

Kendra followed the other guests into the dining room and
perched on the wide window ledge which gave a clear view of the
garden. Several of Sheila's friends in loud frocks to match their
strident voices surged towards the groaning table to fork Parma
ham, salads, antipasti and hors d'oeuvres onto white china plates.

Sheila's signature dish of boeuf bourguignon with rosemary
took pride of place alongside an overflowing bowl of sticky rice.
Kendra wondered if it was possible to be a rice snob. If so, then
she took first prize. Only the finest Persian rice, with every grain
separate and fluffy and coloured with a hint of saffron ever graced
her table. She and Rani had joked about it many times.

Kendra wanted to go home. Greg had promised he was online
from midday. She had to talk to him. It was all she could think
about.

'Have you known Sheila long?' said a woman with a severe
black bob and heavy eye liner. 'She taught my daughter in year
ten. Brilliant artist you know.'

'Kendra teaches social sciences at the Academy,' Sheila cut in,
dipping a bread stick into some guacamole, catching the drip in
her hand. 'Psychology. She's an expert on the teenage brain.'

'Psychology, amazing,' drawled the woman. Kendra thought she
was missing long black gloves and a cigarette holder.

'So you're the one to ask about why kids turn into monsters the
minute the clock strikes thirteen. My Cecilia is simply vile. She
dyed her hair bright purple and has got a tattoo on her shoulder.

She thinks I don't know.'

'Teens are difficult. You have to be patient and let them find their own path through.' Flashing an apologetic smile at Sheila, she made her excuses to leave.

'Jo's making coffees and handing out the truffles. Stay for a bit longer. You can see why I need you,' she said through the corner of her mouth.

'Jo? JO?'

Kendra winced as Sheila's shrill voice shot up the staircase.

Her son and a frail looking girl with waist length red hair sidled out of his bedroom.

'I'm not going to ask what you've been doing but get down here and man this barista contraption. People are waiting for hot drinks.'

'I'm Willow,' said the girl, offering Kendra her cold fingers. 'I'm a white witch.'

'Really?'

The girl sat at the foot of the stairs to examine her silver nails.

'Puppy dog's tails? That sort of thing?'

Willow scrutinised Kendra with dark blue eyes. 'You're hurting. That's why you mock. I make spells to bring people together. Lovers who have parted. Husbands who've vanished.'

'Do you? Right. Well done. I'm sure there's a lot of call for your services, Willow. Pleasure to meet you. Shee? I'm off.'

'Take no notice of her. I don't know where Jo finds them. Last girlfriend was a body artist.'

Kendra was relieved to wriggle out of her dress and pull on some jogging bottoms. David was dozing in front of a natural history programme but Greg wasn't online when she logged on. She banged her fists on the desk and slammed down the lid of her laptop. *Where the fuck are you Greg? We had an agreement.*

'Damn.' She paced the floor in an effort to calm her breathing. 'Damn, damn.'

A week later

Grumpy faces filled the staffroom when Kendra arrived for work. The driveway had been cleared of snow but the forecast promised a fresh fall during the day.

'The part-timer's arrived,' announced Geoff, tucking a newspaper under his arm.

Kendra ignored him as she flicked through her file. The thought of teaching basic human emotions to Year Tens made her heart plummet. They were good students but the subject material seemed dull compared to Kendra's growing interest in the paranormal. She bumped into Maurice who was fiddling with his trousers and peering through her classroom door.

'Are you looking for me?'

'Can you come and see me at lunchtime. We need to have a chat.'

'What about? I'm teaching till one and then I've got a doctor's appointment.'

'It won't take long. My office? It's important.'

The morning dragged on in a miserable January apathy. Mock exams were looming and it seemed that very few of her students had done much work over the holidays. Apart from a lone Santa clinging to a forgotten piece of twine over the doorway, the pale green classroom walls were devoid of the tinsel and paper chains her students had pinned up eagerly before the holiday. Rather than a stimulating place of study, it felt more like a hospital waiting room.

'We've done all this before Miss. I'm fed-up of hearing about the amygdala.'

'Well if you think you're the expert now Marcia, you give us all a summary. Come to the front. Kendra handed a marker pen to the girl with a crop of blue streaks in her hair.

'No. It's not my job.'

'So be quiet then.'

Kendra handed out some test questions while she logged onto her iPad for her daily horoscope. *It's a challenging year especially with ongoing family problems. Nothing will resolve until September. Time for a clear out Libra and a new career.*

Kendra watched her group finishing off their papers or texting on their phones.

'Do you girls ever read your horoscopes?'

'Yeah. All the time!' They chorused.

'Do you ever believe them?'

'Course not Miss. It's just a bit of fun.'

'It sells magazines Miss.'

'Why do you think people read them?'

'Habit.'

'It gives them something to look forward to.'

'For the lesson next Wednesday, research your horoscope sign and make some notes. Let's see how accurate they are.'

'But Miss, it's exam week.'

'So it is. Well, after the exams. We'll go to the staff restaurant for a change of scene.'

Kendra took her time in reaching Maurice's office. 'You wanted to see me.'

Her head of department indicated for her to sit down. She looked for a spare seat while he wriggled around in his badly fitting check jacket and perched on the edge of his overflowing desk.

'How are you getting on? Are the hours more suited to your personal life?'

'Everything's fine.'

'A couple of the girls' parents have been to see me. They're a bit concerned you're not sticking to the syllabus.'

'Really and when did they become the experts? I've been doing some applied work with some of the groups. They're bright and keen. Psychology is a dynamic subject. It applies to their everyday lives.'

'Hmm.'

Kendra watched him snap a pencil, noticing he'd removed his wedding ring. He coughed then asked, 'Any more news on your daughter? Bad business I must say. It must be hard for you and Robert.'

'David.'

'Ah yes. David. Professor Blackmore. How is he these days?'

'Fine. Maurice, what's this about exactly?' Kendra stole a look at her watch.

'Nothing much. I just need to know that your personal worries are not affecting your performance in school.'

'They're not.'

Kendra stood up to leave.

'But if they do, I shall resign immediately.'

Maurice slid to his feet. 'Bloody hell. You can't do that.'

'If that's all… See you Tuesday.'

She'd lied about a doctor's appointment. The urge to get home and phone Alex, a new psychic detective who turned out to live locally was so overwhelming that she exploded at a guard who blew the dispatch whistle for her train as she skidded onto the platform.

A pile of post lay on the hall table as she pushed open the front door. Her heart plunged when she saw the brown envelope from the telephone provider. Hoping David hadn't seen it, she stuffed it into her bag and fled upstairs.

'You're early,' he said, hanging up the coat she'd tossed onto the stairs.

Kendra jumped. How David managed to appear from nowhere was a mystery.

'Weather warning,' she lied. 'I'll be down in a minute.'

When she finally got through to the accounts department, she gave them her bank details in a hushed voice.

'Are you sure this is right? £825.98?'

'Yes, you've made a lot of calls to premium lines Mrs. Blackmore.'

'That's none of your business,' Kendra snapped as she wiped her palms down her trousers. 'Don't send anymore bills to the house and transfer it into my sole name. I want you to email me future bills. You've got my address.'

'We will need Mr. Blackmore's permission to do that.'

'Just do it or I will make a complaint to your manager about your attitude.'

Kendra's body shook. She sat back in her chair and took a long swig of water. A rush of blood to her neck travelled upwards, leaving fiery spots on her cheeks. She looked at the bill again then forced it through the shredder. It was a mistake. She'd write to them asking for a recalculation.

David knocked on her door and handed her a mug. Her hands were trembling as she took it from him.

'I said I'll be down in a minute. I need a bit of space. Horrible day,' she said, unable to meet his eyes.

Kendra listened for his footsteps going down the stairs before dialling Alex's number. She felt confident that he was the one who could find her daughter.

CHAPTER 15.

FEBRUARY 2016

'Come into town with me on Saturday and help me choose a black dress for the 'I Love Brum' design awards. You've not been out for weeks.'

'I don't think so Sheila. I'm hopeless at choosing clothes even for myself.'

'You've been wearing the same black leggings and baggy tops for ages. A new spring wardrobe would lift your spirits. Big prints are in this year. They'd look fabulous on you. Come on. We can try out The Cube. You know that place with the rooftop bar next to the Mailbox? The views over the city are supposed to be amazing. They do a champagne afternoon tea. You've got to keep going.'

'If it will stop you nagging then fine but I don't want to be out all day. I've got some calls to make.'

Sutton Park was getting busy. Dogs were piling out of the backs of cars, barking and jumping as their owners tried to attach a leash. Cyclists in luminous shorts and matching helmets weaved in and out of groups of walkers, striding out with their Nordic poles, pausing to shout out angrily,' you don't own the park, you know'. The two women wandered down towards the model boat pond.

Kendra studied her fingernails. 'I've got a black dress I've not worn. It was for Rani's graduation. It's a 12 to 14. It would fit you.

Just plain but good quality.'

'I couldn't. It seems wrong.'

'It will be sent to charity otherwise. Come round and try it on. I won't be offended if you say no.'

'I've been a rubbish friend over this. I'd forgotten about the graduation. I suppose I thought you've been overreacting and I got really mad over your obsession with psychics. You know better than I do that they're money making frauds and use all kinds of tricks to get you to believe them. It makes me really angry and you're still vulnerable.'

'So you keep telling me.'

'Have you thought anymore about informing the police?'

'No point. David and Adam keep saying she'll come back when she's ready. It's my problem not Rani's. I need to let her go to find her path but I feel so…. gutted. We were friends and we did a lot together. That's all gone. I need to know where she is and that she's safe and not mixed up in something dangerous.'

'The not knowing must be excruciating. I wish I could do more to help. Something practical. Retail therapy isn't the answer but I'm not much good with these things. You're the expert. Maybe you could set up a support group for other parents going through the same thing. By the way, staff room gossip being what it is, Dave Kennedy's been putting it about that you've been logging onto tarot readers on the school network.'

As they climbed the grassy bank, Kendra shot round, convinced someone was watching her through the trees. Was that the light reflecting on binoculars? She tugged at Sheila's sleeve.

'Look. Over there. Can you see that man? He's dived behind the big oak. He's been watching us.'

'Don't be daft. There's nobody there. You're imagining things.'

Kendra took another look. Nothing. Nobody.

'I'd better get home.' She stuffed her clammy hands into her pockets. If Sheila saw how much they were shaking she'd insist on calling a doctor.

They left each other at Banners Gate. Sheila watched her friend race towards the main road as if trying to outrun somebody and it worried her. Something was really wrong. It was like she was possessed by demons. Obsessed, withdrawn and if staff room gossip was to be believed, losing her grip on her work. She'd no idea how to help.

Kendra stumbled on some loose stones as she turned towards home. As the paving stones rushed up to meet her eyes, a man with forget- me- not eyes and cropped white hair caught her by the elbow.

'Thank you. Sorry, I'm in a hurry.'

'Quiet Tinks,' he said to the growling terrier with a wonky ear.

There was no time for Kendra to make David's lunch. The kitchen was littered with open pots of khaki and grey modelling paint, unwashed brushes and balls of screwed up newspaper. She changed her coat and ran back out towards the station, afraid of being late for her two o'clock appointment.

Pacing it out up New Street towards the Museum and Art Gallery, she looked out for Chamberlain Hall. Pausing by a neglected Victorian building with peeling cream and blue paint, she pushed open the door into a sour smelling hallway and peered at a brass plaque on the wall. *Noel Sleet. Visions.*

Kendra climbed the brown wooden stairs to the first floor, avoiding touching the banister, until she reached a door. It had been freshly painted in white. She rang the bell, half turning to leave when a short, balding man wearing a hand-knitted cardigan opened the door. Kendra took an instant dislike to him wishing she'd gone for a walk around the bull ring instead of throwing more money away.

'You must be my emergency two o'clock' he beamed, rubbing his hands.

A brightly lit room in pale green and lemon was a welcome contrast to what she'd been expecting. The latest laptop model lay open on a curved white desk. A water-cooler station stood in the corner of the room. All very innocuous but Kendra couldn't help feeling she'd walked into a spider's web.

'Can I get you a drink? I've got some lovely teas. Camomile, mint, pink grapefruit?'

'No thanks.' Kendra sat down stiffly on one of the Ikea chairs, shifting under his gaze.

'Can you help me find my daughter? Your website said you take on cases of missing people. Yes, or No?'

'I see you like to come to the point Mrs...?'

'Blackmore. Well, can you? I can't take any more of the uncertainty.' Kendra recounted the story for the umpteenth time but she still felt on the outside looking through a hole in the wall.

'Have you contacted anybody else? Ours is a very specialised profession.'

'No,' she lied. 'If you can't help me then tell me now so we don't waste each other's time.'

Noel Sleet leaned back on his chair, steepling his fingers under his chin. She got up to leave. He was playing games with her.

'Why do you need to find your daughter?'

Kendra threw him a look.

'Well wouldn't you? Your child acts completely out of character, has spent months before her degree finals mixing with people that might be involved in some dangerous political activity then sends you a note out of the blue to say Bye Mum. Nice knowing you.'

He picked up a pen as if to write then laid it back on the desk.

'She's not a child and what evidence do you have that's she's mixed up with …'

'God's sake. Is this how you treat all your clients? Even if I was going to commission you, which I am not, I would want testimonials.' Kendra tucked her bag under her arm and made for the door.

'Sit down.'

'Goodbye Mr. Sleet.'

'I'm going to give you the name of a private detective. A colleague of mine. We work in different ways but he might be able to help.' Noel Sleet handed her a card.' I will tell you this. You are the one keeping your daughter away. You have a negative vibe.'

Kendra stopped in her tracks and stared at the back of the door. Slowly she turned to face him.

'How dare you. You know nothing about me. Or Ariana.'

He got up and opened the door to show her out.

'I don't need to *know* anything in the way you understand it. I simply sense your daughter will come back when she's ready but you can send out more positive vibrations. Stop trying to control her. She's a grown woman. Get in touch with Rod. He's good but in my experience people are only found when they want to be. That will be sixty pounds for the consultation.'

Kendra slapped the cash on the table and left without saying anything. She walked back to the station in a daze. Shame burned her earlobes as she mentally calculated how much money she'd spent that week on what she fooled herself into calling research.

The following day

David Kennedy was in the computer room, changing cartridges in the printers, when Kendra poked her head round the door. Seeing her, he smirked.

'Mrs. Blackmore,' he drawled, wiping ink off his hands. 'Have you come to read my stars? He waggled his fingers towards the sky.

'I want a word with you.' Kendra's eyes bore into his. 'I don't know what lies you've been spreading around the staff room but I have a right to use this lab without any interference from you. You're the technician so you have no jurisdiction over me.'

'Oh but I do. I have to make sure that the computers are not being used for illegal purposes. Porn, poker, psychics. You've been on three different tarot sites this week.'

'For your information, I'm writing a doctorate proposal in parapsychology. It was for research purposes. Take this is a friendly warning Mr. Kennedy. You will not talk about my business to all and sundry or I will be obliged to report you for smoking hash on school premises. You know what I'm talking about.'

Kendra tapped her nose before slamming out of the room. She went in search of her reallocated classroom since there was no heating in her own. Her GCSE group shuffled moodily into the lecture theatre which was dark and cold.

'The results of your mock exam were very disappointing,' she told them folding her arms as she paraded across the stage. 'Every year the examiner's reports are full of comments about poor performance in sampling methods. That's why we spent so much time on that part of the syllabus.' Kendra felt a cold mist gathering around her head as she reflected on the times she spent time discussing unrelated issues with this group of bright, eager girls who she'd earmarked for A and A star grades.

'I've put a timetable up outside Room 412. Write your names next to a convenient slot and we will spend twenty minutes going through your paper.'

'It's not our fault Miss,' called out one of them. 'You can't be bothered to plan your lessons properly. My Dad's coming into complain. He wants you sacked.'

'Ladies, collect your papers on the way out and go the library to work through them. We're going to get stuck in and make sure you pass with gold stars.

Kendra saw Sheila in the corridor, her arms full of files.

'Tell Maurice I'm sick. I'm going home. Seems I'm for the chop anyway.'

CHAPTER 16

$\mathcal{M}$aurice didn't hold back when he called her later that day. Unprofessional was one of the kinder remarks he'd made. The verbal warning came shortly after. She in turn had told him to stick his job up his butt. A brief moment of triumph was replaced with a feeling of horror. Never before had she spoken so viciously to anybody, not even her ex-husband when he stood at the door with his cases and told her he was going back to his family.

The snow was sticking to the trails as she tramped through the park to clear her head. Her mind was a knot of confusion. She needed her job to pay off her groaning credit card on which she'd amassed so much interest it made her quake. Hassan had built up debt she'd known nothing about, leaving creditors hounding her for two years. Owing even a penny to anyone brought back the trauma of that time.

Crunching her way round the lake, she churned over the exchange. Maurice had said she was unbalanced and in return she told him he was a drunk. Cold anger stung her lungs as she pushed her way through ranks of naked trees, their black skeletal fingers stretching towards a snow laden sky. Pulling down her woollen hat, she avoided making eye contact with the bullish dog walkers who were striding towards her.

'Bloody kids,' she sobbed into a soggy tissue she pulled from her sleeve. 'Bloody everything.' Kendra felt a choking sensation in her throat. Panicking as she struggled to swallow, she bent over and banged her fist between her shoulder blades.

'Hello? Are you alright?' A man with white hair and a tartan scarf was striding towards her, his black and tan terrier dancing around her ankles as it sniffed the undergrowth. He seemed familiar.

'Yes thanks. I swallowed my mint,' she lied. Looking up with water streaming from her eyes, she said.' 'That's twice you've rescued me.'

His blue eyes smiled. 'At least I'm useful for something.' Bending down to clip a lead onto the dog's collar, he said, 'Do you have time for a coffee?'

Kendra hesitated and looked around. Home was the last place she wanted to be. David would be waiting with his questions.

'I think I need one.'

The path twisted back towards the main road, beckoning them towards the warmth of the wooden hut, which despite its scuffed décor offered a friendly welcome and the best coffee in North Birmingham. As they ordered, she searched her pockets for change.

'It's on me,' he said, handing over a note. 'Let's sit over there. Tinks can watch the birds.'

'I'm Kendra by the way.'

'Marco.' He held out his hand. 'Italian grandfather. Tinks, lie down.'

'Are you a local?'

'Not far away. I come here most days to get out of the house now I've retired. That's a good thing about having a dog. You're forced to get some exercise. I hope you don't mind dogs. I should have asked.'

Kendra smiled. She wasn't sure how she felt about them. David barely tolerated Vesta and the feeling seemed to be mutual. She nibbled on her thumb nail as she fought for something suitable to say.

'If I had a one like Tinks, I'd be very happy.'

'A diplomatic answer if I may say so. I bet you're a Libra.'

Kendra stared at him.

'Ignore me,' he said, tugging at the dog's lead to pull him away from a curious spaniel. 'When my wife was alive, she used to play this daft game of guessing people's horoscope signs. Sorry, I've embarrassed you.'

'No I was just… surprised.' They sipped their drinks in synch, pausing every so often to watch Tinks do his flirting routine.

'Are you a fan of astrology?'

Marco threw back his head and laughed. 'Me? No but whenever I brought home the local paper, my wife would make a beeline for the back page.'

'Actually, I'm quite interested in this stuff for a research project. I teach psychology. Well, I'm not sure if I still have a job.' She went on to tell him snippets of the story.

'The bit about getting hooked on the paranormal sounds an interesting field to study. There's a lot of help for gambling addicts but I've never heard of psychic junkies.'

'It's a behavioural addiction rather than a substance one. Behaviour is my field.'

'The science would interest me. Which bit of the brain is responsible, that sort of thing.'

'Are you doctor?'

'I can't stand the sight of blood,' he laughed. 'I'm a civil engineer. I've worked all over the world but settled in Birmingham of all places. That's because Kay, my daughter, was living here with her family then they moved to Scotland. That's a lesson to all empty nesters. Don't follow your adult offspring around the country.'

'You must miss her.'

Marco was quiet for a moment, distracting himself with feeding Tinks a bit of biscuit.

'I do. Very much but you have to let them go and live their own lives. She keeps in touch.'

'Will you stay? Here?'

'Probably. I'm too old to move now.' They chatted for a while about how much change the city had gone through since the nineties until Marco stood up and brushed the crumbs from his brown cords. 'It's been lovely meeting you but I've got plumbing problems to sort out.' Seeing Kendra blush, he quickly added, 'My washing machine's sprung a leak. Someone's coming to look at it. That's if they turn up.' He gave her a wry smile. 'Maybe we'll bump into each other again. Not literally next time.'

They shook hands and Kendra became aware of his reluctance to let go.

The first thing Kendra noticed as she approached home, was David's scowling face at the window. She could sense his agitation by the way he bobbed his head from side to side. He opened the door before she had time to find her keys.

'Your school has called twice. What's going on?'

She took his arm and led him into the dining room.

'David, please calm down. I'm probably going to be suspended. It's a misunderstanding that's all. Someone's out to cause trouble for me. I'm sure it will blow over.'

'Where've you been?'

'I had to clear my head so I went for a walk. Nothing sinister.'

Kendra tried to marshal her thoughts into a logical order so he would understand but she didn't know what the facts were. Maurice had started yelling at her for not doing her job properly anymore and she'd lost her temper. She gave David a heavily edited version.

'We can't afford for you not to work Kendra. We agreed. My pension doesn't kick in for another year and we need to build our savings.'

'I've got money from Dad's estate. Don't make it sound as if we're on the breadline.'

Kendra felt her palms turn clammy as she agonised about what to say to him. She twiddled her wedding ring. There was so much she wanted to say to him. *Why couldn't he get a part time job or sell some of his telescopes. B and Q hired older workers and it would get him out of the house.*

As David became more and more remote, shutting himself away in his workshops, inventing, modifying, building and trailing in and out for drinks, messing up the kitchen and talking at her about some technical problem, Kendra could feel the stirring of a revolution between them. As she opened the tap to fill a glass with cold water, she pondered on the old rumour that Professor Blackmore had become unmanageable, always wanting to do things his own way, in his own time, never turning up to meetings or socials. Exasperating was how someone had described him.

He followed her up to her study, wiping a black grease mark from his cheek.

'We need to talk.'

'Later. I'm tired.'

'No. Not later. I want to know what this is all about.' He carefully laid down an opened envelope.

'Looks like a phone bill.' Kendra feigned nonchalance.

'Overdue. It's over a thousand pounds. I've been through the numbers and they are premium lines. At first I thought you were gambling but I rang one of them. Do you know what I was asked?'

Kendra felt prickles of sweat form on her top lip. Turning back to her desk she pushed notepads and books into drawers. Before she could hide her deck of tarot cards, David leant over and grabbed them and tossed them in the bin.

'I was asked to put in the pin number of my preferred psychic. I tried, at random, a couple of other numbers. Card readers, angel therapists, astrologers…'

David dropped onto the bed, his expression like a mask of plaster.

'Every number links back to some fraud conning you, us out of money. What is happening to you?'

'Nothing is happening to me. I'm doing research. I told you all this. The paranormal and what drives people to contact these helplines.'

'Helplines? So talking to somebody who says they can lift a curse or bring back a … a lover is helpful?'

Kendra got to her feet.

'My work is none of your business. I don't interfere with what you're doing or tell you I think you are wasting your time making stupid telescopes or whatever. It's your hobby. You spend enough money buying parts on line. I don't question you.'

David pulled on his cheek.

'That's different. We're talking about a few pounds and I've got something useful for my money. You may as well draw cash from the machine and feed it into the drain because that's what's happening.'

'So this is just about the money? I'm using my own money. I do work you know and I don't have to answer to you.'

He sighed and began his ritual thigh slapping, a sign of being unable to express his thoughts. Kendra knew she should step in to calm the situation but refused. It wasn't her problem.

'I know this is about Ariana. I'm missing her too or have you forgotten she's my step-daughter. We have always had a good relationship but I've watched how you've over involved yourself in her life. Telling her what to wear, organising her study times even at university, vetting her friends.'

'Oh I see. You're now going to tell me it's my fault she's left.'

'No. She made that decision so it's her responsibility but maybe if you'd given her more space…'

Kendra watched the tips of her fingers shake like those of an alcoholic going into withdrawal. Feeling a dull nagging in her stomach she went downstairs into the kitchen and ripped open two packets of crisps. When David came down she was stuffing them into her mouth helping them down with a slug of water. Nothing would fill the gnawing chasm she felt every waking minute. Her loss was visceral.

'The phone company called to ask if anybody under eighteen had made calls to those numbers. Kendra, will you stop shoving junk food into your mouth and talk to me. I don't believe this is about research. That's an excuse. You need some help.'

'Ha. Coming from you that's rich. Well I hope you've not relayed your nasty suspicions to my son.'

'No, but I have requested a call bar to premium lines. No more Kendra. It has to stop now.'

She spun round and slapped him on the cheek. Stung, he picked up his box of tools and quietly disappeared into his workshop. Dusting the crumbs from her jumper, Kendra followed him and kicked open the door.

'How bloody dare you? It's not me with the problem David it's you. You're never there for me. You have no idea what I'm going through as the very thought that Rani might be dead rips my mind to shreds every single bloody day but then no, you don't feel anything. You're too in love with these.' Kendra pulled out the slim metal drawers of the cabinet by his desk and tipped the contents onto the floor, one after the other until her rage subsided.

'It took me days to sort those out into size.'

'Who cares about your fucking inductors or whatever they are,' she said picking up a handful and throwing them over his desk. David leapt from his chair and pushed his wife outside, locking the door behind her. She could hear him howl like an injured animal but didn't care. He'd taken away her oxygen, the speck of light in the darkness killing any love she felt for him. *I will never forgive you for this.*

A few days later, Kendra made a call to Caz, the chair of the Midlands Therapy Forum. Finding she had to talk to a voicemail, she ended the call and resorted to sending an email instead with a request for a catch up. The central heating boiler was grumbling away in the airing cupboard as she sat transfixed at her desk, pulling paper clips apart and tossing them into the wastepaper basket.

In her mind's eye, Kendra saw herself as an old woman, looking through old photographs, devastated that the daughter she'd raised and loved had never made contact. She imagined someone had sat on her heart, so great was the pain.

She tried to push the image away as she typed Ariana's name, into a search engine to see what might come up. Still nothing. *How could someone go missing without trace in this day and age?* It had been over six months. *How was she living? Who was she with? Who had brainwashed her into cutting off from family?* The endless loop of questions was driving Kendra crazy. Maybe David was right. She did need some help. She hoped Caz would be sympathetic.

CHAPTER 17

*K*endra was in the Central Library reading the news headlines on her phone as she waited for Caz. A piece about Iran's war mongering caught her attention. She became so engrossed, she didn't see the tall, elegant woman approaching. They air kissed before moving to a private corner in the café.

'Kendra! Good to see you again. We missed you at the last few meetings. Sorry I'm a bit late. Stratford traffic gets worse.'

Next to Caz, who was stretching out her long legs encased in tailored navy trousers, Kendra felt clumsy as if her limbs were arguing with the brain's instruction. After exchanging bits of small talk about the weather, parking, and the continuous upheaval in the city centre caused by ongoing construction, Kendra folded her hands on her lap and looked her former supervisor in the eye.

'The truth is, I'm going through a rough time,' she began, explaining about Rani, her job and how she was feeling.

Caz pushed back her long blonde hair and took Kendra's hand. 'I'm so sorry to hear this. I can't believe it.'

'No. We can't either.'

'How can I help?'

'I'm not sure but I wondered if you knew of any groups that support parents in my situation.'

Caz pulled her perfectly shaped eyebrows together. 'Not off hand but I would say they are needed. I read an article recently about this new wave of mother-child estrangement. It's hurting a lot of parents whose kids go to poorly trained counsellors, who are not accredited, and are told their family is toxic and they need to get away. These are bad messages. I'll send it you.'

'All families have their problems but this is out of character for Ariana. I have a horrible feeling that she's got into some trouble and couldn't tell me.'

'How do you mean?'

Kendra leaned forward and lowered her voice, not wanting to be overheard.

'On top of that, David and I had a big fight. Correction, I picked a fight with him and slapped his face.'

'You didn't.'

'He was poking around in my study and found some evidence that I'd been contacting some psychic websites.'

'And have you?'

Kendra looked round at the people glued to their laptops. The air felt thick like a sticky paste.

'You don't mean ghosts and demons?' Caz put back her head and laughed. Her teeth were unbelievably even and white. Kendra noticed the slight smudge of pink lipstick on one of them.

'No. More tarot and mediums. I'm interested in why people turn to them for help instead of people like us.'

Caz leaned in and looked around. The plump red chair she was sitting on squeaked.

''Cos they're braindead fools, my dear. More money than sense. You don't want to tarnish your reputation with this stuff.' Caz's hand flew to her mouth.

'Oh No. Please don't tell me you've been paying money to hear their drivel? To find Rani?' Caz studied her hard. 'Now that is serious.'

'Occasionally. I can't find any rational explanation so I'm looking outside the box. I can't see anything wrong with it.'

Caz leaned forward and touched Kendra's knee.

'Until …' Caz narrowed her eyes… 'It gets a grip on you.' It's an area of addiction we've neglected as professionals. Wooo woooooo.' Her burst of laughter sounded like a jangling wind chime in Kendra's ears.

'What do you take me for? Of course not. David doesn't understand my work and I don't understand his or him for that matter. He was going on and on about stuff he doesn't understand and he has no idea whatsoever about the mess in my head over Rani. He's not a mother. He's not even her natural father.'

'Kendra, we've known each other, what, ten years? I wasn't going to say anything but…' the tall, willowy woman smoothed down her pale blue shirt… 'You look terrible. Haunted I think is the word.' She burst out laughing again. 'Sorry that wasn't meant to be a joke.'

Kendra bit on her lip and turned her head towards a fracas that had broken out between a library assistant and some teenagers. She felt like grabbing them by the collar and throwing them out.

'Caz,' she whispered, barely holding back another spurt of tears. 'I think Rani might be dead. I think she was kidnapped.'

'Stop it now. Stop torturing yourself. Your brain is exhausted from all this ruminating. You know it stops the production of the happy hormones. You need a distraction to break the cycle. I've an idea.'

Caz raised her finger in the air and nodded.

'At the next gathering of minds, we will spend an hour talking about these issues to see how other professionals would handle it.

Maybe you could write a case study or two and say you've got a client you're struggling to help. Hypothesise.'

'Huh. Psychologists are the first people to see through such case studies.' Kendra air fingered the quotation marks. 'They'll know it's about me. Why can't I talk about this stuff as a mother?'

'Because we need to drag some objectivity back into this.'

"I *am* objective Caz. I know I might not sound it but believe me I am rational under the circumstances. I mean, what would you do?'

Kendra pulled at a torn nail on her forefinger, desperately wanting to nibble it off.

'Not having children, I don't know is the immediate answer. I suppose focus on my work, my husband, friends, hobbies and trust that time will sort it out. Most parents experience some of this when their children go off to university or go abroad to work. You know how selfish young adults can be, not stopping to think how their behaviour impacts other people. Parents are well... parents. Always there. I've not heard of anyone actually writing a goodbye letter though. It is extreme behaviour. Was there no indication at all in advance? No mood swings? Hanging out with strange people?'

'Plenty of mood swings but I wouldn't say Rani's new friends were weird. Not her usual type. She's never bothered with Iranian friends before but she joined some society at the university where some of the women covered. She copied them.'

Kendra felt Caz's scrutiny like sun blazing through glass onto her face.

'Religious? Now that is worrying. Is she Islamic?'

'Not in the slightest. Rani is driven by her thirst for knowledge through science. She's like David in that respect.'

'Mm. I see. Well, it could be an identity crisis. I think my suggestion would help. Send me a proposal and I will look into the funding situation but keep it mainstream. No talk of hobgoblins.'

Caz glanced quickly at her phone. 'I've got to go. James expects me to go to dinner with some boring urology colleagues of his. The last thing I want to do is talk kidneys and bladders.'

They stepped onto the escalator which transported them down to the spacious foyer, giving Kendra time to think about her suggestion. It would distract her from the hotlines and bring her back into her field where logic and rationality were at home.

'Let me think it through. I would like to see Emily and Mae again. We were at York together.'

Caz searched in her bag for her keys.

'I'm parked in the Mailbox. Please don't contact these sites again. Even if it is the name of research. We understand addiction remember. It can happen to the least unsuspecting, well balanced individual.'

She bent down to kiss Kendra on the cheek before disappearing in a cloud of expensive perfume to find her Porsche.

David seemed less tense when she got home. He was whistling, *He who would valiant be*, as he repaired a ballcock in the downstairs cloakroom. 'Good meeting?' he called. 'Sorted?'

'Getting sorted. Did you take the stuff out of the dryer as I asked you to?'

'Dryer? What stuff?' David emerged, pointing his dirty hands towards the sink.

'Your clothes.' He looked blank. Kendra shook her head slowly as she bent down to tug at a tangle of shirts.

'I forgot. I had to go to the plumber's merchants to get another of these...'

'Ok. Ok. I don't need the detail. By the way, I'm sorry about the other day. I shouldn't have taken my frustration out on you like that.'

'S'okay. Your school phoned again. Maurice somebody. He's left a mobile number.' David fumbled in his pockets and pulled out a crumpled bit of paper from amongst the muddle of screws, twine, coins and notes.

'How did he sound?'

'Sound? Normal. He asked to speak to you. That's all.'

Kendra took the paper and disappeared into her study.

'Maurice. It's Kendra Blackmore.'

'Thanks for calling back. Look Kendra, we were both a bit heated. Can we rewind?'

'My resignation is ready to go. It's time for me to move on.'

'You would need a reference and leaving like this isn't going to help.'

'Are you threatening me? It seems bullying is as bad in the staff room as it is in the playground.' Kendra could hear her voice rising but felt powerless to moderate it.

'Look we can sort this out. Don't come back until after half term and we'll have another chat. I'll cover your classes with the temp. She was very switched on and the kids liked her.'

'Good, then you'll have no problem replacing me, will you?'

The second she put down the phone, it rang. Sheila sounded out of breath.

'Jo's mate thinks he saw Rani at Heathrow when he was flying out to Singapore. I know it's not much to go on. He tried to catch her attention but she didn't see him. It seems she was covered from head to foot in black and was hanging around the Emirates desk.'

'Really? Then how could he know it was her?' Kendra thought for a moment before adding, 'tell him thanks.'

'By the way, your name's all over the staff room you silly moo.

What possessed you to call Maurice a cretinous drunk? You're on a good number at Darwin. Three days a week and a total opt out of bureaucracy.'

'Not my finest moment.'

'Kendra, you're not helping yourself. You've become like a woman possessed and it's not going to bring Ariana back. You'll end up getting sacked, more stressed and I'm worried you'll turn even more to these deluded con merchants.'

'You can't be deluded and a con merchant at the same time. One requires loss of reality the other is conscious manipulation.'

'Kendra, I ... can't talk to you anymore. You're becoming strange. If you don't work, you'll slowly drive yourself mad.'

Kendra tuned out Sheila's hectoring voice and stared across the street to where a mother and teenage daughter were having a spat. The girl was walking behind, tossing her long purple hair and glowering at her mother's back. The poor woman looked like a picture from The Downtrodden collection she'd once seen in an art gallery in New York.

'I've got to go. Tony's trying to get through. Think about what I've said. I care about you.'

CHAPTER 18

Kendra had pulled out the bed in her daughter's room to flick the fluff from the skirting boards, aware that David was watching her from the landing. His mouth was working up to saying something.

'Why don't you use the vacuum cleaner attachment? It does a better job.'

She ignored him and bent down to pick up a feather which had embedded itself in the weave of the carpet. She sat back on her heels and turned it over in her hands. It wasn't one of the tiny ones that escape from a pillow but more like something from a white plumed bird, like a dove. She remembered Rani chasing feathers when she was little, saying they were like angels. Kendra placed it on the dressing table and made a wish.

'What time did Adam say he landed?' Kendra hauled herself up and massaged the small of her back. She felt aches and pains most days and vowed to join go swimming but couldn't find the energy.

'Here'll be here this afternoon. You've missed that bit in the corner. Look.'

'Would you go down to Ashraf's and get me a few things I need for the dinner. The list is on the notice board. I need the Persian rice he keeps in stock, not any other kind. I don't feel like going out in this wind. I've got a bit of earache,' she lied, tugging her earlobe.

David pressed a finger and thumb against his brow as he contemplated this unplanned task. Shopping alone made him anxious except if he was going to Screws4U to pick up something he'd ordered on line. Too many bodies, badly organised shelves and the loose spices in Ashraf's made him sneeze. His mind drifted back to the steam engine he was planning to build but became aware of his wife waiting for an answer. He felt an uncomfortable twitch in his eye when she watched him too closely.

'Ok,' he agreed pursing his lips.

Kendra watched him from the spare bedroom where she was putting fresh sheets on the bed. His tatty black scarf was wrapped tightly around his ears and plastic bags spilled out of his pockets. She'd lost count of the times he'd argued against paying 5p for a bag, sometimes arguing his logic with the poor assistant who'd done nothing other than ask the question. He was a good man and he didn't deserve to bear the brunt of her fragile emotional state. Despite him not talking about Rani, she sensed he was unsettled by what she'd done. She squirted polish on a bit of rag and ran it over the beech furniture as she tried to see things through his eyes.

When she first met him, she fell for the calm and logical way he saw the world. It gave her the much needed feeling of security which Hassan had undermined for years. He'd been loud and dramatic. David was thoughtful and considered. As time passed, she noticed he didn't want to socialise, preferring to shut himself away in his workshops, absorbed in some technological project. His passion for building telescopes was amusing but it was all he wanted to talk about.

Kendra had put his withdrawal down to 'Grumpy Old Man' syndrome but when he repeatedly said things without understanding why others got upset with him, she began to suspect there was something more than issues of aging. It didn't matter. He was beautifully eccentric and his intelligence bordered on sheer genius. Kendra was proud of him but he annoyed the hell out of her with his routines and lack of empathy. Fluffing up the pillows and giving the surfaces a final clean down with some lavender wipes, she recalled a conversation she'd had with Sheila over a bottle of wine.

'All men, when they hit the magic four zero, are the same. Moody, argumentative and miserable.'

A loud rat- tat- tat on the door sent Kendra scurrying down the stairs, cloth in hand. When she saw a mop of bluey-black hair and a hint of olive skin through the glass, her first thought was Rani. Her heart fizzed with hope.

'Adam. Oh Adam.' Kendra reached up to hug him, protesting when he picked her up and carried her through to the kitchen. 'I can't believe you're here. You're early and where's Alison?' Kendra peered over his shoulder as if waiting for her to appear from behind the door.

Adam slid out of his coat and grinned.

'She couldn't come this time. Doctor's orders.'

Kendra gave him a quizzical look, his jacket weighing heavily in her hands. 'What do you mean? Is she ill?'

'No she's fine. I like what you've done to the kitchen. Very swish.'

'It's two years since you were last here. Where's the time gone? There's beer in the fridge.'

'Alison's pregnant Ma. Three months. She's had a bit of a scare so she's staying home and doing some audit work for an engineering company.'

Kendra clapped her hands to her mouth.

'That's fantastic news. Are you going to bring the wedding forward?'

THE FUTURE CAN'T WAIT

Adam sat cross legged on the Shiraz rug with his back to the radiator. He pulled back the ring of the lager can.

'Nope. We're going to cut it back a bit and rearrange till after the baby's born. Probably next spring. 'This room looks different? Where's the piano?'

'Rani stopped playing so we decided to let it go. So… I'm going to be a grand mummy. That will mean more trips across the pond.'

'Well that's another bit of news. I've got a couple of interviews in London and one in Bristol while I'm here. Al wants to come home to be near family. Me too.'

Kendra shrieked and clapped her hands to her cheeks.

'You clever boy,' she said, mussing up his hair.

'I thought you'd be pleased. Where's David by the way? Holed up?'

'Gone shopping for the dinner but why don't we go out instead to celebrate?'

'I'd rather stay home and watch a bit of English telly. I don't want to jinx things. I have to leave tomorrow morning for Nottingham so let's make the most of it.'

Adam jumped to his feet as David appeared through the door leading into the kitchen from the garden. He dumped a carrier bag on the worktop before carefully peeling off his gloves.

'Hello,' he said, making no move to shake his step-son's hand. 'I'll be in workshop two.'

A sadness infused with nostalgia fell over her shoulders as she prepared the okra and salted the aubergines for one of the few vegetarian Persian dishes she knew how to make. It was Hassan's favourite dish. He'd insisted that in Zoroastrian philosophy, animals had a soul and consciousness which meant meat eating was forbidden. It hadn't stop him having the odd bacon bap though. Adam had copied his father and hadn't eaten meat for years. If Rani had gone out to see him then why didn't she say?

Adam was flat out along the length of the sofa, flicking through the TV channels.

'Doesn't get any better does it?' he said, settling for BBC news.

Kendra slipped a bookmark between the pages of a novel she'd been trying to read for months.

'Terrorist attacks. I would love to know what's in their heads. I can't believe they're driven by religion. Most of my colleagues think they're drugged to the eyeballs with heroin from Afghanistan. No sane person would be able to carry out such atrocities and have no remorse.'

'It could be a mass psychosis,' added Kendra. 'That can happen. Freud said war was an outlet for the death instinct.

Adam grabbed a handful of crisps and pushed them into his mouth.

'The death instinct? Hmm. I suppose in the right circumstances it can override all logic and reason. It's odd how so many of them are in the same age bracket. Eighteen to twenty-five.'

'You know as much as I do about brain development in the twenties, Adam. Frontal cortex decision making and all that but I don't know if that explains everything. I see it as some kind of collective mania which even Rani may have got caught up in.'

Adam crumpled the lager can and tossed it in the bin. He'd run out of ways to calm his mother's fears.

'She had no interest in any sort of politics. Even Dad got really angry about the Khomeini regime. Don't forget, the Najafi family had lived prosperous and free lives under the Shah. You were there during the regime change. It must have been terrifying.'

Kendra nodded. One day we were in fashions from Paris and sipping champagne in some of the best hotels in the world, the next, being chased by the evil dress police if our stockings weren't dark and thick enough or we were showing a strand of hair. Your Dad did everything to get us out of Iran after the arson attack on the cinema in Abadan. Five hundred people killed in that fire. That was the start of it but it took months before we could get the right paperwork. Every time he went to a different office they told him to come back the next day. That was after queuing for hours. Not much different to what's happening these days. War of ideology.'

'I've been thinking. Maybe Rani *has* gone to Iran to connect with family although I don't know how she'd track them down. She felt more abandoned after Dad left than I did. Maybe she didn't tell you because you'd worry.'

'She was in touch with some of the cousins through Facebook. That's when the regime wasn't shutting it down. It wouldn't be difficult but she knew very well that if she went she wouldn't be allowed out again. Not without your father's permission. She's a dual passport holder but over there it's not recognised. The other danger is the link with the Najafi name. Your Dad was under surveillance at one time.'

'You mean here? Secret service sort of thing?'

'Police. He got mixed up in some political activity. I can't remember the detail now but I do know that the Shah's secret police questioned him at university several times just before the revolution and he got hauled into West Midland police station after he'd been on a demonstration.'

'God Ma. I never knew that. So how come I managed to get into the USA?'

'Because you are my lovely boy,' was all she would say, reaching up to kiss his cheek.

Kendra jumped up as the doorbell rang. Always in the back of her mind lurked the hope that Rani would one day appear on the step and say, 'Hello Mum.' It was her dream. A nightly prayer to a deity she didn't believe in. She'd forgive everything if that came true. She peered down the drive for signs of life but there was nothing save for a dog sniffing its way along the gutter, its owner calling him to heel. A flowerpot lay on its side and Kendra shuddered. Instinct told her someone was trying to unnerve her.

Adam got up to see why she was shouting out.

'Someone keeps appearing Adam... then disappearing. One day it's a tall man in a parka kind of jacket standing by the bus stop across the road, the next a woman in red glasses is following me around the supermarket. The phone rings but there's no one there. Ask David. He's taken a couple of calls.' Kendra wiped her eyes with her sleeve. Adam took her chilled hands and led her back into the living room. He covered her knees with a blanket. The strain was showing in her eyes, dull and listless and circled with purple blotches. He could tell she'd not been eating properly by the state of her nails.

'Ma. You're overwrought. The mind plays tricks in grief. I understand that. Uncertainty can be a killer. The worst of it is... I don't know how to help you. It's affecting me too but I have to keep going for Alison's sake. David told me you'd stopped going to work and what's more concerning, he thinks you're having an affair.'

Kendra felt the hairs stand up on the back of her neck.

'A what? Where the hell has he got that idea from?'

Adam ran his fingers through his hair and grinned.

'I know it's not true Ma. Don't get so worked up. He emailed me to say you were always whispering to someone on the phone with the door shut and he didn't know what to do. He wanted me to speak to you. You think David's not tuned into other people but he's more astute than you give him credit for.'

'I can assure you I'm not. There's no room in my head for subterfuge.'

CHAPTER 19

*A*dam was holding onto the top of the door frame, rotating his neck to ease out a crick when Kendra came downstairs, suppressing a yawn.

'It was a bad idea to stay up half the night chewing the fat,' he said. 'Sorry I was a bit harsh on you.'

'Hmm? Oh about the paranormal stuff. I looked up that professor you mentioned. He wrote that we all possess some kind of hyper sensitive detection device which is why we believe there is something out there; - ghosts, spirits and the like. He'd be a good reference point for my work. Breakfast?'

'Too early for me.'

'However, I don't think the power it has over people can be dismissed,' she went on. 'Who doesn't read their horoscope in the paper from time to time?' She picked up Vesta and gave her a squeeze.

'That's harmless enough. Even I've had a quick glance but it doesn't mean I believe it. The problem comes when people get hooked. It's like gambling or a shoe addiction. I should know. I have to work with people who find themselves caught up in these behaviours and can't see it. I've got a patient who is a hoarder. His house is now uninhabitable but he's in the depths of denial.'

Kendra didn't want an argument before he left.

'Your research should focus on condemning these beliefs or dealing with the obsessive behaviours attached to them. I don't want to compare it with something as serious as anorexia but trying to get people to see the madness of their thinking is like getting a very thin person not to believe they are overweight.'

'Ok. I get your point.'

Adam filled the jug for the coffee machine.

'There's a sucker born every minute. I'm glad you told me that you're not involved with some toy boy but you're going to have to tell David about these phone calls. It must be costing a fortune.'

'He already knows.'

'Right. I need to leave in twenty minutes. Would you iron my shirt?' Course you would.'

Having him at home even for one night had lifted her spirits. They'd laughed, debated, argued and vehemently disagreed but it left Kendra stimulated and afraid she would melt into the grey backdrop of her life once he'd left. David appeared still in his dressing gown, his face drawn and pale.

'Are you feeling alright?'

He stared at her as if trying to translate the words.

'Yes. No. I have a headache.'

Kendra poured him a glass of water and handed him the bottle of aspirin, frowning as he struggled to unscrew the top.

'Let me.'

When Adam came downstairs, in his designer navy blue suit and white shirt, Kendra couldn't resist straightening his tie.

'David's not well. Could you check him out quickly and tell me if I need to call his doctor?'

Adam glanced at the clock.

'Sure Mum. Put that stuff in the car for me would you?'

Kendra wandered around the front garden, noticing how neglected it was in parts. David had a system for his gardening rotas. Weeding, pruning, planting according to his coloured charts he kept in the greenhouse.

'What do you think?' she asked Adam, biting on a thumb nail.

'He could do with a bit of an MOT. Make him an appointment and go with him.'

Turning to his mother, he rested his large hands on her shoulders and looked into her eyes.

'Ma. I can see how this business with Rani has blown you out of the water but you need to take a scientific approach to this. Remember when I was twenty-five? I had an urge to leave the country and go the States. It's not because I didn't love my family but I had to find myself. I believe it's the same with her. This note means nothing. She's being dramatic. She probably felt like that at the time but it will pass. Just give it time. But and a big but, no more psychics and astro babble. Promise?'

Kendra smiled and gave him a hug.

'You're going to be late,' she said, gently pushing him towards his hired BMW.

'I'll keep you posted on the jobs. At least you've got something to look forward to now.'

She watched him go, waving until the car disappeared from view, wishing she could have gone with him.

David was sitting in the winged back chair in the living room when she came back in the house. She could see his head leaning to the side, a magazine sliding from his knee to the floor.

'Shall I call the doctor?' Kendra pulled a blanket round him, feeling his ice cold hands.

'I'll be fine. It's probably a migraine. I need to get my eyes tested.'

Kendra hovered over him unsure of what to do. She couldn't

remember the last time David hadn't vanished into his workshops as soon as he'd finished breakfast. He looked as if picking up a handful of screws would exhaust him.

'I'll nap for a bit. You get on with your work Kendy.' He smiled weakly and closed his eyes.

'I'm going for my walk. Here's your mobile. Call me if you need me. I'll be in the park.'

Kendra pulled on her boots and jacket. Feeling in the pocket for some gloves and loose change, she quietly shut the door and walked pensively towards Town Gate. Half hoping she'd see Marco, she felt a surge of guilt. It felt wrong leaving David on his own but she needed to escape from the house to battle against the magnetic pull of the internet sites. She'd found a way round David's call barring by getting a reading by email and paying for it on her credit card.

Half an hour into her tramp along the muddy trails she felt the strain in her lungs. Two squirrels chasing each other caught her attention. They cared about nothing other than gathering and retrieving food. She smiled at the irony. Supermarket runs, putting it away, bringing it out, chop, mush, cook, eat, and clear away. *Oh to be a squirrel.* She turned towards the lake, the thought of survival on her mind. It took her all her strength to keep her head above water especially now the insomnia was getting worse.

Kendra caught her reflection in a puddle, shocked by how the face staring back appeared as a water-logged mask. Tinks appeared from behind the foot of a towering oak followed by Marco who raised his hand in greeting.

'Hello boy,' she said, bending down to scratch behind his ears.

'Hello Kendra. How are you?'

She looked up, aware that her cheeks were flushed.

'Fine. You?'

'My washing machine got fixed so I'm squeaky clean now,' he grinned.

She matched his pace as they followed Tinks on his familiar trail with the dedication of a sniffer dog. They chatted about the weather and the bad smash on the Aston Expressway. Kendra told him about Adam's flying visit.

'I can't stay long. David's a bit under the weather.'

'Sorry to hear that. I was going to be impertinent and invite you to Chez Marco for coffee. I've spent days spring cleaning as best I can.'

Kendra hesitated. So many forces were pulling her in different directions.

'I'll give him a quick call first.' She turned away and walked in a circle as she waited for the call to connect. Reassured that he seemed better and was tidying up his workbench, she nodded to Marco in acceptance of his invitation.

The Edwardian terrace with its neatly trimmed front lawn and hanging baskets of cheeky viola flowers, smelled of polish and pine disinfectant. Tinks dashed into the kitchen where he could be heard lapping up water. Marco took her coat and hung it on the one of the pegs in the hall, ushering her into his study.

Kendra wandered around the cluttered room, stopping to run her fingers over the spines of an eclectic mix of books. Crime novels tumbled over gardening books on the wall to wall shelving. On his huge desk, books and papers balanced so precariously she had to be careful not to bump against them.

Marco edged his way through the door, cups rattling on saucers, coffee spilling onto them. Kendra took the tray from him and placed it on the low table between the chairs.

'I had no idea you had such a mix of interests. Ancient Greek, Impressionist painters, astronomy.'

'Painting is my big passion these days. It helps me to relax. All men need hobbies, especially if they live alone.'

'David builds telescopes.'

'Maybe he could build something for me. I've always wanted one.'

'Are you happy being retired?'

'Had my wife not been so ill, I guess I'd have carried on working. I do miss the social side of work even though it got very political like most places. It gets a bit lonely being at home all the time which is why I have the dog.'

Kendra shuffled awkwardly on the edge of the chair, spreading her fingers on her lap as she mulled over how much she should reveal to Marco about her real situation.

'I feel I should tell you something. About me.'

Marco watched her over the rim of his cup. He liked the way she pushed strands of her pale hair behind her ears and the fold between her eyebrows when she was deep in thought.

'My daughter Ariana has gone missing. Well, not exactly.' Kendra gave him a brief account of the story. Marco rubbed his cheek. 'I've been trying to find out what would make a home-loving girl with seemingly no worries other than to get a first in her finals do this. I know there are explanations of the need to mature and find her own path but this isn't the way it's done. You read about young women joining cults and things…' Her voice trailed off. 'I turned to psychic detectives and the like to find her.'

'I feel for you,' he said softly, glancing over to a graduation photograph of his daughter. 'It's hard when they go but this is an extreme way of doing it. Did these psychics you consulted… Were they helpful?'

'Not really. I think I've selected bits from the readings and applied it to me. Even a jellyfish is a lifeline when you're drowning.

Some even blamed me and said I was controlling.'

Marco stroked his goatee beard.

'Scaremongering tactics followed by pushing you to fix more appointments is the modus operandi of some. It's a lucrative business designed to get people hooked. I thought about going to the spiritualist church when my wife died. It's not an unusual reaction.'

Being able to talk to Marco so freely about her fears and what ran through her mind in the early hours of the morning as she paced the living room was like the stroke of sunshine on her soul. As the clock chimed the hour she got up to leave. So engrossed was she in the conversation she'd forgotten all about David.

'I hope you don't judge me for being so foolish. I've got some help with trying to break the addiction but it's not easy.'

Marco took her hand and looked deep into her eyes.

'Now why would I judge you? I'm honoured that you've chosen to talk to me about it. I doubt I'm much comfort but I do have two willing ears.'

He scribbled his phone number on the back of an old envelope and handed it to her. Their hands touched briefly. Kendra could think of nothing else but the warmth of his fingers as she strolled home.

CHAPTER 20

Shouldering open one of the scuffed double doors into the academy, Kendra felt a need to run away. She didn't want to be there. Reaching for her necklace she counted the pearls between her thumb and finger. Adam had shown her a way of calming her nerves.

Maurice had calmed down and was all but begging her to return to work. His tactic had been to say a posse of students had presented him with a petition to reinstate their favourite teacher. Despite knowing how manipulative he could be, Kendra agreed to discuss it.

His office was its usual pigsty state. Without apology, he gathered up a toppling pile of papers from one of the armchairs so she could sit down and dropped them onto a corner of the floor. A dank smell lingered in the air making Kendra's nose twitch. She felt sorry for the cleaners.

'We've known each other for many years Kendra, and you know how much I admire and respect you.'

Kendra watched him circle his desk and waited.

'I know you've got personal problems at the moment,' he waved his hand in the air and assumed a look of concern. 'Your daughter and that.'

Empathy. Good start Maurice.

'You're an excellent teacher and you've brought Darwin credit on many occasions. Your students like your style even though it's a bit, shall we say, unorthodox.'

Back handed compliment. Kendra gave a gentle tug to her skirt as she wondered where this was going. She refused to help him out.

'It would keep your mind occupied if you picked up the reins, still on three days a week. Just come in and teach. The bits you like. Hm? What do you think?'

Kendra sensed a false calm in his voice. The Academy was under a lot of financial pressure and couldn't afford to waste money on unnecessary recruitment. Every Friday staff threatened to give notice because they were drowning under bureaucracy and feared the wrath of the Principal who shot out of his office from to time to bark orders to the troops.

She stood up and picked up her briefcase.

'My students have important exams coming up. I will see them through to the end of the academic year but I can't promise anything after that. My husband hasn't been well and yes, you're right, the situation with my daughter is taking its toll on the whole family. I would be grateful if you would not make it a topic of staffroom gossip.'

Her Head of Department reached down to scratch the inside of his leg then held out his stubby fingers to shake Kendra's hand. She shrugged him off, squirming at the idea of him touching her. Sheila was mid-argument with the design technician, stopping when she spotted Kendra by the pigeon holes. Even in the days of electronic mail, someone was still stuffing mail boxes with memos and junk.

'What happened?' Sheila whispered.

'Nothing. I told him I'd stay till the end of the summer term providing everyone leaves me alone to get on with it. I doubt I'll stay after that.'

From the pile of educational catalogues and copies of the Metro newspaper, Kendra pulled out an envelope and felt a stabbing pain behind her ribs. A red overdue notice was stamped on the phone bill.

'Bloody hell. You been ringing sex lines or something?' said Sheila, aghast as she caught sight of the figure. Kendra screwed it up and shoved it into the bottom of her bag, muttering something about an error. At least it wasn't as bad as the last one but David would go super nova if he found out. Walking back to the station, she felt her legs shaking so much that she had to grip the handrail to stop herself stumbling down the broken steps onto the platform.

Relieved to find a bench that, despite it being covered in vile graffiti, hadn't been vandalised, she sat down and slowly inhaled and exhaled aware that the bill was burning a hole in her bag. When the train arrived, she sought out an empty carriage and tried to block out the shaming voices in her head.

A copy of Birmingham Today lay on the seat beside her. Kendra skimmed through it to keep her mind off her fear. An advert caught her eye. *Roisin, genuine Romany psychic, 5th generation.* Kendra stored the number in her phone and as soon as she found a quiet spot in the foyer of New Street station, she called the number and was given an address close by. She pushed her card into the cashpoint machine, not daring to check her balance, and withdrew the cash for Roisin.

'Sit here,' ordered a wide hipped woman with dyed black hair piled on top of her head. A thick silver bangle clanked against the glass table on which stood a large crystal ball resting on a black stand. Kendra noted the stereotype with dismay. She felt foolish sitting in the cave-like room which hung with the expected paraphernalia of the fortune teller; crystals, dream catchers, tarot decks and a sickly smell of incense. The adrenalin that had powered Kendra into this dismal place had dissipated, leaving her with an urge to escape. Roisin lit two candles before pulling out her cash box.

'Formalities first,' she said. Kendra handed over the money. 'Now put your hands on the crystal ball and close your eyes. Don't talk.' Her accent morphed between Dublin and West Midlands.

Kendra did as instructed and felt a hot jolt of energy shoot up her arms. Her instinct was to pull her hands away.

'I'm sorry but this is a mistake. I need to go.' Kendra gathered up her bag and made for the door.

'People don't like to hear the truth do they? Not if it's about themselves.'

Roisin gathered up the notes and put them into a tin which she locked and hid away in the desk drawer.

'Truth? Is that what you call it? Where's your evidence that you can see into the future?'

'I'm not going to argue with you. It's bad for the vibration. See yourself out.'

Kendra walked slowly back into the room, fixing her gaze on the woman's eyes.

'It's people like you that destroy lives on the pretext you are helping them. You give false hope, take their money and wait in your den like a spider waiting for the fly to waltz by. You need to be exposed.'

A nerve in the woman's cheek began to twitch. She covered her crystal ball with a black cloth.

'You're a journalist. I sensed it the minute you walked in. Well let me tell you something lady. You've got dark forces around you. Someone in your family is out of their depth. Now GET OUT.'

Kendra stood on New Street watching people passing both ways like a speeded up film. Her head was buzzing with disbelief and disgust at herself. It was the first time the extent of her addiction was hitting home. Roisin, aka Gail, was on the phone. In a thick Black Country accent she said, 'I'm done for the day. I've made the four hundred quid so if you want to collect your share, I'll be in the Anchor.'

'Are you ok? Can I get you something?'

The young man's eyes were filled with concern as he spotted the woman sitting on the steps which were splattered in pigeon droppings. Kendra struggled to pull his vague outline into focus.

'I'll be ok.' She tried to get to her feet but had no energy. Her joints ached with the effort.

'Here's a can of coke. It'll help if you're low on sugar. You look as if you're about to faint. Let me help you up. Shall I call somebody?'

Kendra shook her head quickly and tried to offer him money for the drink. He waved it away and with a final glance of concern, he hurried back to the council offices.

Two hours later Kendra arrived home to find David more cheerful than normal. He commented on the pallor of her skin, suggesting she was coming down with the bug he was sure he'd had.

'Go to bed. I've got something to finish.'

She drew the curtains in her study and unplugged her technology. Pulling the blanket over her eyes she tried to sleep. Too many disturbed nights were affecting her health. Permanently tired, snappy and miserable, she knew she was losing it.

Images of Rani flitted across her inner eye as snippets of happier times floated in her head like torn strips of black cloud; the two of them sipping vodka and coke by the canal, Rani promising to get her chipped tooth fixed, an argument over an unsuitable dress made up the mosaic of memories.

A familiar sense of being watched made her sit upright, hardly daring to breathe. She put a hand to her forehead to ease the dull pounding above her eyes. It was building up to one of her rare 'crown of thorn' headaches. Her brain raced like a flywheel unable to stop as anger, indignation battled it out with raw grief. Through the crack between the curtains, she saw a man sat in a car opposite the house reading the paper. It was the same one she'd seen on the platform at New Street. She recognised him from the sharp jawline.

Kendra leapt up to the window and scrawling through the icons on her phone for the camera she pointed it towards the car. When she checked the image there was nothing in the file. She clicked again but the car had gone. She needed proof for the police otherwise they'd dismiss her as a crazy old woman.

CHAPTER 21

David shook his wife from a heavy sleep by pulling back the duvet and turning on the main light.

'Wake up. The police are here. They want to talk to you.'

'What? What time is it?' Kendra rubbed her eyes, trying to focus on David's face. His eyes were bloodshot. 'Police? What do they want? Is it about the stalkers?'

'I don't know. They didn't say. I'll tell them you'll be down in two minutes.'

Kendra shot out of bed, dragged on some clothes, her bare feet slipping on the stair carpet as she ran downstairs. Bursting into the kitchen, where two police constables were standing by the window blocking out the light, she asked, 'What's happened?' A hand flew to her mouth when she saw a handbag in the shape and colour of a watermelon slice on the kitchen table.

'Mrs. Najafi?' Kendra stared at the large mole on the woman's chin.

'Blackmore now. I remarried.' She looked from David to the two officers, aware that a panda car was filling their drive.

'Are you the mother of a Miss Ariana Najafi?'

Kendra nodded, words sticking like flies to a jam pot.

'Does this bag look familiar to you Mrs. Blackmore? Maybe

you'd like to take a closer look.'

Kendra didn't need to. She and Rani and chosen it together in the Birmingham rag market.

'It's my daughter's,' she confirmed, sitting down, her feet feeling like lumps of ice on the wooden floor. 'Where did you get it?' *Oh God. She's dead.*

David sat at the table and began doodling on the edge of the Sutton Coldfield Observer. All eyes turned to watch him.

'When did you last see your daughter Mrs. Blackmore?'

'Last July.'

'Has she been in contact with you? Do you know where she is?'

Kendra drew a deep breath and told them the story, careful not to share her suspicions.

'Did you report her missing?'

David neatly folded his newspaper and looked up. 'No we didn't. She isn't missing. She went to London to work then sent my wife a note to say she wasn't coming home again.'

The officer frowned as she wrote something in her notebook.

'Do you have this note?'

Kendra fetched her bag and pulled out the crumpled sheet of paper.

'You say this was out of character? Had there been a row or something? Was your daughter behaving strangely? Mixing with maybe the wrong people? Were you concerned about her?'

The questions were bouncing down on Kendra like apples shaken from a tree.

'Of course I've been concerned. Worried to death.'

'Have a look at this picture. Is this your daughter?'

Kendra took the grainy photograph which looked like something from a CCTV camera. A young woman in a scarf was talking to two men outside a house surrounded by litter. In the background she could pick out a sign over a shop. Halal butchers. She peered more closely, spotted a ring on the right hand. It was gold with a small turquoise stone like one missing from Rani's jewellery collection.

'What gives you that idea?'

'I'm asking you. Is it your daughter?'

'No,' she said handing it back. She felt the colour drain from her face. 'Besides, if it was so what? This person is not committing a crime.'

'We know these two men. They recruit girls to terrorist organisations. You're sure this is not Ariana?'

'Stop. STOP. This is ridiculous. If you know these men then why are you talking to me? You've worked out that because my daughter has a non-English name - no, let me correct that, a Middle Eastern name - that she must cover up and be involved in some recruitment agency for dodgy men with beards that you happen to know? It's racist and outrageous.'

'Kendra. Calm down. This isn't helping.'

'No I won't calm down. 'I've been interrogated by my son, my best friend, and my head of department. NO, NO, NO. She's not been radicalised, nationalised, demonised or any other sort of 'ised'. She went to Birmingham University so she could stay home for God's sake. Nobody knows why she's done this to us.'

Kendra's voice broke as she dropped her head into her hands.

'And was an active member of the Free Palestine Movement. At the university.'

'So bloody what? Is it a crime now to speak out against injustice? What is it you want from us?' Kendra's voice was rising.

'Where did you find the bag?' David sat back and folded his arms.

'It was handed in to the Coventry station a few days ago. A

passenger found it stuffed behind the radiator in the waiting room. The officer with the sleek black hair tipped out the contents; brush, tissues, teddy bear key ring with house keys Kendra's spare car key, photo of Rani and Adam in Boston, bits of frippery; but it was the driving licence that Kendra grabbed.

'This is the only thing that helped to ID the owner. No purse or bank cards. She could have been mugged and the bag got discarded. That's common enough or she could have done this herself in an attempt to put you off her trail.'

Kendra's chest felt as if it was in a vice. 'What are you implying?'

'We're not implying anything. We don't know but we are concerned for her safety. She may be in some danger. Where is her father from?'

'Is this relevant?' David replaced the cap on his pen and folded the newspaper in half.

'Iran... but he's not here. He went back home over fifteen years ago.'

'Could she have gone there perhaps and didn't want you to know?'

'No. I don't know.' Kendra got up to pace the floor, working way at the nail of her middle finger.

'Is your daughter political?'

'As political as you are probably,' Kendra snapped. 'I know what you're getting at but you're out of order. You need to find the person who has dumped this bag then come back to us. I don't know where Rani is. All I can tell you is that her behaviour is completely out of character.'

'If you'd reported this to the police...'

'You'd have laughed in my face.'

Getting to his feet, David said in a level voice, 'My wife needs time to process this development. She's in a fragile state as you can see. We will be in touch.' Business cards were handed to David as he showed them out.

Exhausted, Kendra went back to bed, her head feeling like a copper bottomed pan. The police had asked if Rani was vulnerable. What they really meant was gullible. Open to suggestion. Her daughter wasn't even impressionable. Her stubborn streak had been the source of fierce battles when she was a child. Rani would take the road never travelled if it meant asserting her independence. She'd resisted peer pressure to take drugs, go to London to study and no doubt the many other temptations young people faced every day. When David came to check on her, she said, 'Do you think the police are implying Rani's dead?'

'No. They didn't say that. The probability is that the bag was stolen and dumped. It's a coincidence and nothing to do with the contents of the note. It's easy for the mind to make false links. We can only draw conclusions based on evidence.'

'And what about that photograph? Were they trying to trap me into admitting something?'

David sat beside her and nibbled on a piece of toast.

'I don't know but stop speculating and don't stay in bed all day. You won't sleep tonight.'

Kendra shuffled on to her side, feeling the mattress press deep into her ribs. She wanted to stay there but not alone.

'Come into the workshop with me. I need to fix one of the lights. The wiring isn't safe. You can read or listen to music.'

Kendra knew he was doing his best to be understanding.

'I wonder how many other parents go through this. Missing children who are never found, adult children who go on the streets or get caught up in some horrible situation like drugs or prostitution.'

'Stop torturing yourself. Come on. Keep your mind busy. Shall I show you the plans for my new telescope?'

'Alright.'

'No more talk of terrorist groups. Please. You're sounding like a stuck record. Nine hundred people are reported missing every day but most come back eventually. I read it on the Missing Person's website. We can post something on there. Maybe say you're ill and she needs to get in touch. It's not a lie.'

'I misjudge you sometimes. It's a good job one of us has our head screwed on.' She reached up touch his cheek.

David grinned. 'Put on something decent. You're starting to look like Sutton Coldfield's bag lady.'

'Thanks,' she muttered as she headed for the bathroom.

David was in the middle of a complex equation when the phone rang. Annoyed at the interruption, he paused to answer it. It was an update from the police which he relayed to Kendra as she towel dried her hair.

'The CCTV showed a white male in a hoodie stuffing the bag down the back of the radiator on platform 3 at 23.11 on December 23rd last year. It is most likely this was a mugging or a theft for Christmas money. They had over seventy similar reports across the West Midlands.'

'And that's it? No offer to put out a search for her knowing that she might have been injured?'

David frowned and shook his head. 'They can only tell us what they know.'

'Then they should have known this before they came here. They had a hidden agenda, knowing Ariana's background.'

Kendra glared at him, a hundred responses spinning through her head. He'd already returned to his work.

'I'm going out to the park. Adam's emailed to say Alison's gone into hospital with sickness. It looks like the stars are conspiring against me - and don't take that literally.'

The sight of oak trees gave her a mental boost. Here was something that grew tall and strong gathering wisdom and magic through its many seasons. It was the symbol of immortality that had the most impact as she stepped over their thick knotty roots, gleaming from the rain. A sudden urge to throw her arms around one of the trunks, loving its deep ridges and a faint smell of apple cider vinegar brought a comment from a faceless voice.

'Lucky tree.'

Brushing off bits of bark from her coat, she looked around and saw Tinks snuffling in the undergrowth.

'Hello. It's you. I thought it was someone trying to be funny.'

'Oh dear. I thought it was funny. Tinks stop it. He's after the mushrooms. You must think I'm stalking you. Hey, that was almost a joke!'

'It's always good to see you.'

As they walked, Kendra told him about the police visit and how angry she was feeling.

'They implied that my daughter was tied up in some underground recruitment agency for... oh it's complicated and you're not my dumping ground. Sorry.'

She gave him an apologetic smile and didn't object when he linked his arm through hers.

'You sound very stressed. Let's enjoy nature and we can talk later. Isn't this place beautiful? Look at those daffodils. *And then my heart with pleasure fills and dances with the daffodils.'*

'You are full of surprises!' she teased.

'For an engineer you mean.'

They laughed at Tinks trying to get the better of a Great Dane.

'Small dog syndrome,' they said in unison.

'So many people who don't know Birmingham think it's a

wasteland. Somewhere dirty and gritty, full of smoking chimneys and children running around in rags like in Oliver Twist. Just look at all this wonderful parkland.'

'Well Suttonians don't see this as Birmingham but I agree. We have so many well-tended parks. It's like living in the countryside.'

'And the canals give us the seaside feeling,' he laughed. 'I was one of those people. I resisted moving here for months.' He bent down to clip the lead onto the terrier's collar. Shall we tramp together then go back to mine? I'll save my etchings for another day,' he said with a grin as they disappeared deeper into the woodland.

'Did you run Ariana Najafi though the computer?' Sally Ray leant over her colleague's shoulder to study a print out.

'Yeah. No arrests but there's something on a Hassan Najafi. It could be the father. He was an anti- Revolutionary in the seventies when the Shah of Iran was deposed. Arrested for breach of the peace on a few occasions and having a stash of cannabis on his person. Intelligence had a file on him.'

'That's interesting. So the daughter could be up to something. I thought the mother was on the defensive.'

'We'd better not tell her he was suspected of bigamy. He had a wife tucked away in Iran.'

'She seemed very fragile and that husband of hers… Weird or what?'

'We'll keep an eye open. Nothing more we can do. If she wants to file a report, we can take things further.'

CHAPTER 22.

A slim book in an eye-catching rainbow cover rested on the edge of the coffee table in Marco's back room. *Necessary Loss; Healing the Grief.* Kendra flicked through it, noting a sentence or two which resonated with her.

'I searched that book out for you. It was given to me when Kay got married and left home and it was a real help when Lizzie died. I hope you don't mind.'

'No, but why?'

'I may be speaking out of turn but I can see the sadness in your eyes even though you hide it well. I'm sensitive to these things.'

Kendra didn't know what to say. In the warmth of the room, the pains in her back gradually eased out. She rested her head against the back of the chair and looked around. The eclectic mix of furniture, spoke of legacy; 1950's sideboard with a few scratches, a walnut inlaid desk, a red and orange wall hanging with a South American design and a Turkish looking rug. Kendra loved it all. The comfortable silence was broken only by Tinks sniffing around her ankles.

'Don't let him on the sofa. Lie down boy. Basket.' Marco pointed to it and the two males locked eyes.

'Tell me about your daughter. Ariana? What is she like?'

Marco poured them a brandy. 'Take your time.'

'You'd be a good therapist. I like to think of her as a modest genius. As early as primary school, she was into inventing things and coming up with revolutionary ideas. She'd talk to David about the wonders of the universe until I had to drag them away from their telescopes to get some sleep. I thought she was happy but then she screamed at me one day saying I'd pushed her into doing a course she hated. Astro-physics. She lived and breathed it. I didn't understand what had changed.' Kendra's eyes moved to an array of photographs on the mantelpiece.

'I don't know much about this other than from my own experience and bits I've read but young adults go through a rebellious phase far more dramatic than the teenage troubles. They need to shape their own identity. There's a very good book by Gail Sheehy. Life Passages. I'll look it out for you. See how eclectic my reading tastes are?' He smiled. 'But then I'm preaching to the converted. Sorry. I remember how Kay was.'

'Yes I know, but when it's your own daughter who disappears and weeks later sends you a note to say she's done with you…'

Marco raised his untamed eyebrows in sympathy.

'I'm so sorry. That must have been terrible for you. It's extreme but haven't we all done something similar? Cut off from our roots for a while so we can grow into our own skin. I'm mixing clichés here but you know what I mean.'

Marco settled himself back in the chair as Kendra unburdened herself.

'It's what my son says. It's ironic isn't it? The development of the young adult brain is my speciality. It neurologically repositions itself during the early twenties and that has an impact on behaviour. It's always been the case but there is something extreme and selfish about this generation. It's like they've been robbed of any empathy for other people.' Kendra paused to sip some water. 'I couldn't imagine doing this to my parents. I phoned once a week and maybe a letter.'

'Ah. Technology. That's what's changed. Even Kay prefers to send a quick text when I would like to speak to her on the phone. She calls me Noah.'

'I'm beginning to feel old too. Out of touch. At one time the spirit duplicator was complicated enough. Now I can no longer keep up with it all. We'll be having chips embedded in our hands one of these days. That'll be the way we communicate. Beam videos from our palms.'

'We've never made so many strides so quickly. I wonder if it impacts on brain development. All this Facebooking and gadgetry can't be good. I worry about my grandchildren and hope Kay won't give in and buy them tablets or phones when they are in nursery.'

Tinks padded over to give Kendra one of his special cute looks.

'The studies are being done now so I guess we will see,' she said. Technology abused. Imagine if we were sent videos in technicolour of massacred soldiers in the Great War. Maybe it would have ended sooner.'

'Or is it a case of what we don't see, we don't grieve over. Now those poor families of hostages in the Middle East struggled to avoid seeing pictures of their loved ones in orange jump suits about to be beheaded.'

A heavy silence fell over the room. Neither could find words to express the horror at what they were feeling over the frightening unravelling of world events. It was Marco who broke the silence by getting up to open the French windows to release a wasp into the garden.

'I don't like killing insects if I can help it. It was something I learned from the Buddhists when I worked in Cambodia. How's your proposal coming along?'

Kendra frowned and tugged on her fringe. Marco went on.

'For your doctorate? The supernatural and why people believe?'

'Oh that. I don't really know whether to carry on with it. I got hooked on calling up psychics and the like, not realising I was becoming addicted. I doubt I could be objective enough.'

'Maybe addicted is a bit strong? Obsessed? I can understand how that happens when someone is under so much stress. It's like grief. Your rational mind tells you your loved one is dead. Gone for good but a part of you says something else.'

'Cognitive dissonance. It came to a head when David found out. It was an ugly scene but it brought me to my senses although I'm not completely free of it.'

'Withdrawal you mean?'

'Sounds ridiculous doesn't it?'

'Don't be so hard on yourself. This isn't your fault.'

Her phone vibrated in her pocket. She checked it and sighed. 'It's David. I'd better go home.' Marco helped her into her coat and handed her some books.

'Have a browse through these, especially the Life Passages one. You might find something that resonates.'

Marco took her hands and rubbed life back into her cold fingers. 'You're grieving and the pain is very real. Come anytime. I'm always ready to listen.'

'You're the only person who takes me seriously. I appreciate that Marco.'

She stepped out into the chilly air. The sun had gone behind a mass of grey cloud. He squeezed her arm and watched her walk down the path before closing the door. Wishing he could do more to help, he looked up a number in his diary.

Kendra retraced her steps through the park towards home, deep in thought. If Rani was going through a phase, then maybe she wasn't to blame. Adam was right. She'd soon come to her senses but as Kendra turned into the drive she pushed that idea away. Her daughter was still accountable for her actions. Shock was giving way to anger.

CHAPTER 23

David caught a glimpse of the postman, reaching down into his cart to pull out a bundle of letters and a small parcel.

'Gave me a bit of a fright there boss,' he laughed, as David opened the door and stared down at him from the step. 'Here you go,' he said, plugging the buds of his headphones back into his ears.

David studied the envelopes, frowning as he shook the package. He couldn't remember ordering anything for the steam engine he was building. Turning it over he saw his wife's name in thick black lettering. He put it aside on the kitchen table and returned to his workshop to look for a piece of paper he'd mislaid. Kendra had shouted at him as she'd left the house for work and he was feeling too rattled to do much.

He couldn't cope with emotional outbursts and chose to calm things down by not confronting her. He didn't know why it made her angrier. Once, when she'd called him names for letting a pan of soup dry up, he'd grabbed it by the handle and thrown it hard against the kitchen wall. He sat at his work bench, brooding for the rest of the morning.

Kendra was watching the rain drip off the trees as her group of life skills students worked their way through some questions about

Troubled Feelings.

'Mrs. Blackmore. What does this mean? I catastrophize when I feel anxious?'

Kendra threw the question out to the group.

'You think the worst is going to happen even when there's no evidence for it.'

'Well done Shelly. It's called cognitive distortion.'

'Oink, oink,' sniggered a girl in full face make-up who sat behind her.

'Shut your face.'

'Ladies. Respect. Here's an example. Who thinks they will fail their GCSEs?'

A number of hands hovered in the air.

'What is your evidence?'

'I didn't do well in the mocks,' said one with a smug look on her face. 'That's plenty of evidence.'

'It just feels like it,' added the girl sitting next to her.

'So it's based on a feeling. Do you know for sure that's going to happen?'

The girls at the front looked at each other and shook their heads.

'Joanne, you're very quiet at the back. What do you do when you feel anxious and negative about something?'

'She eats chocolate.'

'I'm talking to Joanne. Jo? What happens when you eat chocolate?'

'She gets fat.'

'I'm warning you Marcia.' Kendra turned to the rest of the girls whose eyes had zoomed onto their doodling.

'Let's take this further. Would it be a catastrophe if you did fail your exams? Let's compare it with young people fleeing a war zone.'

'My dad would kill me so yeah it would be.'

'You can't compare it with boatloads of people coming here to get benefits. My dad goes mental when he watches the telly.' A loud popping of gum punctuated the stream of invective which received nods of agreement from the girls in the room.

Kendra felt as if someone had struck her across the mouth. She knew it was a bad analogy as soon as the words left her lips but to be faced with such unashamed prejudice in a school that prided itself on teaching tolerance was shocking. Barely controlling her outrage, she told them to finish the worksheets and hand them in first thing in the morning or risk penalties.

'I don't believe it,' Kendra said out loud to the staffroom which had begun to fill up with people, steam from the kettle and the crackle of newspapers. 'For all the boasting about inclusivity this school is supposed to be noted for, I've got students showing their true colours against refugees.'

'Well they've not picked it up from us. It'll be the media or listening to their parents,' said one of the part time teachers as he scrolled through his phone.

'That's right. Blame parents again,' cut in Sheila, pushing her way to her desk. 'Some of us work hard to raise our children to reach out to others irrespective of background yet we still get the shit thrown when something goes wrong and I don't agree that schools don't contribute to some of the hate we're starting to witness. We're becoming complacent.'

Kendra was wishing she'd kept her mouth shut. Pushing some papers round her desk, she noticed a stiff cream envelope from the Honourable Caroline Whitely. Stuffing it in her bag to read on the train, she gathered her files together and made a discreet exit to escape the toxic rhetoric.

The train back to Sutton Coldfield was jammed with commuters blocking the doorways oblivious to people trying to get out at

New Street. An altercation between an elderly man and a gang of teenagers attracted Kendra's attention. One boy pushed the man backwards onto the platform, jeered on by his friends. Too caught up in their own lives, other passengers stepped over him as he tried to pull himself to his feet. Kendra leapt out of the train to help him.

'Are you alright?' She helped him onto a bench.

The man brushed himself down and pulled up the right sleeve of his jacket to examine some small cuts which oozed blood.

'A bit shocked. I was minding my own business then bang, out of the blue, those kids started on me for no reason. I'm eighty-one you know. I don't understand what's happened to this generation. We never treated old people this way.'

Kendra handed him a pack of tissues as she guided him towards the escalator. In the foyer she bought him a drink.

'My grandson died in Afghanistan. He was the kindest boy you could want to meet. His mother didn't want him to go in the army,' he paused and dabbed at his eyes. Kendra let him talk, keeping her eye on the clock. Once she was sure he was feeling better, she said goodbye and made her way back down to the platform. She was struck by the coincidence of meeting a stranger who had taught her more about resilience than any textbook. His grandson would never walk through their doors again but her daughter would. One day. She had to hold onto that.

'There's a package for you,' said David, pointing to it on the table.

She picked it up, noticing the dark rings around his eyes.

'I'm going to have a soak. You sort out dinner.'

David slipped off his glasses and wiped them on the edge of his gardening jumper.

'Me?'

'Yes please. You've been home all day.'

'But I don't know how to.'

She spun round on her heels. 'David, you can make telescopes, circuit boards and calculate missions to Mars so I am sure you can work it out.'

As she watched the water shoot into the bath, frothing up the globs of bath essence into a lavender floss, she knew her husband would be sulking in the kitchen. Kendra didn't care what he did as long as she could lose herself in the fragrant steam if only for a few moments. As she sank deeper into the water, she closed her eyes for a few moments to block out the day.

Ignoring her husband's constant calling up the stairs, Kendra tore into the packing with a pair of nail scissors she found hiding under a tangle of pens, memory sticks and a couple of pink curlers, to find a gold box decorated with a picture of the archangel Michael, his huge blue wings pointing upwards. Kendra's fingers grazed the embossed lettering. Angel Cards. All promises to Marco and Sheila to stop consulting oracles were suspended as she held the cards to her chest and asked for the traditional blessing as written in the instruction leaflet. Feeling a strange heat shoot through her arms to her fingertips, Kendra was sure the angels would answer her requests. She closed her eyes and brought Rani's face into focus.

'My darling girl. I miss you so much. I hope the angels are looking after you and will give you this message of love. Please call me and tell me you are well.'

'Kendra. Kendra! The pan has burned dry and the potatoes are black. I forgot about them. Are you coming down?'

Bloody hellfire!

Kendra placed the cards carefully back in their satin wrapping, fearful that now she'd made the connection according to the rituals, it would be lost.

'What was in the parcel?' David picked out some seeds from a red pepper.

'Nothing important,' she said, 'and stop doing that.'

They moved around each other like skaters fearful of a collision. Kendra emptied the washing machine while David did the crossword. Their home had lost its sparkle over the months as it waited expectantly for a new development. Conversation was stilted and touched only on safe subjects. Kendra was losing a connection to her feelings while David focused on his physical ailments. At some level he knew he was losing her. Kendra knew she was losing herself.

CHAPTER 24 ⟳

*K*endra shook the contents of her workbag in search of the bottle of Calm Down herbal tablets Sheila had suggested for panic attacks. She placed it at the back of her tongue, worked up some saliva and swallowed hard, shuddering at the bitter taste.

The in-surgery counsellor her doctor recommended had made copious notes when Kendra told him she was being watched. She couldn't convince him that she really *had* seen the man in the park, slinking behind a tree when she turned round and he *had* watched her from across the road when she reached up to draw the curtains. He'd talked to her about the complications of grief as it related to the loss of her daughter but Kendra shook her head.

The effort of getting dressed for work then navigating the swarms of commuters pouring into New Street station was too much to contemplate on a drenched Monday morning. From her bedroom window, Kendra watched the water from an overflowing pipe gush down the pavement as children on their way to school were pulled away from tempting puddles by frazzled adults. Every cell in her body squealed in pain since she'd made a conscious effort to stay away from the lure of the psychics. It had been two weeks and three days and three hours since she'd last checked her horoscope or telephoned a hotline for a quick reading. Kendra referred to the latest entry in her journal. *Feeling ok today. Slept 6 hours. Improvement. No appetite.*

The crumpled letter from Caz lay on the windowsill, the ink smudged from the damp. Kendra read it for the third time.

'Come to our next meeting at Carrs Lane Counselling Centre where you can raise the issue of psychic addiction. We can see where it goes from there. Talk about your personal journey. By the way, it seems 'channelling', whatever that is, seems to be another wave of madness hitting the vulnerable. Click on these links. May be your research idea isn't so off the mark after all. Call me soon to talk it through.'

As the letter dropped from her hand, Kendra went straight to her study and logged on to the YouTube links. All thoughts of calling the academy switchboard to report her lateness were overridden as she watched a demonstration of a young woman seemingly in a trance and talking in a strained voice of an older American man. The woman's face was distorting as she writhed on the chair, her head tossing backwards uttering messages purported to be from some Greek philosopher.

After five minutes of watching this spectacle, Kendra flicked to the comments at the foot of the video and read the rapturous feedback of the followers. Kendra felt uneasy at the group think which reminded her of the story about 'The Emperor's New Clothes'.

She ran the video again, looking for some psychological explanation for the woman's behaviour. Making a note to look into it further, she called the Academy to say she was on her way. An empty train was waiting in the station. As she settled into a window seat, she realized Caz was right.

So many vulnerable people, especially the bereaved turned to psychics and mediums for help and reassurance that their loved ones existed somewhere in some form. In crisis, human beings

THE FUTURE CAN'T WAIT

needed comfort and to be told everything would be fine in the end. Kendra knew that from her training and her own personal experience yet some had told her things they couldn't have possibly known. *Your daughter has an unusual heritage. She's just scooped a prestigious award.*

'You've missed all the action,' said Sheila, a demon grin on her face as she pulled Kendra into an empty classroom. Keeping her voice low she went on, 'Maurice has finally flipped. He was caught coming out of some seedy lap dancing club last night on the Hagley Road with his proverbial pants around his ankles.'

'Proverbial pants eh?'

'He was snapped with some women in French maid outfits on Broad Street. The boss is in uproar. The video is all over social media, linking it back to here.'

Kendra clutched her bag to her chest. Maurice was like an irritating mosquito in her life but she wasn't going to get involved with the hand flapping over his latest escapades. She knew he was lonely since his wife left taking the twin boys and that his drinking was becoming a problem but as she told Sheila, 'I'm a psychology teacher, not his therapist,' whenever one of the staff urged her to *do something about him.*

'But aren't you shocked?' Sheila searched her friend's face for signs of horror.

'No. Nothing shocks me these days.' She flicked through a pile of papers on her desk.

'Oh, I found this in the travel section of the Sunday papers. It's a feature on Iran. Top tourist destination for 2016. Ironic really considering the relationship we've got with the Arab world.'

Kendra cast her eye over the front page before promptly handing it back.

'Iranians are not Arabs. I do wish people would educate themselves. They are Indo-Europeans.'

'Sorry. I didn't know that.'

'We're going to end up with some serious divisions in this city if we throw stereotypes around in a place where we are supposed to be teaching critical thinking. I've got a class.'

'So much for trying to be nice,' Sheila muttered under her breath.

Letting the door slam behind her, Kendra disappeared down the corridor to her classroom, in no mood for small talk. She wanted to do her job then leave.

'What's up with Kenny?'

'Leave it Alex and don't let her hear you call her that. She's stressed like the rest of us slogging it out in this place.'

'Oh yeah? Kendra Blackmore doesn't believe in stress. Remember that article she wrote about employees making wildly exaggerated claims of mental distress? The insurance companies loved her. I bet she made a shit load of money from it.'

'You're stirring it. We all know you don't like her. Maybe it's because she can see right through you Alex. To see the nasty foul mouthed person you really are under that swaggering exterior. You know something? The reason I'm getting out of this place is not the kids. I feel sorry for them. It's the politics. That and the childish antics of the staff.'

Kendra spent the morning's double lesson fighting off the memories of the good times she and Hassan spent in Shiraz before his family gathered the power of a small government to drag him home.

She tried to engage her group in a discussion about the pituitary-adrenal system, blundering her way through some examples, wishing her students would show some interest. Her eyes swivelled towards the clock as another wave of panic gathered momentum.

'Is there a problem today? Have you all actively decided to fail your AS level? Maybe I'm boring you?'

Two girls at the front played with their hair. A nervous giggle broke from a girl at the back.

'Martha? Would you like to share the joke?'

'No joke Miss.'

'Well, what we don't cover in this class will be given as extra homework. You want to be treated as adults but you don't attempt to behave with a modicum of maturity.'

'We are listening Mrs Blackmore.' Shelly looked around for support from the class.

'But?'

'We think you don't like us anymore. In fact, we think you've given up on us.'

Kendra opened her mouth to reply then closed it. Slipping off her glasses and moving from behind her desk she said, 'Thank you for having the courage to be honest about your feelings. I'm sorry you feel I've let you down. I've had a lot of family problems and haven't been as focused as I should be. Personal and professional life should be kept separate.'

'But you can't do that Miss. You're human,' protested Martha. Her black curls streaked with overtones of fashion grey bounced around her shoulders.

'It's something you will all have to learn when you start your careers. Putting the mask on and going out there to perform as if nothing is wrong is the hardest thing we have to do.'

'But what if someone in your family dies?'

'You get compassionate leave for a while then you go back to work. It isn't healthy to indulge your emotions for too long.'

Kendra flinched at the irony of what she was saying.

Stacey was on her feet. Being under average height, it was the only way she felt she could be noticed. Two red spots burned on her cheeks.

'Only a robot could control emotions like that.'

'Duh Stace. If you were a robot, you wouldn't have any feelings.'

'Stephanie. What have we said about sarcasm?'

'Sorry Miss. Is it your daughter? We heard she's gone missing. Is that why you did that lesson with us?'

'You don't have to hide your feelings with us Mrs Blackmore. It must be really hard for you.'

'All behaviour has a knock on effect so we have to consider that when we choose to act. Now we need to move on with the lesson but I will tell you the story sometime. Now, let's put the pituitary gland to one side today and look at the biology of emotional control.'

The room began to pulsate with a fresh energy and a new understanding.

'That was a great lesson Miss,' said three girls who normally sat at the back swiping away at their forbidden phones.

'Why was that?' Kendra finished wiping down the whiteboard.

'Cos it's relevant to us. Stuff we need to know about. It helps me deal with my mum when she goes off on one.'

Kendra smiled. 'Glad it was useful.'

Sheila poked her head round the door, her mouth puckered into an apology.

'They seemed very buoyant. Not another exploration into the male mind?'

'Not qualified to teach that. Sorry I snapped. Seeing those pictures of Persepolis brought back some painful memories.' Kendra dived between the tables to retrieve scraps of paper for the recycle box.

'How do you fancy trekking up to Selly Oak and go to that food store you used to like. Sells dates and rugs and stuff. You could sniff around to see if anyone knew Rani. It's close enough to the university. Jo wants to check it out as a possibility so we could leave him there and have a mooch round.'

Kendra carried on tidying up the classroom, pulling down poster size diagrams of the brain as she thought about Sheila's suggestion. 'No carpets,' she said firmly. 'I've a loft full of them. Saturday maybe?'

'It's a date. I've got a meeting with the curriculum heads now. See you later.'

A couple of days later, waiting for a break in the never ending deluge of rain, Kendra pulled on a cagoule and checked on David before she set off for the park. Marco was happy to walk in all weathers but doubted he would be out as Tinks turned his nose up at getting wet. Tramping along the muddy paths, Kendra found herself comparing Marco, who talked to her and could empathise, to her husband. David was only comfortable with facts and formulae. Feelings and people were messy things to be avoided.

An emailed pinged its arrival on her phone.

'Ma, Skype me on Sunday. Not heard from you. Called home this afternoon but David seemed a bit dazed. Is everything ok?'

CHAPTER 25

BOSTON

$\mathcal{A}$dam sat at in his office, a pile of folders neatly stacked on his desk, staring at the letter in his hand. It was brief, written in Farsi with a few English words in American spellings dotted in between the flowing script. He tapped the end of his pen against his teeth wondering who he could get to translate it for him.

A search of Facebook had brought up the names of a couple of cousins whom Adam hadn't seen since his last visit to Iran as a child. Having made contact with them, he'd asked for their home address on the pretext of exchanging some photographs. In a throwaway line, he'd written, 'I hope Ariana is enjoying her time in Shiraz. Please ask her to get in touch.' It was bait and it seemed to have worked.

'Hey Reza, how you doing? Can you spare me a minute?'

Adam was rushing to an appointment when he spotted a colleague striding out of the elevator, a briefcase in his hand.

'Literally one minute. What's up?'

'You read Farsi don't you?'

Reza rocked his head as if to say, well sort of, maybe.

Adam pushed the letter into his hand and watched his dark eyes scan the writing.

'Sixth grader!'

'What do you mean?'

'Well apart from your address written in a mature, English hand, this quote has been written either by a child or a foreigner.'

'What does it say?'

'Well there's a bit of a philosophical poem by Rumi about needing to be patient but that doesn't seem to be linked to anything and... Um... your father's got lung cancer. Sorry to hear that. A bit of criticism about your mother keeping you and your sister away from the family. Says your Dad tried to visit you in 2008 but immigration refused his entry visa in the UK.'

'Is that it? Does it say anything about my sister?'

Reza studied Adam's stricken expression and shook his head, handing back the letter and resumed his soft whistling down the wide corridor with its pale yellow walls covered in Disney characters en route to the paediatric ward. A hundred questions spun round in Adam's head like bits of mosaic making it difficult to concentrate on his most difficult patient of the day. His biggest dilemma was should he tell his mother anything at all knowing her fragile state of mind?

It was almost noon on Sunday when Kendra answered his Skype call, peering at his grainy form and irritated by the number of times the conversation got lost in the ether. David sat at the dining room table, carefully unfolding a science supplement to one of the Sunday broadsheets.

'I can't concentrate,' he told her, rubbing his hand across his temple.

Kendra moved into the living room and closed the door. Adam gave her a selective account of the letter.

'And that's it? Your dad tried to get back in the country and was deported? Why?'

'Ma, I don't know. Ali has closed his Facebook account so I can't go back and ask. Seems Dad is very ill so it's possible Rani found out about it and wanted to see him. It is logical don't you think?'

'Oh God. She'll never get out again. There was case in the news of a woman who went to visit family and is now in jail. The authorities make up stories about spying and find someone to pin it on.'

Kendra's voice cracked in terror. 'My baby girl. Oh my God. We'll never see her again. The pieces fit. I spoke to a remote viewer. She said Rani was somewhere hot, covered in black...'

Adam's head dropped into his hands wishing he'd kept his mouth shut.

'Stop this Ma now. Get a grip. It's pure speculation with no evidence. You're overwrought and it's not helping anyone. Let's keep to the facts. Did she have an Iranian passport?'

'Yes. No. I found a half completed application form in her drawer.'

'OK. She needs an Iranian birth certificate for that and they are not easy to get since she was born here. The embassy have to issue them and I presume Dad would have to be involved somehow. It's not like here or in the UK. It's complicated.'

'She could have travelled on her British passport. That's not here.'

Adam shook his head, adjusting the webcam to create a clearer picture.

'She's classed as a dual national. She would have to travel on her Iranian one so I think it's unlikely. Nobody is going to tell us if she did travel so we have to rely on her to get in touch. There's nothing more to be done. If she has gone out there without doing her homework, then to be honest Ma she deserves all she gets. I'm running out of patience.'

'And she needs an exit visa! Only your father can provide the permission for that. Oh Adam. What a mess. Stupid, stupid girl.'

Kendra tugged a handful of tissues from the box and blew her nose. 'I'm going to go out there myself. I can travel on a British passport.'

'Are you crazy? The world is teetering on a precipice. War could break out and involve us and Iran. No. Absolutely not.'

Adam closed his eyes and pressed his knuckles into the corners. His head was pounding from a late night out with the boys and Alison's heaving noises from the bathroom were jangling his nerves.

'I've got to go. Don't do anything foolish. OK? We'll talk soon. Love you.'

Kendra stared at the blank screen, frozen to her seat for several minutes, trying to process what she'd heard. Too many questions and no answers. Kendra knew what Iran had been like in the early eighties. The moral police swarmed the streets, especially those looking for violations of the strict Islamic dress code. People disappeared for voicing an opinion against the regime. Family members betrayed each other. Places of public execution were being built. The revolution was almost forty years old and she doubted anything had changed despite the new wave of tourism. At the time, foreign wives were unable to leave the country to visit their own families without the permission of their husbands.

Kendra needed to talk to someone and went in search of her husband. The fact she had to prepare for two classes the next day pushed her to skim through her notes, scribble a lesson plan on some scrap paper, and shoehorn everything into her bag before dumping it by the coat stand in the hall.

She pressed her ear to the door of his workshop before entering the dingy space, lit only by a couple of lamps on his chaotic workbench. She waited for him to set down his magnifying glass and assume his *I'm busy* face.

Keeping to the bare facts, she told him about her conversation with Adam while he twiddled a micro screwdriver between his fingers. Resisting the urge to push everything onto the floor with an angry sweep of her hands, she said, 'That's the last time I am going to share anything with you that doesn't involve money, food or postal deliveries. You have no interest in anything outside your own needs or how something is directly affecting you. It seems to me that you tolerate me being here as long as I am useful to you. You don't care about how I feel and never have done.'

Bending over to look into his eyes she added, 'Maybe it's time to call an end to this marriage.'

David reached over to plug in his soldering iron.

'I don't understand why you get so upset over things you can't control Kendra. It wastes energy. Your logic has been compromised by this emotional rollercoaster you insist on riding. You don't talk about anything other than Ariana. You're obsessed.'

'She's my daughter!' Kendra screamed.

He turned back to his drawing and pencilled in some notes in his tiny writing. He began his whistling, a sign he needed to be left alone. Kendra's eyes blazed. Turning away from him, she kicked a box out of the way and slammed the door. She needed to see Marco but not before she'd sorted out her neglected appearance. At least he would listen.

Hair by Janine was full of mid-week specials. Kendra managed to squeeze in an appointment even though she'd promised to write up the overdue proposal for Caz. As Janine chatted away about her hair needing some warmth with caramel and honey tones, Kendra transferred a few ideas onto her iPad.

'I haven't got much time today so whatever is quickest,' Kendra said.

Janine made a moue of disapproval but called a trainee to take Kendra to the basin for a 'thorough wash'. As she waited for her hair to take the colour under a crackle of foils, she flicked through some magazines. An article in Destiny caught her attention. Sasha, a white witch was offering her services as spell caster for donations only. She talked about the need for patience as it takes time for spells to work and karma might mean that what was being asked for might not be granted. Kendra wanted to circle the poor grammar and spelling with a red pen.

She met Marco by arrangement in the park where they stopped to listen to a school choir rehearsing. 'You look nice.' Marco turned to the terrier. 'Tinks stop digging. You'll have those bulbs out. I wondered if you'd been mown down with this virus that's been going around. I've escaped this time but my neighbour's been so ill for weeks.'

'Oh work gets in the way of life and David's not been too well again.'

'I've been down to The Cotswolds to see my family before they go off to Canada for a year. Brandon, my son in law, does a hush-hush job so he's moved about a bit. Ottawa this time.'

'It's supposed to be a beautiful city. You'll visit them?'

'If I'm invited. It's not too far,' he said in a distant voice giving Kendra the feeling that Canada's capital was on another planet. 'Shall we go back to Chez Marco?'

Tinks sniffed his way along the grass verge on the way home. As Kendra soaked up the sun in Marco's back room, the dog slid his paw onto her knee, head on one side in expectation.

'He's getting cheeky,' said Marco, giving him one of his dog treats. Kendra met Marco's eyes for a few seconds and smiled. 'I hope you don't think *I'm* cheeky as well, inviting you here,' he said. 'I've missed your company.' Marco gathered up a handful of pens on the desk and returned them to the holder. 'I'd started the big tidy up but didn't get very far.'

'I relax when I come here. I love it as it is.'

'That's good. Any news?'

Kendra brought him up to date, expressing her fears that Rani might have gone out to Iran to see her father.

'She sounds too sensible for that knowing that it could be dangerous. We have to trust our children as they grow up. We give them the values and I believe they are always deeply buried with them even though they make mistakes. Brandon does a dangerous job and can't tell Kay about it. He tries to keep her safe. I worry how she would cope if something happened to him but I have to trust the universe to look after them both, as soft as that might sound. I do have this philosophy. When the time is right, things come right.'

'I used to believe that too. I thought I knew about people and what drove them to behave in certain ways. Then look what happened to me. I shouldn't be teaching psychology at all.'

Marco took Kendra's hand and rubbed her fingers. 'You are much too hard on yourself. You are a strong woman and people need you. Sharing this experience with other mothers, parents, would be a tremendous service. Maybe the universe is trying to tell you something after all.'

'You're good for me,' Kendra said, her words lost in his kiss.

CHAPTER 26

When she called on Marco a week later to return the books she'd borrowed, he was wearing a smock-like garment covered in paint. She noticed a streak of blue in his left eyebrow.

'Come and see my etchings,' he winked, showing her into the front room which had always been closed off to keep the dog out. 'By the way, I'm sorry I overstepped the mark the other day.'

Kendra smiled, not knowing what to say. She'd felt guilty but pleased that someone had shown her some affection. Several canvases of different sizes were propped up against the wall, the smaller ones laid out on a sideboard for Kendra to view.

'Interesting. Love the bold colours.'

'All abstracts become interesting when you don't know what they represent. I don't either to be honest but it doesn't matter.' His face lit up as he showed her a half-completed canvas resting on an easel. 'I have no idea what this is going to be. I'd never painted in my life until Lizzie died. It was somebody at a widowers' support session suggested getting out of my comfort zone. I tried different classes and if I'd worked harder I could have followed my dream of painting seascapes but as we are bang in the middle of Birmingham…'

He squeezed a blob of yellow paint into a tub, added a drop of water, mixed it and handed Kendra a small round sponge.

'I thought we might finish this one together. Dip it in the paint and squeeze on the canvas, anywhere you fancy. Twist it into a circle.'

'Me? I can't paint. I got thrown out of the art class at school.'

'I'm giving you permission to co-create with me. It doesn't matter what it looks like. That's the beauty of abstract. Well, my version of it. Come on before the paint dries up.'

Kendra took off her jacket and allowed him to tie a plastic apron around her waist. Following his instructions, she held the sponge close to the canvas.

'Go for it. Be brave.'

She pressed hard on a space in the middle, twisted the sponge clockwise and released it. A golden ball with a furry bit around the bottom stared back at her.

'So, what do you think it is?'

Kendra stood back and put her head on one side.

'A bit of a mess.'

'Sun? Human cell? Alien life form? You see it can be anything you want it to be. It doesn't matter what someone tells you it is. It's your own world when you paint.'

'Mm. Ok, it's a balloon which can take off in any direction and find a new path. You're going to tell me this is straight out of my unconscious aren't you?'

'I'm not the psychologist. Is it?'

'No, although I did feel a bit spacey for a minute or two.' They giggled and made woo-wooing sounds. Holding her gaze for a fraction, Marco handed her a stump of bristles that looked like an old shaving brush.

'What colour do you like?'

'Blue. Any sort.'

Marco mixed some more paint in a yogurt pot and suggested she carried on filling the canvas with any shape she fancied.

'But it's going to ruin your work,' she protested, pushing hair away from her face.

'Who defines ruin?'

For an hour, they painted, joked and laughed. Kendra felt on a high as if something huge had been lifted from her shoulders.

'What are you thinking?' Marco opened the window to let in some air.

'About what it means to be happy. I can see why you took up art. Stops the swirling thoughts.'

'Now we've finished our masterpiece, we must sign it.' Marco signed their initials in the corner of the canvas. K and M. To Kendra, it felt like an admission of adultery.

'We deserve a glass of wine. Sit in the garden and I'll bring it out. Don't look too closely though. I've not done very much to it this year.'

Kendra fingered the filigreed pattern on the patio table as she watched Tinks race around the lawn after a squirrel.

'Maybe I should take up a hobby. I've always been too engrossed with work and raising a family to have time for myself.'

'Churchill found painting to be very therapeutic. He said it rested an overworked part of his brain and put a different part to work. He too said it was the act of doing it and not the results that mattered. Try one of these. I made them this morning.'

He bit into a cheese biscuit, flicking the crumbs from his shirt. Tinks raced back to study his every movement. Kendra sipped her wine and looked down towards the bottom of the garden where she could see a pavilion- like summer house, nestled behind some overgrown trees. David had built something similar in their garden but it had never been used. It gave her an idea.

Time slid by as they chatted about art, world events, life and death and whatever came to mind.

'I must go. Thank you for a lovely afternoon. You've given me back some confidence.' She kissed his cheek as she left.

Her creative afternoon had pushed away her worries about her daughter if only for a short time. The art teacher at school had made it clear that Kendra couldn't draw a straight line with a ruler. She loved the way Marco had encouraged her to express whatever was in her heart. *If you feel blue. Paint blue.* No wonder art therapy was growing in popularity.

The evening was warm and full of promise. Kendra logged onto You Tube to find some Art for Amateurs videos. A local man had over 20,000 views for his lesson on Sutton Park in watercolours. Kendra was so absorbed in watching him mix the colours and explain the techniques of painting a spring sky that she didn't hear David moaning in the kitchen. When she found him bent over the work surface, paint sloshed over the floor, she helped him to a chair and mopped the sweat from his forehead.

'It's a bug. I'll be fine.'

'But you've just got over one David. Your breathing is shallow. I need to call the doctor.'

He raised his hand in protest. 'No,' he gasped. 'I'm fine apart from my vision. I'll lie down on the sofa for a bit.'

It was a few days before he was back to himself. Kendra didn't comment on how he was dragging his right foot when he walked, deciding to keep a close eye on him instead. She was telling Sheila about it over tapas in a new bar in Sutton town centre when she got a funny feeling that she needed to go home. She tried ringing David but he didn't answer.

She ran through the house calling his name. The light was on in the workshops but no husband. She noticed some overturned metal trays, their contents spilled across his workbench. Willing herself to stay calm, she skirted the edge of the garden, calling his mobile and shouting his name. Frustration bubbled over. The car was on the drive so he hadn't gone far. Maybe a walk? Yes, he must have gone to the garage to get the paper. Kendra talked to herself as she ran around the garden shouting, 'David? David!' One of the neighbours, who was cutting his hedge, looked up and gave her a sour look.

As she bent down to wind up the hose, she spotted a black wellington poking out from behind the greenhouse.

'Oh no. Please God no.'

Her husband was lying on the stony ground, his right arm bent under his back. Kendra's immediate thought was that he was dead. A strangled scream escaped from her throat as she dialled the emergency services.

'Kendy?' The voice was weak and seemed to come from far away.

'I'm calling the ambulance.'

'No. I'm ok. I fell. Help me up.'

Kendra shook her head as she noticed how frozen the right side of his face seemed to be.

'You can't move until you've been checked over.'

David struggled to lift his upper body, grabbing Kendra's arm to steady himself as he pulled himself into a sitting position.

'My arm feels numb and my head aches but I'm ok. I need to lie down in the dark for a bit.'

He leaned on Kendra as they shuffled back into the house where she could help him onto the sofa. Drawing the curtains, she helped him out of his jacket and placed a cushion under his head.

'I'm calling the doctor. This keeps happening and it's not a bug. You've got a nasty cut above your eye.' She didn't tell him he was slurring his words.

'Wait a few hours. Please. Let me nap for an hour then call.'

David slept throughout the evening and well into the night, waking only for glasses of water. Kendra dozed on the reclining chair, unable to rest until she was sure her husband was out of danger. By the following morning, he seemed better, although tired and unwilling to talk. He sat watching Sky news on repeat, shaking his head at the media saturation of global mayhem and violence. He ignored the plate of savoury snacks she brought to him at intervals, even pushing away a bowl of pistachio ice cream and chocolate sauce.

Kendra was due into work the following day but didn't know if she dare leave him on his own. Watching him doze, she picked up her iPad and sent some urgent emails, drew up a work plan for her students in case she had to stay home before disappearing into her study to play with her set of tarot cards.

Kendra had read somewhere that fear wasn't just a feeling. It was something you could smell. At that moment she couldn't shake the sensation that somebody was hiding in the room. A curtain rustled in the breeze, knocking some papers to the floor. Vesta appeared in the doorway, hissing and arching her back. *The cat knows more than that useless counsellor.*

In a shaky voice she called out, 'Who are you? What do you want with me?' Sweat ran down the small of her back as listened to the thudding of her heart. Kendra knew all about the mind disconnecting from reality to cope with trauma but this was no delusion. She felt threatened and when the scream finally came it bounced off the ceiling and down the stairs.

'Kendra, what's that noise? What's going on? I feel better and the headache's gone.' David appeared in the doorway.

'There's somebody in here. I know it. I'm being watched.' She grabbed his jumper and forced him to open the wardrobe door.

'Calm down. You must have had a bad dream.'

'I've not been asleep. I'm telling you. Why are you looking at me like that?'

Kendra backed away from him and with trembling hands, seized a pocketknife from her desk, warning him to back off. Something in her gut told her that he knew something about her daughter's disappearance.

'It's you isn't it? Rani's gone because of you. What have you done with her David? Tell me or I shall call the police.'

'Don't be ridiculous. You're overwrought and your mind is playing tricks. I've been reading up on it. Professor Campbell has written a piece on this…'

'Stop lying to me,' she said through gritted teeth. All of a sudden, she stopped and looked around. On his instruction she put the knife back on the desk and followed him downstairs. 'I'm sorry. I don't know what got into me.'

CHAPTER 27

'I don't understand. Why are you going walking in Wales this weekend on your own? I thought we'd planned to do that together in the summer. Pembrokeshire Coastal path. Remember?'

David shuffled around, tapping his hands on the worktop as he waited for the microwave to ping. One of his tuneless whistles escaped from his lips until he caught sight of Kendra glaring at him. Focusing on the plastic tub sailing round on the glass plate he said, 'I need a break. From all of this. We need a break from each other.'

'I've said I'm sorry for accusing you… over Rani. What happens if you get ill again? The doctor confirmed you had a mild stroke and could have another.'

David opened the microwave door, tasted the soup before spooning it into a bowl with slow, deliberate movements. He placed a slice of bread in the toaster and reached into the fridge for the butter. His movements were slow and deliberate.

'David! I'm talking to you. This is serious.'

'Don't make a drama out of it Kendra. It's only for a few days. Walking is the best thing for me right now. On my own.'

'I see. Well, make sure your mobile is topped up.' A plastic bottle crackled in her hands. 'And give me some contact numbers of where you're staying.'

'Do you know where the rucksack is? I'm taking the train to Aber then buses from there. That's all I know. I'm an adult Kendra. I will do what I like, when I like.'

Kendra studied him, baffled by the sudden changes.

'It's in the garage, squashed onto the top shelf. Have you checked the weather? I heard West Wales was expecting some bad flooding. Marco said…'

'Who's Marco?' David's knife clattered to the floor. 'Are you having an affair with him?'

Kendra turned away from him to wipe a cloth over the draining board. 'A friend.'

'Isn't that what they all say? He's just a friend? When I get back, we need to talk. Take this time to think about what you want from your life.'

Kendra threw a bottle of bleach into the sink, her jaw set like a rod of steel.

'And what's that supposed to mean? Do I have to be trapped in this house while you spend your whole life in your shed, barely talking to me? Maybe Ariana's the lucky one. She could walk out.'

David cut his toast into squares and waited until Kendra had finished.

'You don't tell me anything these days and keep disappearing for hours on end.'

'Don't turn this back on me. When I do try to share things you show very little interest then forget. I find myself going over and over the same ground with you to the point of exasperation. I've given up. Marco is someone I met in the park where he walks his dog. Sometimes we meet for coffee and have conversations. Something you and I don't do. He listens I talk. I talk he listens. That's what communication is and before you ask the question, no there's nothing going on between us. I can talk to him about Rani and how I feel. That's important to me if not to you.'

Kendra threw open the internal door to the garage to look for his rucksack, slamming cupboard doors and kicking a row of neatly lined up petrol cans out of the way. She wanted to trash the shelves on which David had piled up labelled boxes of ancient bits and pieces going back to the seventies because he couldn't bear to get rid of them. She was sick of it all. Sick of him. Sick of life.

Kendra dragged it into the kitchen, shooing away the cat as she tried to make a bed out of it. David was standing by the washing machine peering at the dials, a soap pod in his hand.

'Where does this go?'

'In the drum. Turn the dial to number 7. Fast wash. It saves money.'

David ran a hand through his hair.

'Have I done something wrong? You seem upset.'

As she emptied a pouch of cat food into Vesta's bowl she thought about how to answer him. No matter how many times or ways she tried to explain her feelings to her husband, he absorbed the knowledge with the same level of understanding as if she told him the gutters needed cleaning.

'I'm not upset,' she said. 'Just worried about you.' They embraced awkwardly as they listened to Vesta lapping up some water. David raised his wrist to check his newly repaired watch, unable to resist giving the winder a twizzle.

'Look, it's as good as new,' he said, a beam of satisfaction lighting up his face. 'Where are you going? I need you to help me pack.'

'Shopping. I'm sure you can manage.'

Squinting against the bright sunshine, Kendra walked the mile into Sutton town centre with the intention of browsing the art and craft shop. Once inside, her eyes fell on the bewildering rows of paint, racks of brushes in every size and shelves piled with every craft item imaginable; wool, felt, paper, glitter, stencils…a real cornucopia.

'Fancy meeting you here.' Marco's deep voice made her jump. 'These brushes are good quality but I've got lots of spares if you don't want to spend money. I've come in for a palette knife.'

'There are times, Marco Cappolini, when I think you are stalking me,' she joked, tapping him on the arm. 'Will you help me choose some colours? It's too confusing.'

'Titanium white is a must,' he said popping a tube into her basket. 'This paper is good quality too but don't buy the canvases. I've got loads. I can give you a lift home if you don't have your car. I was hoping you might come round for another art session soon. I've got a new idea you might like to try out. I really enjoyed the other day.'

'Me too. That's why I've decided to do some more. It's good therapy,' she added, taking him up on his offer of coffee. Kendra blew on the hot liquid before lifting the fancy glass cup to her lips.

'David's going walking for a few days. On his own. I'm worried in case he has another stroke.'

'I can understand that but maybe it's what he needs right now. You can come and keep me company if you have time.' A fleeting shadow crossed her face. 'As long as it wouldn't cause any problems for you.'

She felt the warmth of his hand on hers, knowing she should move it away, but relishing the feel of her heart beating a fraction faster. It had been a long time since she'd experienced that.

'I've got a heavy week at work but I'm sure I can find an evening. I could bring some food round. I'm not much of a cook I warn you.'

Major upheavals to the cross city line the following week meant Kendra was late for work two days running.

'Your class is about to go super nova,' grumbled Maurice who was filling up the main entrance.

'I'm sorry. I had to get three buses and…'

'Ok, Ok, I've had enough transport dramas today. You better go and take control of 5G.'

'Shut up,' Kendra shouted above the din in the classroom. 'What on earth do you think you are doing? I don't expect this behaviour from people who fool themselves into believing they know so much about people they don't need to apply the rules to themselves. Sit down NOW.'

The classroom sunk into a sullen silence apart from a fly buzzing against the window. The floor was strewn with what looked like confetti some of which had settled in Marcia's hair.

'All of you report to me after school. After such poor mock exams results I would have hoped you'd have the intelligence to spend your time more wisely than wrecking the equipment.' Kendra pointed to the flipchart lying on its side then swivelled her gaze to the whiteboard.

'Marcia, clean off these disgusting drawings immediately. Jenna, pick up these marker pens and the rest of you clean the floor around your desks. What is happening to you people? I realise your brains haven't developed a sophisticated level of cognitive control but this is a BLOODY DISGRACE.'

Kendra felt the blood pound in her temple as she swiped through the files on her computer. Her fingers stuck to the screen as she tapped hard on the page to make it open. She wanted to walk out and never return but knew that she would destroy any chance of decent references. Maurice would make sure of that.

'We're going to carry on discussing impulse control. It's page 92 in your books. I hope you appreciate the irony 5G.'

The double lesson was completed in an atmosphere of muted whispers, anxious hands tentatively raised to ask questions amid an undercurrent of resentment from all sides. As the lesson drew to a close, Kendra apologised to the class for losing her temper.

'This is not the right way to handle a frustrating situation. It's important to remain calm, assess things and ask questions.'

'You were late Miss so it was your fault.'

Marcia gave Kendra one of her famous dagger drawn looks.

'Yes, I agree I was late but it was your responsibility to behave in a mature manner. Wrecking the classroom was your decision. Nobody made you do it.' Kendra made sure she included everybody in her admonishment. 'Before we finish, would anyone like to share a personal experience of when you lost control in your personal life? Yes, Joanna.'

'My mum goes on and on about the state of my room. It's my room not hers. She went in one day and cleared it all up. I couldn't find a thing and I swear she went through my personal drawer and my diary.'

'Ok. How did you handle it?'

'I ran downstairs and grabbed her by the hair.'

A collective intake of breath broke the tension of the story.

'I was tired and stressed out. My friend's being bullied on Facebook ...'

'How did your mother respond?'

Joanne fiddled with her pencil case.

'She walked out of the room but I know she was crying.'

'And how you do feel about it now?'

'I don't want to talk about it.'

'Ashamed? Guilty? Powerful?'

'I don't fucking want to talk about it. OK? Stupid bitch. No wonder your daughter buggered off... to get away from you.'

The tall girl with the butterfly tattoo on her wrist shoved everything in her bag and slammed out of the room. Kendra wanted to go after her and grab her by the hair. She would have to file a behaviour report. The world seemed to be full of angry young people, hell bent on trashing their futures.

Slumping into an armchair in the staffroom, she picked up the crumpled newspapers to scan the international news section. There was nothing positive to offset the torrent of bad news spewing out across the globe. Before returning it to the rack, she couldn't resist a peek at her horoscope for the day. *Partnership is the word today Librans. Endings and beginnings. When you look back in months to come you will be shocked.*

She scanned the nonsense of the day for Cancer. *You've hurt someone at home but with fiery Uranus urging you on you are where you are meant to be right now. You're on a mission.*

'Yes Ariana, you damn well have,' she muttered as she started a pile of marking.

Watching the teachers dash in and out of the staffroom, arms laden with exam papers, angst etched deeply into their faces, Kendra knew that despite her good deal with Darwin Academy, her teaching days were coming to an end. It was time to move on.

THE FUTURE CAN'T WAIT

CHAPTER 28

'Sheila? Do you fancy coming round? I'm on my own. David's gone walking in Wales for a few days.' Kendra paced the patio as she waited for an answer. She was unable to settle to do anything useful.

'Give me an hour. I've got a few jobs to do, including pinning Joe to his chair to revise. He's clearly taking your advice to heart and doing nothing. Shut up Shap. And the bloody dog's getting on my nerves.'

Kendra made a sympathetic noise before hanging up. A couple of seconds later her mobile beeped.

'Hello. It's Marco. Is this a bad time?'

She felt a rush of blood to her right ear as her fingers twiddled round the gold stud.

'How are you?'

'Ridiculously nervous for an old man ringing a lady he'd like to invite out for lunch. Burger, caviar, tempura. Take your pick.'

'Well, thank you. It can't be today but maybe Sunday? David's back on Monday I think. I've not been able to get hold of him.'

'You sound concerned. Something I've learned over the years. Most of the things we worry about don't happen and if they do, we have the reserves to deal with them.'

They made arrangements to go to Alessandro's. Kendra felt ridiculously excited. Like a love-struck teenager on a first date. To get rid of her excess energy, she set about cleaning up, psyching herself to remove something Vesta had brought in.

'What *is* that smell?' Sheila sniffed her way through the kitchen. 'Hopefully not dead mouse.'

'I'm supposed to be on the 5:2 diet and today is a 500 calorie day. Hey ho. No mouse for me. You look full of the joys of spring. Must be this man friend you're sneaking out to see in the park.'

'No sneaking out. Heard from Tony?'

'Don't change the subject Mrs. Blackmore. I want to know more. I've seen you two going off piste, heads practically cemented together.'

Kendra gave her a look. 'Can't people be friends without all the insinuations?'

'Have you… you know?'

'What?'

'You know… got to know him better. Come on Kendra, stop being coy.'

'Cheek. No and it's none of your business anyway.'

'Go on. Say it… we're just friends.'

Kendra threw a tea towel at her friend.

'What about you? How's the sewing school going?'

Sheila sighed heavily and folded the cloth into a square.

'It's not taking off. Rich is talking about emigrating to Canada and Jo is going to be the death of me. As for Tony, he says he might stay on in Florida for another year and wants to know if I'll go out, knowing full well I can't. Why is life so bloody complicated? Sorry, I shouldn't be complaining.'

'You mean because I've got it much worse,' Kendra worried away at a torn nail until Sheila smacked her hand.

'Ouch!'

'I was going to say you seem a bit more relaxed these days and if your friend is helping with that then I'm all for it.'

'I'm ok. I'm trying to follow Adam's lead and get on with my life and that means leaving teaching. I can't carry on with the nonsense that goes on at Darwin. Even my students are becoming unmanageable.'

Sheila slid off the stool and walked round the kitchen, rubbing out the ache in her lower back, making a mental note to book a yoga class.

'Maurice will go nuts. What will you do instead?'

'Set up a specialised counselling practice for young people and their families. We've got a summer house that never gets used which could be turned into a suitable place with a bit of insulation and tarting up. There's a separate entrance and the downstairs loo is accessible.' Kendra reached for a folder and pulled out some hand drawn plans.

'Looks great. What does David think about it?'

'I've not discussed it with him. He's not been himself lately which is why he's gone off on his own for a bit. We're not getting on at the moment.'

They talked about Jo's resistance to study, his plans to become a musician and Rich's new Canadian girlfriend. By listening to Sheila's story, Kendra began to see how much parents wanted to control their adult children's lives, including her. Where she saw concern, Rani saw control. Like Jo. The more Sheila went on about his future, the more he resisted.

She'd given enough lectures on the need to let go of children to find their own path, remaining in the background as support but it seemed that she and Sheila had become helicopter mothers. The worst possible kind of parenting.

Kendra mulled this over as she later pottered in the garden, dead heading and watering the plants as per David's detailed instructions.

The salmon pink petunias sat perkily in their pots next to the tomato plants which had an abundance of fruit ready to ripen. When she finished, she went back into the house to fetch a small canvas and spent the afternoon poring over a crude painting of a burgundy and yellow pansy, its cheeky face smiling at her efforts.

Kendra missed Adam's call on Sunday morning as she had already left to meet Marco. She saw him leave his house and turn to double lock the front door. Tinks was at the window barking and whining, his head turning from one side to the other.

'That dog tries to make me feel guilty every time I go out without him. He's not used to being left in the house on his own.'

Marco smoothed down his tousled hair and adjusted his collar. 'I picked up a walking map from the visitor centre. This two miler looks easy enough.'

'Visitor centre? I didn't know there was one. Shall we have a wander up there to work up an appetite?'

Half an hour later it began to spit with rain. Kendra had chosen a pair of rarely worn shoes which were cutting into her heel and noticing her hobbling back along the path, Marco offered her his arm. Convinced she heard somebody calling her name, she stopped in her tracks and turned round.

'What's wrong?'

Kendra shrugged. 'Nothing.'

'We'll stop off and get my car. You can't walk into town in that state unless you prefer to change your shoes?'

'Car please. I should have known better.'

'On second thoughts, I could carry you.' A mischievous grin spread across his face as he unlocked the passenger door and helped her in. The restaurant was half full when they arrived but as Marco caught the eye of the manager, they were quickly ushered to a reserved table by the window. She was surprised to hear them exchange a few words in Italian.

'We have to hand over mobile phones. Company policy.'

'Where did you learn Italian?'

'I spent three months in Milan,' he explained. 'Now, I'm very boring when it comes to food. A bit of antipasti, linguini and clam sauce, no pud because of my cholesterol. Good job we're not courting as that would be a real turn off.' He grinned and poured some wine into their glasses as a live quartet played discreetly in the background.

They ate in silence, pausing to taste from each other's forks until Kendra puffed out her cheeks and patted her stomach. She sneaked her fingers around to undo the button on her skirt.

'Wow. That was heavenly,' she sighed, nodding at the offer of taking coffee in a private lounge reserved for friends of Alessandro's. They sunk down into squishy leather sofas, luxuriating in having the place to themselves. Marco stretched out his legs and let out a deep sigh of contentment.

'The last time I did this was just before Lizzie got very ill. We went to a place in London after her consultation. We tried so hard to be optimistic but we both knew she was on borrowed time. There are times when the future can't wait and times when it has to.'

Kendra drew him out about his life, realising that she'd dominated most of their conversations with her problems.

'Do you ever feel she's around somewhere? You know, looking out for you?'

Marco shook his head. 'If you mean do I believe in the continuation of the soul or spirit...'

'I would call it consciousness.'

'No. I don't think so. Obviously we don't know and I resist becoming an evangelical skeptic but I think it's wishful thinking. The brain fears annihilation so creates experiences which make us believe life goes on. The smell of a loved ones perfume suddenly filling a room, a perceived voice in our ear are products of a distorted sensory system which I believe is brought on by grief. This is why I've been concerned about you contacting psychics. They play on these fears. I'm assuming you've given that up now?'

Kendra averted her gaze and fiddled with her wedding ring. She respected Marco too much to lie.

'More or less,' she said, feeling sweat pool in the palms of her hand. 'Only when I think about Ariana. Safer than alcohol,' she added.

'You mean it's a coping mechanism? I was hoping that introducing you to painting might help with that.'

'Oh it has.' She told him about her attempt to draw flowers.

'Remember Churchill? It's the doing of it that's the therapy,' he reminded her gently. 'The result doesn't matter. Breaking a habit can be tough and you're allowed to have false starts. I know how sad you are about your daughter but believe me, when the time is right she will come back.'

Kendra had spent most of the lunchtime with her shoes off.

'How are the blisters?'

'Better. I've padded them out with loo roll.' She turned to face him, her eyes glowing. 'Would you teach me some Italian? I might take a trip to Venice sometime.'

David was sitting on a grassy bank overlooking the sea when he pressed the ignore button on his phone. He didn't want to speak to his wife at that moment.

Clouds scudded across a clear sky and the only sound was that of a child shrieking as the wind puffed out his red kite and tossed it into the air. He folded over the pages of the Telegraph to find the crossword he'd started earlier in the day. Chewing on the end of his pencil he tried to focus on some of the clues but nothing came to mind. He'd noticed that his thinking had become slower, his mind full of fog and it frightened him. He tried a few sips of stewed tea from his flask before pouring it onto the grass. It tasted bitter as did the square of chocolate he found lurking in his pocket. The guesthouse he'd booked was still a mile away and he wanted to press on before it rained.

As he tramped along the coastal path, he relished the respite from the domestic dramas that had interrupted his peaceful life. The idea of renting a remote cottage, never to go home again, was appealing. Pulling up his collar against the dribbling rain, he bent down to photograph a clump of sea campion for his collection.

Pausing to look down on the tiny glistening islands below, a couple with a large dog waved at him from the beach. He ignored them and strode on, sweating, shivering and desperate to close his eyes.

CHAPTER 29.

$\mathcal{A}$lthough Kendra had given in to Caz Whitely's insistence that it would be a cathartic exercise if she spoke at the May gathering of trainee psychotherapists, she wasn't happy about it. David was still in Wales so she had no real excuse. She walked along the side of the canal in Brindley Place, dodging a large group of tourists who kept stopping to consult their guide books. An attack of indigestion prompted her to pause and pop out a couple of chalky tablets from their foil package. A woman shuffled along a bench so Kendra could sit down.

As she waited for the hot and cold spasms to pass, she thought about telling Caz she didn't feel up to the doing her talk but knowing how persuasive her former supervisor could be, dropped the idea. By the time she reached the Carrs Lane Centre, she noticed the hem of her black skirt was drooping. Her pink shirt had a sweat stain under the left arm. Caz, in her tailored white dress with a big blue belt emphasising a tiny waist, came towards her, hands outstretched.

'For an awful moment I thought you might chicken out. Come and get a drink. You look hot and bothered.'

'Look, I don't really want to talk about myself so I'll keep it general.' Kendra assessed the people in the room, raising her hand to the few she recognised. She wanted to freshen up but Caz was checking the time and ushered things along.

'Stop worrying. I'm sure everyone will be fascinated by your story. Bring it alive with some anecdotes. I mean if someone like you can get hooked on fortune tellers, then think how easy it is would be for other people.' Kendra shuffled under her penetrating gaze. 'Take a few minutes to gather your wits. There's Izzy. She looks fabulous.' Kendra felt even more of a mess. 'You remember her don't you? Her book on the millennial generation is doing really well. I'll leave you to sort yourself out.'

Kendra fumbled through her notebook, feeling a prickly heat rise from her throat when she couldn't find the right place.

'It is a bit stuffy in here. I'll throw open some windows.'

Kendra looked up to see a tall man with the most striking green eyes she'd ever seen. He winked at her.

'Padraig O'Brien. You must be our special guest. This *will* be interesting.' he grinned. 'I come from a long line of fortune-tellers.'

Kendra felt a rush of air fan her cheeks. She was about to reply when Caz clapped her hands, making two gold bangles clang together and ordered everyone to their seats.

'Thank you everyone for coming. I know how busy you all are. I think you all know each other but it would be helpful if you could introduce yourselves briefly to our guest speaker, Kendra Blackmore. Jane would you begin please?'

Kendra felt her mouth go dry the moment Caz gave her the nod to begin.

'I'm a psychic junkie.' She waited for the words to sink in. 'In recovery.'

She heard the sharp intakes of breath but was drawn to Padraig's eyes, encouraging her to continue. She filled them in on the background.

'How did I get into this situation? Like for most people, it was triggered by trauma and a difficulty in accepting that my daughter was gone. The psychic industry was ready and waiting for my call. My many calls I should say. They gave me something to cling on to.'

Kendra relayed her feelings, how the addiction got hold and ways in which she fought against it. She stayed calm and unapologetic. Caz passed her a glass of water before inviting questions.

'Psychic addiction isn't something any of us have come across before. From what you're saying, it's on the increase.'

Kendra nodded and quoted some figures from her notes.

'I'm Celine Baker. Did you know you had a predisposition for compulsive behaviour? I mean had you had problems with drinking, gambling, cleaning that sort of thing?'

'Definitely not cleaning,' she laughed. 'As I explained, my daughter's actions threw me into a blind panic. There have been days when I struggled for breath. Nobody was giving me any answers or explanations so I would say it was a desperate need for some certainty that pushed me in that direction.'

'Joanne. Your question?'

'Your field of expertise is the teenage brain. Did your knowledge not help you in understanding that young people can be impulse driven with no thought for the consequences? I find it strange that you should turn to psychics when the answers were at your fingertips.'

Kendra breathed in and out through her nose, slowly as instructed by her yoga teacher. It was a few seconds before she answered.

'You are quite correct. I did. However, when the emotional brain takes over it can be difficult to draw on logic and rationality.'

The questions continued to roll in.

'Addicted people are hard to dissuade from a position because of an entrenched denial. Were you in denial at any point? Even when the huge bills were rolling in?'

Kendra looked across to see a dark skinned woman in a neat black suit leaning forward and watching her intently. Her pen was poised to take notes.

'I knew exactly what I was doing. The problem was that as soon I felt the anxiety build up, I needed another fix. It's like any behavioural addiction. Like buying a hundred pairs of shoes.'

'But there are better ways of dealing with anxiety. Cognitive Behavioural Therapy for example. Why did you not go down this route or grief counselling?'

'Is there a twelve step programme, say Psychics Anonymous? *Do you think your daughter is still alive?'*

Caz caught Kendra's expression and brought the session to an end. Getting to her feet, she formally thanked Kendra with a round of applause.

'If any of you would like to sign up to a workshop to follow through on this fascinating issue, I will be sending out details over the summer.'

Haunted by the renewed fear that Rani might indeed be dead, Kendra needed to get home and hide in her bunker. She could hear Caz's heels clattering down the corridor after her.

'Kendra. Wait. You were brilliant. I'm sorry about that. She's new, inexperienced….'

'And crass. That's a question some thoughtless journalist might ask. I was hoping for some understanding. Not an interrogation.'

'Let's have a debrief.'

'I must go.'

Kendra felt light headed as she trudged her way back to New Street station, stopping only to buy a paper. The front page of the Evening Mail screamed out the horrors of the day; extreme violence in the US and France. Talk of the Brexit referendum seemed to be everywhere.

'Do you think your daughter is still alive?' The words stabbed her in the eyes. How could somebody be so insensitive? Kendra tried to call Marco but it went to voicemail. An urge to ring Kevin from Stars and Planets took hold. As she grappled with the voices in her head, she hummed loudly until a woman on the platform told her to shut the fuck up.

She missed David not being at home. Even when he was tucked away in his shed, fiddling with his bits of wire, she knew she could call on him. Now the house felt deserted and unwelcoming. Vesta was far too busy watching every movement of a young blackbird to bother with her. She switched on the radio for some company and trawled through some of her favourite art sites before remembering to water the plants and dead head the roses. Anything to stop her from dialling the hot lines.

CHAPTER 30

'Look out. Alex is on the warpath. His briefcase has gone missing and he's beside himself. He's already cross-examined me with the subtlety of a bull on steroids.' Sheila was rifling through her desk in search of her bank card while Kendra watched her from her chair with the rickety back leg.

'Where the hell is it?' A wad of papers slithered to the floor. As Kendra bent to retrieve them she spotted the corner of red plastic peeping out.

'Here. Why are you in such a flap?'

'Major Roy's meeting is in half an hour. I heard him giving Maurice a bollocking the other day. He's after blood.'

Two hours later, Kendra was holding her head. It felt as if someone had sliced through it with an axe. Calls for voluntary redundancies, poor exams results, bad Ofsted report and now a police enquiry into money taken from the school bank account by a cyber fraudster. The Principal had marched up and down the raised dais, pausing to smooth down his Brillo pad of a moustache and glare at the assembled troops before going off on another yelling rampage.

'I came into this profession to teach not sign up to a boot camp,' muttered Kendra, gathering up her bag.

'You can't go before he's finished,' hissed Sheila, pinning her down by her arm. 'He'll go into orbit.'

Kendra looked round at the stony expressions and muscle twitching cheeks of her colleagues. Maurice mopped his brow as he tried to catch Kendra's eye. Ignoring him, she whispered something to Sheila who rolled her eyes. The moment the haranguing was over, they tagged onto the crowd jostling to get out.

'God that was painful. People conjure up this false idea that we have an easy life. Home by four. Long holidays. They've got no bloody clue.'

'I can't wait to get out of that place. Maurice can dangle his carrot somewhere else.'

'Oh puh-lease!'

'My head's like an avalanche waiting to topple. I can't give the kids what they need. It's not fair on them and it exhausts me so much I end up in bed most nights by eight. They need someone better. That supply teacher, Alice, who stood in for me, was the sort of person they need now. I'm going to suggest it to Maurice. I've been carrying round my resignation for weeks. If I get it in tomorrow, then I won't need to do more than a few weeks. I really want to go now.'

'Come on, I'll give you a lift. You look all in. Oh shit. What's going on here?'

In the car park, a gang of teenage boys had lined up to prevent three of the Muslim girls from leaving. One was sobbing as she fixed her scarf while another was spewing as much foul language she was getting. Only Khadijah tried to broker peace by remaining calm and reasonable. Sheila's face darkened as she charged into the fray.

'I know you,' she said to one of the boys. 'You're Adam Dale.

Your father's a magistrate.' While Sheila fought down the urge to slap him round the head, Kendra was filming the event.

'Piss off bag lady,' he called out.

'Kendra, go and fetch Roy. He'll sort this out. Girls, you get in my car.' Turning back to the group, rapidly diminishing in numbers, she cornered the ring leader. 'No Oxford for you. I will make sure of it.'

Roy came striding out, Kendra running in his wake.

'Let's go,' she told Sheila. 'He's about to explode.'

They dropped the girls home with the reassurance that everything would be done to prevent a similar situation occurring again.

'Unbelievable,' Sheila muttered as she pulled back out into the road. 'That lad rows for England and has been tipped for great things. What possessed him?'

Kendra turned to look at her. 'Frontal lobe thingies?'

'You heard about that pregnant woman stabbed in Sutton town centre the other day? Violence and hate everywhere. It's like a collective madness. Nowhere feels safe.'

'It's the reason I wanted us to move out of Birmingham. Maybe go to the coast. It's why I suggested to David that we go down to Pembrokeshire to check out some places but... well he decided to go on his own.'

'No idea of when he's coming back?'

'He's even less communicative than usual. I told you about the mini strokes?'

'Mmm. It's time for him to slow down. A move would do you both good but I'd miss you.'

They stared ahead, each busy with their own thoughts.

'I can't do it through till I know about Rani. Suppose she came back and we've gone?'

Sheila cut in front of a white van on the Coventry Road and returned the two finger gesture from the driver.

'That's the first time you've talked about her in ages. You have to do what's right for you. It seems that's what she's doing.'

'I might not talk about her but she's still there in my head, day, evening and night. The night sweats are frightening. It's when I am sure she's being held hostage or she's hiding from the bombs in Syria. I know it's fanciful but it has happened to other girls who got lured by …. Oh I don't know what.'

Sheila pulled up outside Kendra's house.

'What is it you say to me all the time? Where's your evidence? You're exhausted and your head's in a mess. David's not helping but there's Adam. You have to listen to your son. He's the one who knows about these things.'

'I know he keeps telling me it's a phase and I've read so much about young people disappearing for a while to find themselves or whatever but Rani didn't need to do that.'

'You don't know that. All that stuff with her father and the pressure on her to get a first and maybe… maybe being half Iranian at this time got to her. I don't know what it's like to have a mixed heritage but it's bound to bring its own problems. If that scene in the car park is any indication of what she might be facing then I can understand why she needed to get away. It's not for ever Kendy. It's because she couldn't tell you how she was feeling. She didn't want to hurt you.'

Kendra spread out her fingers on her lap, disgusted at how the nails had been bitten down to the quick. She pushed her hands into her jacket sleeves.

'What sort of mother does that make me then? I know you think this is my fault. So does Adam.'

'I'm no perfect mother either. We do our best with the knowledge we have and it's still isn't enough. Pulling apart is nature's way of ensuring the young of the species can live independently. I didn't make peace with my mother till I was around thirty. I kind of grew up emotionally even thought I was an adult from about fourteen. Black eye shadow and fags. Now that's really grown up.'

'Thanks for the lift. I'll try to get hold of Adam. I've been so wrapped up in myself I've forgotten to ask about his life.'

It was late when she managed to talk to her son. She'd tried David's mobile several times, frustrated when it diverted to voicemail, so by the time she connected with Adam on Skype there was an edginess in her voice.

'Did you send me a post card of a penguin by any chance? One came today with an obscure message. It might be from Rani. It's got an American postmark.'

'Not me Ma. Maybe Alison did. I'll ask her when she comes home but don't stress over it. It could be a bad joke from somebody who knows about your situation. That Farah woman? You said she lives in New York.'

'I could get it fingerprinted.'

'Ma stop it. Put it in the bin. Please. I've rung to see how you are not to talk about my crazy sister.'

Kendra jumped on his words.

'So you *do* think she's crazy.'

Adam ploughed on.

'I got the job in Bristol. Alison is so excited and she's feeling much better. Thanks for asking.'

'Sorry love. I'm so glad. It's going to be wonderful being able to see you more often.' Bristol was on the up and up. Maybe it was somewhere she could start a new life with or without her husband. Then Marco's face popped into her head.

'We will probably live somewhere near the sea. It's all going to work out fine, you'll see. How's David?'

Kendra filled him in. 'He's not himself.' They talked about the effect of mini-strokes, the upcoming referendum and the American election.

'We want out of here before things go completely mental. There's a storm brewing. I've gotta go. Speak soon.'

A pop up invited her to call Charente from Global Psychics for a free reading. *So accurate you'll be amazed.* Kendra felt hot and cold shivers run through her body as she tore her eyes away from the screen but her fingers lurched towards the keyboard.

David had stayed in his room in the bed and breakfast for several days pleading a virus. The owner had wanted to call a doctor but he'd refused, saying he needed to make tracks home. Her constant tapping on the door to bring him tea and food was met with a gruff thanks and a reassurance that he would be leaving as soon as he felt well enough to travel.

He sat at the small table by the window and gazed down the bank towards the cathedral, sipping water to cool his burning mouth. He was unable to think about anything other than the searing pains across his brow. He worried about making the long train journey home and what he would say to Kendra. He'd finally made his decision and hoped she'd understand.

After another restless night, he got up early, packed his rucksack and went down for breakfast. He planned to take the bus to Haverfordwest railway station but as he looked through his timetable, the numbers danced in front of his eyes.

'I have to go into town so I will drop you at the station. I won't hear of you getting the bus. I want to make sure you're alright. Now here's a pot of tea and some toast since you don't want a good Welsh breakfast. I'll be ready in thirty minutes. Are you going to let your wife know what time you arrive in Birmingham?'

David grunted as he spread jam on his toast, dropping the knife from his right hand the fingers of which felt stiff and numb. He bent to pick it up, grabbing the table leg to stop him from fainting. Once in the car with the window wound down, colour returned to his cheeks.

'You sip plenty of water and take those pain killers. Close your eyes and don't try to read. Please ring me to say you've got home safely.'

David watched her dumpy figure in an ill-fitting pair of trousers walk beside the train as it slowly pulled out. She waved before returning to her van.

The journey became more stressful as people piled on at major stations, their bags pressing into his knees, a stale smell of cheesy crisps in the air which irritated his nose. He scowled at a girl who was shouting into her phone. As the train pulled into New Street, David felt a tingling in his right hand. He threw his rucksack over his shoulders and with a heavy heart headed for the taxi rank. The thought of being back in the house, being pummelled with questions, made him want to catch the next train back to the Welsh coast.

CHAPTER 31

By the time Kendra arrived home, David was slumped in his chair in the living room, the contents of his bag spilling out across the floor. Alarmed at the awkward angle of his head which disguised a partially closed eye, she tried to rock him awake. He groaned and gave her a glassy stare. She touched his forehead with the back of her hand. It was cold but sticky.

'David,' she said gently. 'Can you hear me?'

Drawing on her basic knowledge of first aid, she lifted his eyelids to check the pupils.

'I'm calling the doctor.' Kendra stabbed the pre-set button as she sat on a stool next to him, holding his hand. A hundred hammers banged away at the back of her eyes as a recorded voice intoned that her call was important and somebody would be with her shortly. She was about to hang up and dial 999 when a curt voice came on the line. Relieved that a doctor would be with her within ten minutes, she filled a glass of water and helping her husband to sit forward, she held it to his lips. He spluttered and lay back, exhaustion etched across his face.

Dr. Ongololo, the locum, confirmed Kendra's suspicions of another mini stroke, reassuring her that the effects would wear off in a day or so. The doctor ran a hand over his bald head.

'You say this isn't the first time?'

Kendra told him briefly about the other episodes. 'This seems worse though. Shouldn't he be in hospital?'

'I need to see his notes. Keep an eye out for confusion and deterioration. His vision might be a bit blurred for a while and he'll probably have a headache. Call 999 if he gets any worse,' he said, unlocking the door to his people carrier.

Kendra looked out of the French windows at a garden in need of some loving care. The roses were past their best and it saddened her that her favourite Shropshire Lad, hadn't bloomed at all that year. It had been a wedding present from David. They'd argued about where to plant it. He'd skulked back into his shed and she'd stomped off round the park. It was the first time she'd witnessed how ill equipped he was to talk through differences, preferring to withdraw for days. He hadn't been an easy choice of husband with his strange ways but she had always loved him. Now she was deeply concerned about his health. Her first thought was to call Medical Psychics Inc in the States but instead fetched a bucket and mop to clean the hallway, singing along to an eighties song on Heart FM.

Relentless self-talk kept her mind focused and reduced the grip of the addiction. She was getting better and that made her feel good. Shafts of sunlight poured through the house and across David's sleeping face. Satisfied that he was comfortable, Kendra headed out for a quick walk. To avoid talking to anyone, she took a different path over some rough ground, before skidding on a patch of mud and falling against a tree trunk. Blood trickled down her temple. As she stumbled to her feet, the skies darkened and released a deluge. People were running to their cars holding plastic bags over their head. She needed to go back. Something felt wrong.

She couldn't dislodge the powerful feeling of dread which echoed in her footsteps as she battled up the hill towards their house which stood on an angle like an awkward full stop at the end of the street. It was the first time she realised how ugly it was. She fumbled with the lock, cursing when the key wouldn't turn.

David shuddered as he opened his eyes. Kendra sat next to him, water dripping from her matted hair onto his trousers. As she looked into his eyes, fearing the emptiness that stared back, she touched a faded burn mark on his chin, squeezed his calloused fingers but he remained silent and unresponsive.

Kendra sat back on her heels and caught sight of her reflection in the window and was shocked. Deep lines had dug in around her sunken eyes making her look as if she'd rapidly aged. She pushed back her hair which hung in soggy strips around her face as her tongue caught a drip from her nose. For a moment she felt paralysed.

Kendra pulled her gaze back onto her husband whose limbs had begun to twitch, his fingers stiffening as he juddered forward in his chair. His eyes rolled up towards his forehead. Frantic, she dialled the emergency services, her hands shaking so badly she dropped the phone.

'Ambulance,' she gasped. 'Urgent. My husband's unconscious.'

Stumbling over the address, she shouted as she was asked to repeat the details. 'You're wasting time.'

Kim, the operator told her to stay on the line until the paramedics arrived. Sitting at David's feet, her head on his knees, she talked to the woman with the thick Black Country accent about her husband, her life and her guilt at not looking after him properly. She found herself pouring out the story about Rani, sobbing as she thought of losing her husband as well.

Ten minutes later a blue light and piercing siren punctured the

↫ THE FUTURE CAN'T WAIT

cold silence in the house and ended her conversation. Kendra rushed to greet two heavy set men in green uniforms who wasted no time setting up their equipment whilst a young woman who looked no more than a teenager took Kendra into the kitchen where she hunted round for cups and tea bags. 'I'm Grace. Tell me what happened.'

'I don't want tea for God's sake. My husband needs me.' Kendra snapped, running back into the living room, oblivious to the exchange of glances and a slight shake of the head from the bald man.

'Your husband's had a major stroke. It must have been very quick. Has he been ill at all?'

'No, yes.' Kendra clapped her hands to her face as reality began to sink in.

'We'll need to take some details then we need to arrange for someone to come and stay with you.'

'What? I'm going to the hospital with my husband. I'll get my coat. You're wasting time. COME ON.'

'Mrs. Blackmore. Your husband, David, is dead,' said Grace in a voice so soft it was barely audible. 'I'm sorry for your loss. Can you give me the name and address of his GP?'

Kendra clapped her hand to her forehead as she tried to recall the information.

'No. You're wrong. It's another mini stroke. He's had a couple recently. Why aren't you trying to resuscitate him? This is all wrong.'

She began to pace the floor, returning to shake David. 'Wake up. Please.'

'I'm going to give you something to help with the shock and Grace is going to stay with you for a while.' The paramedics went into a huddle in the hallway leaving Kendra to spend a few minutes with her husband. She heard the words *post mortem and death certificate.*

'This is all my fault,' she sobbed, trying to rub life into his stiff fingers. 'If it hadn't been for Rani...'

Grace helped Kendra to her feet, catching her as her knees buckled under the enormity of what had happened. Another sudden loss. She couldn't bear it. It was as if she was covering her eyes during a particularly frightening part of a film, her brain knowing it wasn't real and that it would soon end.

As the men worked quietly in the background, Kendra was led through the back door into her husband's beloved garden where she took gulps of warm air. The rain had stopped. The sun had the gall to smile down on the wet grass. It made Kendra want to lash out.

'You have a lovely garden. Which was your husband's favourite bit?'

The words seemed alien and disconnected.

'He likes the rose garden but our favourite one didn't flower this year. I don't know why.' She refused to talk about her husband as if he didn't exist. Kendra began to shake as the shock took hold.

'Maybe that's something you could work on for next year. For David. Show me the rest of the garden.'

They walked slowly down the path, Kendra barely able to lift her feet or open her mouth as Grace admired the multi-coloured lupins and deep blue cornflowers. They watched a blue tit pause to drink from the bird bath David had made with Rani. It was too much for Kendra who turned on her heels and ran back inside. The outside world felt threatening and hostile. She wanted Grace to go.

'Where have they taken him?' Her voice cracked.

'The General. Do you have family or friends nearby?'

'Sheila. I'll call Sheila but I have to speak to my son.'

Grace lightly touched her shoulder. 'Can he come round?'

'No. He lives in Boston but he needs to know.'

'Just the one child?'

Kendra hesitated. A photograph of Rani in a black prom dress sat on the windowsill. She picked it up and put it in the newspaper box. Lifting her chin, she looked at Grace's puzzled expression.

'Yes. Just the one.'

In the kitchen, Kendra pretended to talk to Sheila on the phone, despite knowing she was away on a conference.

'My friend will be round in an hour. You can go. I need to sleep. Thank you for everything,' she said, feigning control. 'I'll be fine.'

No sooner was the woman out of the door then Kendra poured a large measure of brandy into a mug and gulped it down. Her eyes flickered and closed as fresh waves of grief wrapped themselves round her neck and dragged her into the bowels of the earth.

CHAPTER 32

The shock and fallout of the UK referendum result floated over Kendra's head as she struggled to accept her husband's sudden and shocking death. Veering between an overpowering sense of injustice and a devastating personal guilt, she spent the next few days alternating between thumping the cushions, crying and slumping motionless on the bed. Neither the curtains nor the windows had been opened since David's death. The darkness provided some safety from the frightening place the world had become.

The thought of having to call Adam exhausted her to the point she numbed her nerves with brandy and slept fitfully most afternoons. Pain ravaged her body as it processed the shock. After Rani, Kendra didn't think she could take any more blows.

Dirty clothes were strewn all over the bedroom floor interspersed with cups of cold coffee. Uneaten sandwiches in a plastic wrapper lay on the bedside cabinet, courtesy of Sheila, who had gone very quiet when she heard the news. For several days she'd posted a handmade card through the letterbox which said, *Thinking of you, or You know where I am.* It was Sheila who insisted she must make the call to Boston. She pulled on a pair of rubber gloves and glanced around the kitchen.

'I am going to spend the morning cleaning up and you are going to have a long soak in the bath, put on some clean clothes and not those disgusting pyjamas again. Then you are going to call Adam at his work. It's an emergency Kendra. Someone has to take control.'

Kendra did as she was told, agreeing not to lock the door.

'You might pass out and I couldn't cope with any more tragedy. Being selfish that is.'

The two women looked at each other and hugged. Both were too choked to speak. Back in the kitchen, Sheila began the daunting task of scrubbing the counters, getting grease off the hob, and mopping the floors. She bent down to pick up Vesta who was following her everywhere.

'Come on, let's sort your bowls and bed out. It'll be ok,' she murmured, her eyes filling up. She kissed the cat between its ears.

Towelling dry her hair, Kendra picked up the phone and laid it on her lap while she thought about what to say.

'I don't know how to tell him.'

'He's a doctor. You tell him the truth and ask him to come over. If you don't do it, I shall.'

'He's really busy and can't leave Alison at the moment.'

'Kendra. Stop prevaricating. Just do it. Now. Please?'

She had to wait while Adam was paged. Sheila flicked a cobweb from the window as they waited.

'I'm coming straight over,' was his immediate response. 'Alison is already back with her parents. Has there been an autopsy?'

'It was a cerebral aneurysm. He had no chance.' Kendra held a tissue to her nose. 'I feel it was my fault.'

'Leave the soul searching till I get there. In the meantime, I think you should put something on the net so that Ariana might see it. I would be surprised if she wasn't checking on us from time to time.'

She squeezed the tissue into a ball and tossed it towards the bin.

'No. Absolutely not. She's no longer part of this family. Had it not been for her none of this would have happened.'

Adam heaved a deep sigh as he checked his watch. If he was to make it out of Boston that night he needed to tie up some loose ends.

'Good. Now that's one job done. I told you he'd be straight over. I'll make you some breakfast. You look washed out. Sit in the sun for a bit. That always gives me an energy boost.'

It was easier not to argue with Sheila when she was in her officious mood. As she sat on the patio, she felt she was seeing things through a pane of frosted glass with the sound turned down. Even the birds seemed subdued as they hopped along the length of the gutter. The door to David's shed was partly opened and for a moment she waited for him to appear with an empty mug in his hand. Grief had shaken her to the bones so that she no longer knew her own mind. First Rani, then David. Will it be Adam next or the baby? Is this a punishment for something?

Sheila appeared with a glass of water and some painkillers.

'For your headache. I wish you'd eat something to keep your strength up.'

'I'm sick of food. I can't go on much longer like this. It's like living through a long eclipse of the sun. Huh, if David were here he'd give a long lecture on that not being possible.'

'Keep the faith that things will work out. Rani will be home…'

She waved her hand dismissively.

'I don't want to talk about her. She made her choice.'

Sheila folded and unfolded the cloth in her hand before Kendra told her to stop fidgeting.

'What's bothering you?'

'I'm worried that you'll start contacting these mediums again to get in touch with David. You know they're all about taking your money. They're no more psychic than my fingernail. I went to see one many years ago. When Tony's business was on the brink. I believed all the crap she came out with because I wanted it to be true.'

Sheila glanced quickly at her friend to assess her reaction.

'I know. You're right. I'm done with all that. Marco… Oh God. I've not told Marco.'

'You don't need to. I bumped into him when I took Shap into the park. I told him. I'm sorry. He was genuinely upset and passed on the message for you get in touch when you're ready. Maybe I shouldn't have done that but it came out. You know what I'm like.'

Kendra couldn't help but smile. 'Thanks. I'm going to pack up all that stuff of David's in the hall and take it into the charity shops. Those poor kids in Syria need all the help can get. I can't face coming in the front door and seeing them. Thanks for your help. You're a mate even though you're bossy.'

'Are you going to be alright if I go now? Is there anything I can do? Funeral baking, that sort of thing.'

Kendra rubbed her cheek. Her gums were tingling from excessive teeth grinding.

'No wake. Just a private ceremony somewhere. Probably the park. I can't think about it right now. I won't be back in work anymore. I'm working out my notice on compassionate leave.'

'I'm really sorry.'

They clung to each other for a moment. There were no more words. Kendra shivered in her cardigan as she watched Sheila's car disappear into the traffic.

With a manic energy, she spent the rest of the day clearing out from the cupboards the foods that only David liked. A bereavement counsellor had once told her that it was important to get on with the practical stuff and let the grief work its way through.

Tubs of ice-cream were tossed into the plastics bin without being emptied while tins of custard and rice pudding were stacked in cardboard boxes for the Salvation Army hostel. She moved onto the wardrobes, stuffing clothes and personal items into black bags, putting aside his wedding suit for his funeral.

Working methodically through the drawers, Kendra felt nothing, thought nothing, wanted nothing other than for it to be over. Her own doctor, who'd visited shortly after David's death, had talked to her about the stages of grief and how people often got stuck in the depressive phase especially when they'd already experienced one major loss. She'd argued with him stating she needed a prescription for sleeping tablets, not a lecture.

Kendra's nerves were so raw she had to keep any sound to a minimum. Even the sound of someone chomping on chewing gum set her teeth on edge. Hurrying through the supermarket to buy food for her son's arrival was such an ordeal she let rip at someone for being too slow at the checkout, catching the eye of the security guard hovering close by. When he helped take her bags to the car, she broke down telling him that she'd just lost her husband. Every time she said the words they seemed to come from someone else. The man told her his name was Ray and he could empathise. He'd lost his five-year-old to cancer.

'If it wasn't so damn politically incorrect, I'd give you a hug,' he said, slamming shut the boot. 'You take care.'

When Adam arrived, letting himself in with his own key, he saw his mother sitting in a wingback chair overlooking the garden, stroking an old gardening cardigan belonging to David.

'Ma?'

Kendra turned to see her tall, bronzed boy, filling up the door frame, his expression empty of his usual mischief.

'Adam.' He bent down to kiss her cheek.

'Look at you. You're so thin,' he said, enclosing her narrow wrist with his finger and thumb.

'Always the doctor,' she smiled weakly. 'There's plenty of food but you'll have to help yourself. I've run out of battery.'

Adam disappeared into the kitchen, returning with a tray of snacks and mugs of tea in the hope his mother might eat with him.

'You've got me for as long as it takes so we can sort everything out together and talk until your tongue falls out. I'll just give Ally a quick call to say I've arrived ok. She's in the worrying stage at the moment, especially with heightened terror threats. Logan was swarming with police. So was Birmingham. It's not difficult to create fear amongst the people.' He stretched out on the Persian rug and rested his head on a cushion, reminding her so much of his father.

'Have you thought about funeral arrangements,' he asked, zapping through the TV channels.

'No. I can't get it into my head that he's gone. He seemed so fit even though he lived in those workshops lost in his own world. I know we didn't have much in common but it seems so empty without him wandering about with a screwdriver in his hand or rummaging through the freezer for ice-cream. It's the little things…'

Adam turned down the sound and let her talk. He knew how important it was to listen and validate people's feelings. His mother seemed like a fragile bird but he knew she had deep reserves of strength. She'd need to draw on them in the coming months.

'He was good to all of us,' she went on. 'Dependable. The doctors said it could have happened at any time yet I feel responsible.'

'There was nothing you could have done.' Adam watched

Vesta stalking something on the lawn, her ears twitching. Kendra followed his gaze, startled by a shadow in the in the shape of a man in a broad brimmed hat. It fell directly across David's workshop. She held her breath as it seemed to grow longer. The arms of the figure reached out to her.

'Ma, what are you looking at?'

'Er nothing. Sorry.'

'You look as if you've seen a ghost. Not that such things exist.'

Kendra withdrew into her head and she recalled the day she came home to find David dead. The guilt was ripping her apart.

'I should have been here but I went off stomping through the park. I was frustrated and angry with your sister again. Sometimes I think I've let go of it then it comes back like a smack across the face. If I'd not spent all my waking hours worrying about her David would still be here.' Kendra drank deeply from a glass of water. 'I don't want her at David's funeral even if you do make contact. It's too late now. I'm done with her.'

'Now you know that's not true.'

'I mean it Adam.'

Her son changed the subject by opening up his laptop and showing her what he'd created on the flight over.

'Have a look at these templates. It's for a condolences page. Hopefully some people who knew him will find it. We can add details of the funeral when we've sorted them.'

'Do we have to do this now? I'm tired. You choose.'

Kendra closed her eyes as she listened to the tapping of the keys and Adam muttering to himself. Vesta climbed onto her chest and after padding around to find a comfortable spot, settled down in the crook of her arm. For a brief moment, she felt safe and hopeful. Her boy was home.

CHAPTER 33.

*A*s Adam explained to Claire, the funeral celebrant, the need for something simple and connected to David's love of science and nature, Kendra shifted uncomfortably in her seat. She heard the words but they slid around her brain like children losing their footing on a patch of ice. Rubbing her scratchy eyes, she leaned forward and tried to focus. Her mind was whizzing with images of David's face before he left for Wales and his need to be alone. *Did he know something then? Was he trying to protect her?*

'Is there anything you would like to read at the ceremony? Maybe a letter or a poem. Something that meant a lot to both of you?'

Claire's voice was gentle but pressing.

'Maybe,' said Kendra. She thought of the one and only letter he'd sent her. A few lines to say that he loved her because she was practical and not a frilly woman.

'You don't have to read it out yourself. I can help with that. What about music? Any favourites.'

'I don't see how that's going to work in the park.' Kendra stiffened. As pleasant as the woman was, she wanted her to finish and go. 'David wasn't into the fluffy side of life as he called it. His hobby was making telescopes. You don't understand him. Nobody did.' She caught sight of an old wine stain on the fringes of the rug. David had immediately got down to clean it with salt. Now she felt the sting of neat salt being rubbed into her wounds.

'He believed we got recycled back into the earth. He once tried to explain the physical process of death to me but it was horrible.' She stole a look at Adam. 'He said the brain surges in activity after death, giving off hormones and that's why people have got this idea that consciousness is separate from the brain.'

Claire was adjusting the waist band of her trousers.

'Did you share those views?'

'Mum. Let's move on.' Adam pulled out some papers from his file and handed Claire a photograph and a mock-up of the service they wanted, making it clear that it was to be a private funeral by invitation followed by a cremation attended only his mother and him. He unfolded a map and pointed to a spot he'd marked in black.

'Do you just have the one child?'

'Yes,' Kendra said quickly. She didn't want to be led down the path of talking about Ariana.

'Here. Queen's Coppice. It's well hidden from prying eyes.' Adam stabbed his finger onto the map.

'Not there,' Kendra blurted out, remembering the last time she and Marco had walked around there arm in arm, briefly kissing her when she poured out her heart about her daughter. 'Make it Streetly Wood.' She pointed to a spot alongside Thornhill Road. 'It's just as private.'

Kendra looked to her right and smiled.

'David's agreeing,' she said. 'He's there. Look. Hammer in hand.'

Claire coughed and found she couldn't stop. She pulled out a bottle of water and put it to her lips. 'Sorry about that.'

Quickly assessing the situation, Adam brought the meeting to an end. His mother was lapsing into hallucinations through sleep deprivation.

'My mother is exhausted. If you need anything further, here's my mobile number.' He handed the woman a business card as he showed her out.

'I'm not crazy. I saw David for a second. He was smiling and nodding.'

'Ok. I believe you. It will pass. David's gone. You said so yourself to that woman. We need to stay grounded Ma.'

Kendra wrapped her arms around her shivering body and walked towards the summer house, shielding her eyes from the glare. Her son put on some shoes and followed her, worried about what she might do. She'd talked manically about there being no point in life, not realising how much her words stung him but his experience told him there was no point arguing with her. Grief affected perception and only time would heal. It was no cliché. Nature had her methods.

'You can think what you like Adam but it's not the first time he's been in touch. It isn't my brain going into protective mode. He comes to reassure me. In fact, I think he's been warning me before his death. It's beginning to make sense now,' she murmured to herself. She stepped into the dark room and sat on the chair she'd brought from her parents' home. She rocked back and forth, each creak sounding loud in the hollow space.

Adam felt his muscles tense. He punched a fist against an open palm.

'Is that what these psychics told you? This bull about being able to contact the dead?' Kendra looked away from him and continued to rock. It was getting on his nerves.

'Scientists think they know everything but they don't know much about the brain.' She gave him a hard stare. 'Just because you can't see radio waves doesn't mean they don't exist. I'm tired of people dismissing things they don't understand. Not everything is confirmation bias.'

Adam picked up a stray football that lay by the side of the summer house and threw it over the fence with such force, it smashed against the neighbour's shed.

'OK I accept that but why would you of all people spend thousands of pounds to consult charlatans who are only in it for the money. Maybe there are people out there with special abilities but not those who man the phone lines waiting for the next punter. I'm sorry. This isn't the right time.'

'Maybe it's because I was desperate,' she shouted. 'David never understood the total devastation I felt when I got Rani's note. Practical, down to earth David said she'd come back in good time. It was alright for him…' Kendra marched back towards the house. Much as she loved her son, she wanted him to leave her alone because she knew he was right. Nothing got past Adam and he wasn't afraid of cracking walls of denial.

'David could turn off his emotions, if they were ever turned on in the first place and count his bits of rubbish in the shed to keep him calm but he was never really there for me Adam. That's the truth.'

Mother and son glared at each other for a moment before they were interrupted by Sheila poking her head into the garden.

'Is this a bad time? The front door was open.'

Her eyes rested on Kendra's good looking son. His striking colouring and warm manner set her heart racing.

'It's fine. We were having a discussion about the funeral.' Kendra invited her to sit down. 'You look about to burst.'

She perched on the edge of the sofa, looking hesitantly from one to another.

'This might be the worst time possible but Jo's got a bit of a lead on Rani.'

Kendra raised her hand and shook her head.

'I'm not interested.'

'Tell us,' Adam cut in.

'It's not much but he found a post about her on one of his friend's Facebook accounts. I don't know how these things work but you know how they're all connected through this stupid friends and likes business. Anyway this so called friend had put something up about Rani being married. There's no picture or evidence so it might be someone fooling about but the post wasn't in English.'

Kendra stopped fiddling with the loose thread of her cuff and looked up.

'Jo put it through a translator thing but it was blocked. Here, I've photographed it.'

Sheila scrolled through her phone and handed it to Adam.

'Hmm. Can you email it to me? We've got too much to do at the moment without chasing my sister. But thanks anyway.'

Kendra told her about the service in the park. 'I hope you'll come.'

'It sounds so… like David. Oh Kendra.' Sheila pulled a tissue from the box on the table and blew her nose. 'All I can do is make food for you and I'm sure your freezer's overflowing with stuff you can't eat right now. It's what we do though isn't it? In a crisis. Drink tea and make food nobody wants. Keeps the hands busy I guess.'

They talked for a while as his mother dozed. Adam showed Sheila out, his shoulders hunched. 'Thanks for your support. Mum might not say much but I know she couldn't manage without you right now.'

Turning back inside, he said, 'Right Ma. You're going to put on some shoes and show me this famous Streetly Wood. Never heard of it.'

Kendra had to run to match her son's long stride as they took the route along the edge of the wood before slipping in through the Milking Gate entrance. It started to drizzle which, as it grew heavier, soaked through their flimsy jackets. Kendra felt the water drip down her neck. She pulled up her collar and led them down to a clearing in the woods not overlooked by housing or visitors' cars. Hands deep in pockets, they looked at the grassy rectangle bordered by large headed daisies.

'It's a bit rough,' Adam commented as he walked between the oak trees, peering through the dense canopy of leaves.

'It's natural. It's how David would want it even though he was obsessed with keeping total order in the garden. It was just his way.'

'Ok. Why this spot in particular?'

His mother pushed the wet hair out of her eyes and gave him a blank look. 'It's the most private I guess.'

As they made their way onto the main path, Kendra stopped in her tracks. A small dog with familiar tan patches was snuffling in the grass, cocking his leg against different trees with no regard for his owner struggling to keep up. Marco, in his familiar tartan scarf came into view. He was leaning heavily on a stick.

'Come on Adam. I don't feel too well.' Kendra was trying to turn her son towards a different exit.

'That man's calling your name. Do you know him?'

'Please Adam. I need to get into the warm. I'm soaked.'

Tinks began barking madly in the background when he saw Kendra. Marco hobbled towards them.

'I heard the news. I'm so sorry. You must be Adam.' Marco held out his hand. 'It's good you're here.'

After the brief introductions, Kendra explained about the funeral.

'If I can help at all...'

'Yes you can actually,' said Adam suddenly. 'If you're a regular in the park, maybe you could keep prying eyes away. We could give you an official marshal badge or something. That would be really helpful.'

'Adam! Marco isn't our butler.'

'It would be my pleasure. Tinks will see them off won't you boy? If you want to borrow him you can. Dogs are a great source of comfort.' Marco fumbled in his pocket for a dog biscuit. 'Good boy.'

Kendra nodded and clutched her son's arm.

'We must go. Adam will let you know once everything's finalised. Bye Tinks.'

CHAPTER 34.

The day of David's farewell party, as Kendra insisted on calling it, coincided with Turkey's military coup. Adam stood in front of the TV, zapping through the news coverage when his mother joined him, a thin gold chain in her hand.

'David bought me this as a wedding gift.'

Adam fastened the tiny clasp around her neck, giving her shoulders a gentle squeeze as she centred the diamond studded heart.

'Are you ok Ma? Bit of makeup maybe?'

Kendra punched him gently in the chest and asked if her dress met with his approval. She asked people to avoid wearing black as it was a celebration of her husband's life and he didn't like black.

'That turquoise really suits you Ma. It's bright and optimistic. Maybe a belt? There's nothing left of you.'

Kendra rested her trembling hand on her son's cheek. Without him she would have melted into a puddle.

'I found this on the doormat when I came down.'

She slit open the cream envelope and pulled out a card. *In all chaos there is a cosmos, in all disorder a secret order.*

'Carl Jung,' she murmured, slipping it into her bag. 'It's from Marco. That's so kind. He never got to meet David.'

'Well, fourteen people have confirmed for today but you've had so many messages on the site. Nothing from Ariana though. I'm sorry Mum.'

Kendra shrugged as she eased on her boots, as despite it being summer, the ground was muddy from so much rain. A black hearse pulled into the drive.

'Ready Mum?' Adam helped her into a raincoat and guided her to the cars. Seeing the plain wicker coffin with its simple wreath of spring flowers made Kendra gasp. She could barely think that her husband lay in there, cold and lifeless. Grasping Adam's hand, she felt her terror of funerals running at full strength.

About a dozen people gathered in the clearing in Sutton Park, shielded by cohorts of broad leafed chestnut trees, the odd gold leaf heralding autumn. A grey squirrel watched them from a safe distance. Kendra could see Marco and Tinks in position on the rugged pathway and was about to pick her way over clods of horse dung to speak to him, when Claire emerged in an olive suit and a chunky yellow necklace, along with a suitable funereal expression. 'We can take this as slowly as you wish.'

'Let's get on with it,' Kendra said, raising her hand to Marco as he began to turn away the curious and downright nosey from the clearing.

The coffin was laid on a trestle table covered with a green cloth as a few bars of Beethoven's pastoral symphony, pumped through speakers connected to Adam's mobile phone. As the celebration of her husband's life began, Kendra stood like a stone statue in a swirling grey mist. She glanced through a gap in the trees, half expecting Rani to jump out like she used to as a child and say, 'Hello Mum.'

Adam spoke kindly about his brilliant but eccentric stepfather, throwing in some amusing anecdotes which made the frozen faced onlookers break into a laugh. Kendra loved him even more. He was so easy with people. Like his father had been before the Revolution. His profile reminded her of Justin Trudeau; Wild bluey-black hair, a smile in his eyes that was all inclusive, a gentleness that belonged to another era. A few bars of Frank Sinatra got people smiling and chatting as the hearse made its way to the crematorium.

'He certainly did do it his way,' said an elderly man leaning on a walking frame. He introduced himself as David's former head of department. 'Once he'd got an idea in his head there was no stopping him. Terrible team player but brilliant mathematician. Takes all sorts to build a world,' he sighed. 'I'm sorry we haven't met before, Mrs. Blackmore.'

Adam ushered her towards other people who were waiting to exchange a few words.

'Beautiful ceremony. I've never heard of a humanist funeral before. So fitting for him.' She introduced herself as David's former secretary.

Words crafted to console and comfort were uttered by people she didn't know or couldn't place. She felt they'd all read the same book. *How to behave with the recently bereaved.* Kendra made herself smile and respond in the way that wouldn't alarm people when really she wanted to run into the depths of some cave.

'I could strangle that daughter of your's,' said Maurice, tugging his jacket around his ever expanding stomach. He suppressed a burp. 'Come back to work. We need you and you need work. Moping at home isn't going to do you any good.' He patted her arm then wobbled his way back to the car park.

'My Head of Department,' Kendra told Adam unnecessarily. 'Tact personified.'

Sheila had been holding back with Jo until the mourners had taken their leave.

'It was lovely. Perfect. You sure I can't do anything?'

'Cast a spell? Work a miracle?'

'Ma, don't work yourself up. Not today. Maybe Sheila would like to come back to the house after the cremation. Say, in a couple of hours?'

Sheila looked from one to the other, uncertain how to respond.

'Well if it helps Kendra.'

'Come. We can get drunk together.'

Kendra walked over to join Marco who seemed small and lost amongst the trees.

'Thank you for today. It must have brought back some bad memories.'

He looked deeply into her eyes before giving her a gentle hug.

'You get off to the crematorium. We can talk another time.'

Turning from him, she dug deeply into her reserves to do the most awful deed of her life.

When they returned home, Kendra lay on the sofa and stared up at the ceiling. Too exhausted to unzip her boots and too numb to think. She dozed, listening to Adam in the kitchen. The radio hummed in the background. She wanted to turn it off but couldn't muster the energy.

Adam checked on her before quietly unlocking David's shed to sit at the workbench, strewn with drawings, boxes of components, stubby bits of pencil, wires, tapes and stuff he'd no idea about. When he was younger, he'd found David hard to relate to. The only time he'd seen him animated was when he showed him one of his inventions. He would talk non-stop for hours about the finest detail, not realising that it wasn't appropriate.

He knew his mother had been driven to distraction by some of his behaviours but Alison could say that about him. Adam was against pinning labels on people who thought or behaved differently from the normal, arguing that normal covered a wide bandwidth. As a doctor, his job was to help them to manage their symptoms and find a place in society.

He flicked through some papers covered in equations and doodles, noticing his mother's name on the corner of a large drawing. Had he been worried about her maybe after Rani's disappearance but didn't know how to deal with it? He idly picked up books, put them down, and shuffled through magazines for the sake of something to occupy his hands.

A folded piece of paper fell out from between a pile of astronomy leaflets advertising a lecture on gravitational waves at Birmingham University. He bent down to pick it up from the dusty floor. His heart leapt into his mouth as he read the scribbled words.

David. If you'd not interfered I would not have taken such drastic action. Look after Mum. Ariana.

What the hell did she mean? He read it again, knowing that if he showed this to his mother she would go into a total meltdown. Sitting in the half light, the smell of damp rising into his nostrils, he tried to unpick what his sister might mean. Had David done something to his sister? Inconceivable. Maybe this referred to some sort of betrayal. Was he a spy and worked for the intelligence services on the quiet? Was somebody really watching the house? What was Rani really up to and how did that involve his step-father?

Adam's head began to throb. Tugging off his glasses, he pushed the heel of his hands against his eye sockets and let out a deep sigh. Pocketing the bit of paper, he pushed open the door and turned the key. His mother was fast asleep, her mouth open, snoring lightly, pausing to turn over and stretch out her legs. He bent down to remove her boots and pull the blanket up over her shoulders.

In the kitchen he made a pot of strong coffee and punched out a number on his phone. Alison sounded sleepy but more like her old bubbly self when she answered. It was the right decision to go to her parent's farmhouse in North Devon even though he was missing her.

'How did it go?'

'Ok. Mum's flat out. I'm going to stay on a bit longer if that's ok. She's talking about seeing David sitting on the edge of her bed. She says he's trying to tell her something.'

'That's a normal grief reaction isn't it? Mum said that about Granny when she died. Said she could smell roses everywhere and that it was a good sign. It went away after a few months.'

'Hmm. Maybe.' Adam blew kisses down the line and hearing his mother stirring, said a quick goodbye.

Kendra's nose followed the strong smell of Brazilian coffee and handed over a mug to be filled. She frowned.

'What's on your mind, love?' Kendra suppressed a yawn.

'Let's have a wander round the garden. You might want to get somebody in to help with this. Or move?'

The once glorious displays of geraniums, petunias and pansies in pots had shrivelled from neglect. Adam paused to turn on the hose to quench the dry compost. Tomato plants were struggling to produce some fruit that was now ripening. Kendra noticed how much the lawns had grown to the point they looked shaggy and unkempt. Dandelions were thriving alongside the aggressive march of the bindweed's white trumpets. It was David's domain and it hurt to see it go to ruin.

The squawking off a crow overhead frightened her. She was sure it was an omen of more bad luck.

'There's going to be some terrible things happening in the world soon.'

'Ma, there's always something going on. We carry on through the world's craziness. More terrorism, economic woes, climate change. You can't control it so you need to let go of it. Focus on you.'

'It scares me Adam. The thought of being alone in this house.'

Her son, stopped pulling up weeds in a patch by the patio and frowned.

'But you don't need to be here. Sell up and come down to Bristol. We need your help. It would be good to get away from all the memories and have a fresh start. I was assuming that's what you'd do.'

Kendra thought about Marco. It was time they talked about the future.

'If Ariana ever comes back and I am not here…'

'That's a feeble excuse. She will find one of us if she really wants to. My name is always in the public domain.'

He gave her a curious look.

'Is there something else keeping you here? That man, Marco for example?'

Kendra gave him a look as if to say 'don't be ridiculous'. She fetched a garden bag and helped him bag up the weeds. She felt torn between going to be with her son and his family and staying to be near Marco. Life was growing ever more complicated.

'I know the experts say don't make any drastic decisions after a bereavement but I think moving to Bristol would be the best thing for you. In fact, it's a doctor's order.' His eyes darkened he wrapped his fingers round the folded paper in his trouser pocket. There was always a point in life when a difficult choice had to be made to protect somebody. Whatever the note was about was immaterial now.

A letter from Iran, a post card to his mother from America, this obscure note to David from his sister might or might not be connected but one thing his training had proved time and time again was that the mind was capable of making links where none existed and producing false beliefs especially when it was in distress and overwrought. Grief, especially in his mother's case had become multi-faceted. He wasn't going to add to it.

'Let's go out for a drive. I'll have a wash first.' He showed her his grimy hands.

In the upstairs bathroom, he tore those few incriminating words into shreds and rooting for the matches his mother kept for her candles, set fire to the bits of paper in the basin.

CHAPTER 35

*K*endra waited until her son texted to say he was boarding his flight to Boston before she phoned Marco. Adam had helped her sort through most of the paper work needed for probate which David had methodically filed in date order. Surprised that his step-father had left him and his sister a small legacy, not enough to be life changing, but in his case to furnish a new house and have some left over, he wondered what would happen to Rani's share. He appraised the solicitor of the situation who told them that a notice would go into the London Gazette advising his sister to get in touch.

'You'd be surprised who comes out of the woodwork when money's involved,' he said, the weight of dealing with obstreperous and greedy people trying to claim familial links with the deceased, bearing down on his hunched shoulders. 'There's a fixed time of three months so let's see what happens.'

It wasn't hard to believe that David had amassed so much money over the years when his frugality at home was legendary.

'You'll be able to buy that dream cottage by the sea,' were her son's last words before he flew off.

Looking out into the empty street at the water gushing towards the overflowing drains, she dwelled on that idea, knowing that she would miss Marco who had become an important part of her life. Pembrokeshire was out of the question although she did think about visiting the bed and breakfast where David had spent his last few days.

The thought of having to empty the house, move and start a new life was debilitating. David's workshops were overflowing with stuff she had no idea how to sort out. Eventually she plucked up courage to call Marco.

'Hello. How are you? I've been thinking about you.'

'I'm ok. Adam's gone back so I feel at a loss.'

'Come round and have a natter with a crazy old man. We can go walking or I might brave the city centre if you want to do some window shopping.'

Kendra groaned. 'I couldn't think of anything worse. Would you come round here? I need a bit of help with something.'

Not only did the micro print on the instruction manual for the new mower make no sense, it strained Kendra's eyes trying to read it. She didn't want to rely on Marco but so far her path to technical independence had been fraught with disappointment.

She'd managed to put a new fuse in the plug of the kettle which had given her some satisfaction until a smell of burning panicked her into yanking it out of the socket. Then she realised some chicken was burning under the grill. Putting four new batteries in the remote control took ages as she tried every combination possible before a green spot of hope flickered in the corner of the TV. Dealing with the simplest of tasks had become overwhelming.

The afternoon sun burned down on her neck as she pushed the mower into a corner and went in search of some sparkling water. She'd stopped drinking alcohol after a crying fit in the pub. Sheila had bundled her into her new car, a guilt gift from Tony, where Kendra had thrown up three Bacardi and cokes. Sheila had called her a silly arse and had sprayed the car with air freshener.

She placed the glass on the patio table and kicking off her shoes, flicked down her sunglasses and turned her face to soak in fading warmth. The jangling of the doorbell brought her back to her feet. Marco stood on the step, grinning, his arms wrapped around a bucketful of colourful dahlias.

'They're gorgeous. Don't tell me they're from your garden.'

'Yes. They're my favourite flowers. See this red one. Bishop of Llandaff. They've done really well this year.'

Kendra showed him into the garden while she hunted for vases.

'Is there another one of these going?' he asked, pointing to her drink.

'Sure. Maybe you can make sense of that mower. The manual's like reading Greenlandic.'

He laughed, his blue eyes lighting up as he watched her move gracefully into the kitchen, her lemon skirt swishing around her tanned calves with their well-defined muscles.

'You don't have to do the mowing, just work out what all the paraphernalia is. David was so meticulous about keeping the lawns neat even if it took him from dawn to dusk to cut them with an ancient push mower. I feel I'm letting him down.'

The air was warm and still. Soon it would be autumn and the dark nights would be upon them.

'So, how's the new business idea going?'

'It's hard to concentrate yet if I don't fill my days with something I shall go crazy. The website's done thanks to Jo so people can pay on line for sessions on the digital diary. Adam was really helpful in getting the ideas bedded down. Whatever did we do without this technology?'

Marco grinned. 'We managed.'

'I had to change the name to Emotions in Crisis. I don't like it but it's what the marketing people call a sexy title. I feel a fraud though. I mean I'm still all over the place but maybe helping others will help me in the long run.'

'Any takers yet?'

'Yes I'm surprised. The site has had a lot of hits in the first few days and someone got in touch who wants a phone discussion first. Something to do with a son at university who is about to drop out. He's training to be a doctor but keeps flipping out. His mother's words not mine. That's all I can say. Confidentiality and all that. I can't help him unless he contacts me himself but hopefully I can navigate his parents through their feelings and find ways to cope.'

Marco nodded as she talked.

'The difficulty in these cases is that the families want the therapist to coach or fix the person they think is mad, bad or sad but they've got to present in person. Many people don't want to be helped or don't see there's a problem.'

'I think this is a great idea. You'll build a practice in no time. Didn't Jung coin the phrase 'The Wounded Healer?' If you think about it, many people who go into the healing services have experienced wounds of their own.'

'I've come across that. It does make them empathetic, especially if they are helping people with unresolved childhood issues. It's a bit like survivors of disease or tragedy who go on to set up support groups.'

'It's a good time to be setting up your business and being of service to others. You have a lot to offer.'

'This idea of the counselling consultancy has been brewing at some level for a while. I love teaching but I'm up to here with the bureaucracy and the politics within the education system.' She slapped her hand against her temple. 'When I first trained my attention was focused on the students. Not anymore.'

'Maybe to reach this point you had to go through these dreadful personal experiences.'

Kendra clapped her hands to her mouth, her pupils dilating to the size of bluey-black marbles.

'What's wrong?'

'It's Rani's birthday.' She's been gone over a year now. A whole year since I've heard from her. Sometimes I smell her perfume, it was musky and something she got from a Dubai importer who sells it in Grand Central.' Kendra couldn't believe she'd forgotten the date. 'It's like she's died but there's no body. I know it's morbid but what else am I to think?'

'Come here.'

Kendra felt herself being gently pulled into his arms and for several minutes they stood locked together. He kissed her forehead, smoothing back her hair as he wiped a tear from the corner of her eye. She felt small against his broad chest, rising and falling steadily beneath his shirt. The buzzing inside her head began to lessen as Marco pressed his cheek against hers and whispered, 'I'm here for you.'

Tears turned her black mascara into clumps which she tried to wipe clean with a serviette.

'Now I look like a panda,' she sniffed as she scrubbed around her eyes.

Marco placed his hands, roughened from years of gardening, at either side of her face. 'And pandas are beautiful creatures.'

A sudden trill from the house phone cut through the charged atmosphere. Kendra slipped away to answer it but the line went dead.

'Are you getting nuisance calls as well?' Marco was studying the controls on the mower as Kendra dialled 1471. It was a London number. She tried to call it back but it rang out, giving her a strange feeling that she was calling a phone box. *Do they exist anymore?*

'Are you ok? You've gone very pale.' Marco was removing the grass box for emptying.

She nodded, picking at the edge of her frayed shirt. Something about the dead call bothered her.

'I'm upset that I can't celebrate her birthday. We always did fun stuff together in the day before she spent three hours in the bathroom getting ready to go out with her friends.'

'But we can celebrate! We can make a cake and a card. Take your power back as they say. You've got the paper and paints. You can write how much you love her and hope she will be home soon. Maybe she'll pick that up via the collective unconscious.'

'Are you teasing me?'

Marco turned on the mixer tap with his elbow and scrubbed clean his hands, while Kendra rooted through the pantry for ingredients. 'Not at all,' he assured her.

She pulled out a small pair of steps and reached up to one of the top shelves in search of some candles. Together they shared the baking, laughing like playmates in the school yard as Marco put his floury hands on her cheeks. They cut out and coloured in butterfly shapes to stick on some yellow card, crafting a verse and decorating the cake in chocolate and sugar flowers. Marco left Kendra to write her message to her daughter.

'I've enjoyed doing that. Therapeutic. Maybe I could incorporate craft into my session as a way to express feelings.'

She held out the two cards for his inspection before placing them ceremoniously on the mantelpiece.

'I feel a bit guilty,' she confessed after they'd tasted the cake.

'For feeling happy?'

'Hmm. It feels disrespectful.'

'I know how that feels. The Victorians had it right. Wear the colours of mourning, black to grey to colour then get on with your life. We have to do the same. Guilt won't bring David back. Nor Lizzie. They would want us to get on with our lives and if that means eating cake, then let us eat cake!'

Marco spun her round and pressed his mouth down onto hers, wrapping a skein of her silk- like hair around his fingers, shocking them both with the intensity of supressed passion. Kendra tuned the radio to Heart FM and wrapping her arms around Marco's neck, led him into a slow dance, pausing to kiss and celebrate life. Kendra took his hand, winding her fingers through his.

'I might be moving away and I… I'm going to miss you if I go.'

'Let's not think of the future,' he said softly into her hair. 'It has a way of taking care of itself.'

CHAPTER 36

As she watched hordes of people run for the commuter service into town, Kendra was relieved to be out of the rat-race. She wondered how her students were getting on with Miss McKyntre, a no nonsense, do-it-by-the book teacher who played hockey at the weekends and drank green tea in the staff room from her own flask.

The comings and goings of parents taking children to school, reminded her of the times she walked Rani to St. Luke's. They'd played games on the way, pausing to look at the pink cottage with the white shutters while they made up a new story about its occupants. In her mind's eye, Kendra watched her daughter's long plaits bounce along with her schoolbag as she ran happily into the school playground to meet her friends.

Reminiscing was not helping her to prepare for her new on-line client, a harassed mother frightened of her young son. The tap in the shower had become loose and she was about to call for David to fix it when the truth hit her once again. She perched on the edge of the bath, feeling like her head was being held underwater. The sounds from the street were muffled as she nursed her bag of sadness. It was times like these when the clocks seemed reluctant to move on. Every time Kendra wanted to push through the fog it felt like an act of betrayal.

In his painting room, Marco was mixing a palette for a stormy seascape when his mobile rang. Seeing it was a London number he was about to reject the call but the number seemed familiar.

'Hello?' He dropped his brush into some water and hoped the freshly squeezed acrylic paint wouldn't dry up. 'Can you speak up it's a bad line. Oh Scott! Thanks for coming back to me. How's life in the world of spies and counter terrorism?'

Marco sat down as he listened carefully to what he was being told.

'So this Dari person. Who is he? Are you allowed to say? And you said the girl's name's Royah? Her father's a friend of the Najafi family in Shiraz?'

Marco scratched his chin as he noted the information.

'OK. I understand. No, I won't say anything. I know you're putting your neck out and it could be dangerous.' Marco picked his words very carefully. 'We'll have to hold on to that then. Scott, I appreciate your time. I know Brandon was reluctant to ask you. No, it's not much but it brings some hope. Say hello to Mel for me. The baby must be growing up.'

Marco laughed and swished his brush round in the water.

'My goodness. She's ten already! Ok Scott. If you hear anything else…Her mother is on the verge of a breakdown with all this.'

Kendra felt anxious as she waited for the Skype call. She wondered what Marco was doing.

'Hello Anna. Thanks for calling today. I'll run through the agreement first then you can tell me your story.'

Lighting up a cigarette, a young mother in a grubby T-shirt, spilled out her fear in between yelling at a crying toddler. The more upset she got, the more she broke into her Black Country dialect.

'Why do you think he kicks and punches you, Anna?'

'Cos he's a frigging nutter like his dad. The doctor says he's got ADHD but I don't want him on tablets. The two young'uns are frit to death of him.'

'Does he hit them as well?'

Anna stifled a sob, running her hands through her lank hair.

'Yes,' she said in a small voice. 'He bosts up their stuff and shouts. I cor purrup with it no more.' Anna put her hands over her face and sobbed.

Kendra waited for her to become calmer.

'Who do you think is running this relationship? You or Cain?'

Anna sat back in her chair and folded her arms.

'Yo bein funny?' She glowered at Kendra.

'Not at all. I'm trying to get you to think who's in charge. Who has the power?'

Anna thought about it as she lit another cigarette.

'He has I suppose. His dad buggered off a year ago and Cain says he's the man of the house now.'

'He's taken on a big responsibility in his own mind. Maybe he's modelling his behaviour on his father, thinking that's what he must do. However, it's no excuse. He's eleven years old and a child. Do you do things together? I mean just the two of you?'

'Like what? He's always out with his mates. The only time he talks to me is when he wants summat like money or food. I aye got no cash to spare and that's when he goes ape.'

'He needs some attention. Positive attention. Not shouting at him. Let's see what we can work out.'

After an hour, Kendra closed the conversation, leaving Anna with a task she needed to complete before the next session; that of spending an hour of quality time with her son. They'd agreed on making a kite together and going to the local park to fly it. Anna had suggested making up a picnic with Cain.

'And get him involved in making the cakes,' Kendra added, thinking back to the fun she'd had with Marco. 'He needs your love Anna. More than anything.'

Kendra wrote up her notes but felt her counselling had been inadequate. Patronising maybe but at least the poor mother had crushed out her cigarette and given her son a hug as he came in the room. His face had split into a beaming smile when she told him about the plan. That was some success.

A tempting pop up appeared in the corner of her computer screen. *The most remarkable psychic in the world.* Kendra clamped tight her jaw and quickly powered down. A message beeped on her phone.

Ma. All sorted for the move. Arrive LHR Sat.

Kendra stabbed out a quick reply.

Wonderful. Keep me posted.

As she closed her file, she felt David massaging her neck. She could smell the wood glue he used for his model making. For a moment Kendra believed it really was him.

She held her breath as the sensation grew stronger. She felt her hair being parted at the nape of her neck and a kiss like a spray of perfume settled on her skin.

When Marco called round to cut the hedge, she told him what had happened. Tinks jumped up beside her and licked her hand. He tried to get on her lap before Marco shooed him to the ground.

'It's all those chews you've been giving him. He thinks you're a push over. Down boy.'

'Am I that gullible Marco? Is that how you see me? I know I've been a total fool over this but I really sense him near me.'

Marco squeezed her hand. 'No fool.'

'You told me you experienced something similar when your

wife died. You could smell her perfume?'

Marco picked up a trowel and pushed it into the earth to dislodge deeply rooted weeds. Lizzie's face sprung into his mind but it was a like an out of focus photograph.

'It was just my imagination, as the song goes. Sadly.'

"Do you think we go on somewhere else? The existence of consciousness outside of the brain? I'm in two minds about it.'

'Very witty.' Marco carried on turning over the soil. 'I think most people feel there's something after death at some point. The brain is so fearful of dying that it builds a bridge between reality and hope.'

Kendra studied his profile as he mopped his brow with his sleeve.

'Do you fear your own death?'

He shook his head. 'I fear loneliness more than that,' he said simply. 'Jung said, and I've been reading a lot of his stuff since I met you, *"shrinking away from death is unhealthy and robs you of the life you have left."* We have to get on and make the most of things. We owe it to those who've gone. My wife told me to find somebody to love.'

Kendra felt herself blushing. She blew on a dandelion clock to hide her feelings. 'Pass me that slug repellent please. I just hope snails don't have existential crises.'

CHAPTER 37

*K*endra's online counselling service was growing faster than she could manage. By the time she'd finished clearing her inbox for the morning, replying to cries for help in dealing with hostile daughters-in-law, moody teenagers and grown up sons who had moved to Australia to find themselves, on top of deleting a growing tirade of trolls spouting their venom, it was nearly lunchtime. Kendra's diary was filled with appointments for the next few weeks which provided a healthy distraction.

She'd arranged to meet Sheila at the station for a trip to the rag market. It had been years since she'd had the luxury of browsing the stalls and feeling the lovely fabrics. Sheila wanted to buy a bundle for her Saturday sewing class for teens.

'We've started with long, loose tops in plain material so they can stylise them with fashion belts and chunky necklaces.'

'Sounds complicated to me,' said Kendra, tutting at a young mother jostling her ankles with a pushchair that looked more like a mini space ship as they boarded the train.

'I can teach you. It's such a simple pattern.'

'David was the one who was good with his hands but I'll pay you to make me a few tops for the autumn.' Kendra pored over the pattern. 'These look really comfy now that the middle age spread is back.'

The once fresh weather had turned humid again, as they wandered through the crowds, trying to peek from behind some well-padded women, at the huge bails of materials and fancy trimmings. Sheila got stuck into some serious haggling with the Indian stall holders before being offered "a very good price" for some turquoise and lemon polyester mix.

Kendra shuffled to another stall where a woman with a strong Irish accent was selling vintage clothes. Watching her friend's performance had reminded her of stressful times in the bazaars in Shiraz. It was where she and Hassan had experienced their worst arguments. She wanted to pay the price. He shouted that she was insulting a culture of thousands of years by not bartering.

'Cheap as chips,' beamed Sheila stuffing the brown packets into her fabric bag. 'I need to get some cottons and bits then we'll grab a drink somewhere by St. Martins. Are you ok? You look hot and bothered.'

'It's so humid in here. I'll wait for you by the entrance.'

'Ok. Why don't you go up to Coconut and sit on the terrace? I won't be long.'

Kendra's legs were aching by the time she walked round looking for the place Sheila had mentioned. She found a seat and ordered tea and a glass of lemon water. The waitress screwed up her face and disappeared without a word. *Is this rudeness everywhere or just here?*

She watched people sauntering in and out of the two halves of the Bull ring shopping centre, amused by the contrast of women's clothing; miniskirts over leggings and others in full Islamic dress. In Iran, few women covered their faces. Instead they went to all lengths to turn their long coats and scarves into fashion statements, often risking a severe reprimand from the dress police. Kendra wondered if that still happened, although judging by the recent movement of men wearing the hijab and posting selfies to support their wives, she doubted it.

Stirring milk into her tea, she remembered the night her sister-in-law was pulled over because she was showing some of her long luscious bleached hair beneath her scarf. Susanna didn't care. She'd drive with her windows down, the latest pirated copy of some Eighties boy band blasting out.

Kendra became aware she was being observed by two girls in jeans and headscarves. One was checking her phone in its pink case.

'Mrs. Blackmore?'

'Yes,' Kendra replied, frowning as she studied their faces. She thought they must be former students from the academy.

'I'm Maryam Sadaneh, this is my sister Shuku. We were at Birmingham Uni with Rani. She used to come to the Persian society meetings.'

Kendra's hand slipped from her cup, yelping as the hot liquid gushed onto her lap, scalding the insides of her thighs. Dabbing frantically with a wafer thin serviette, she felt a thousand ants run up her arms.

'Can we help?'

'I'm fine.'

'We'd better go. Sorry to bother you.'

Kendra got to her feet, banging her knee against the edge of the table.

'No, please, wait. I want to talk to you.' The moment passed as they disappeared into the throng of shoppers. The surly girl brought her the bill and twiddled her lip ring as Kendra counted out the money into the saucer. Kendra ran into the crowds, her eyes scanning the scene for two turquoise scarves. Her phone trembled in her pocket.

'Where are you? What's happened?'

'Sheila? Sorry. Give me twenty minutes. There's something I have to do. Meet me in Grand Central.'

Dashing in and out of fashion boutiques before realising her efforts to track down the only real link she'd had with her daughter in a year were as futile as clutching at clouds, she took another call from Sheila and reassured her she was on her way. A wave of nausea caught the back of her throat and noticing a sign for the Ladies, she dived in. Behind the locked door, her ears picked up the low murmurings of two women by the washbasins.

'Maybe she doesn't know about Rani,' said one. 'She seemed really shocked to see us.'

Unable to leave at that moment, Kendra strained her ears, desperately wanting to call out.

'We can't get involved,' said her sister, waving her hands under the blast from the dryer. 'We don't know anything, remember? I told you it was a bad idea to approach her.'

'But we should say something. Do you know where she lives?'

'No.' Maryam scowled and rearranged her scarf. 'I would take this off if it wasn't such a cool fashion accessory. Come on. We've got some serious shopping to do.'

Sheila's impatience got the better of her as she texted Kendra to say she was on her way home and could she please explain what the bloody hell was going on. Marco was at the station to meet Kendra after receiving her tearful phone call. Putting his arm around her shoulders as he led her to the car, he asked if she wanted to go straight home. When they got inside, Kendra leaned on the breakfast bar, rubbing her temple in circular movements to ease the tension. The muscles in her shoulders had knotted into tight bands, causing pains to shoot up her neck and through her head. She yelped as Marco kneaded the muscle between his fingers.

'You need a proper massage,' he said, pouring sparkling water into a glass. 'What's happened today to get you into this state?'

In recounting the story, Kendra remembered she need to call Sheila.

'Mmm.' Marco thought back to the conversation he'd had with Scott and was on the verge of saying something.

'Let her calm down. You sit in the garden and I'll open this wine. This weather isn't going to last much longer. The autumn forecast is storms and turbulence.'

'They know something. I'm sure of it. They looked... well... guilty. If I'd not spilled the tea over me I would have found out.' She watched a ladybird crawl across the patio table, wishing she had such a simple, orderly life.

'All in good time. It's easy to force bits together when they don't really fit.'

'Just when I think I've got my head sorted, something comes along and bang... knocks me off balance again. I've never met those two women before and Ariana never mentioned their names. I would have remembered. I'm convinced they know something about Rani. I suppose I could track them down on social media.'

'And torture yourself some more?' Marco turned on the outside tap and filled a bowl with water for Tinks who lay in the shade, his pink tongue hanging out. 'Focus on something positive. Have you heard from Adam? How did the move go?'

'Ok. He's not started the new job yet. I can't get over the idea of him being a consultant psychiatrist. We'll be sorted if we get dementia,' she said wryly.

'And the baby?'

'Due in a few weeks, although Alison's sure it's going to be early. They're excited about becoming parents. Little do they know what lies ahead,' she muttered, refilling her glass.

'I think we all make a mistake of owning our children and forgetting that our real role is to raise them, give them values we hope they will take forward and then we have to let go. Nobody tells us the pain of that, which reminds me, I'm going to Canada for Christmas. My daughter's expecting another baby which is due on Christmas Eve.'

Kendra took his hand and smiled into his eyes. 'Now there's a coincidence. Congratulations.'

'You could come with me. We can book a cabin in the woods or something. Log fires, friendly moose poking their heads through the door. Silly me. You will want to be with your own family and there's me thinking life got less complicated as we get older.'

Kendra shook her head, trying to decide if this was the time she should let him down gently.

'Marco?'

'Tinks, get down off that wall. Look, he's after that cat. Funny how he sticks his nose up at Vesta when she's around but anything else cat-like and he's twitching.'

He leapt off his chair and grabbed the terrier whose body was stiff with anticipation. A low growl rumbled in the dog's throat as Marco bundled him into the kitchen and shut the door.

'I hope you don't mind. That's his regular punishment. There's somebody coming up the path.'

'Sheila? I'm sorry about earlier.' Kendra stepped back to let her friend in. 'We're having a drink on the patio.'

'I can see that.' Sheila's eyes burned into them both. 'Next time you want to ditch your friends to nip into bed with your Latin lover, have the decency to let me know. I bought you some material. If you don't want your tunics, I'll use it for cushion covers. Bye.'

'Sheila! Wait. It's nothing like that.'

Kendra stood rooted to the spot as if surveying the devastation from a mild hurricane.

'What was all that about? I know she's got a temper but that was uncalled for.'

Marco snipped away at David's favourite lilac tree with a pair of rusty secateurs he'd found in the greenhouse.

'This should restore it to health. That pond water looks a bit murky. Shall I clean it out for you? I've got some really good stuff at home.'

'Marco, I -' Kendra pushed her sunglasses onto the top of her head and perched next to him on a bit of rock. He carried on with his task.

'You don't have to say anything. I know you're not ready for a relationship. Neither am I. I would like us to be friends. Companions. I'm too old to be your Latin lover.' Marco threw back his head and laughed. 'Although I'm very flattered.'

CHAPTER 38

'That blog piece you wrote about teenage brains being still under construction and parents expecting too much from them was brilliant. I've put it on my Facebook. It helped me be a bit more lenient with Jo and it's paying off.'

'So you're talking to me again?'

'Don't be daft. We're friends. I suppose I'm a bit jealous of Marco replacing me.'

Sheila slipped her arm through Kendra's as they walked into the woods on Cannock Chase, Shap bounding ahead, pausing to bark at anything moving through the undergrowth. The torrential rain had been unprecedented but now the sun was poking its grinning face through the trees.

'You don't begrudge me having a male companion I hope. Marco can't replace David but he does communicate with me… listens and talks and… understands how I feel. He doesn't judge me.'

'I know,' Sheila squeezed her arm as they navigated their way around thick, squelchy tracks of mud churned up by mountain bikes and horses, which led deeper into the trees. 'I'll be glad when Tony's back. Christmas time he said. It's not the same having Skype conversations. I've started to really miss him.'

'And all those annoying habits you moan about?'

'Especially those. David's death has made me look at myself more closely. Nagging Tony into doing repair jobs when he's clearly knackered from work, the sulking when he falls asleep straight after sex. I refuse to talk to him for at least two days. I know I'm not reasonable either and it takes time apart from someone to get some insight into that and to swallow a dollop of pride to admit it.'

'"*Ego is the only requirement to destroy any relationship.*" I saw that on one of those wall hangings they sell in gift shops. I could say the same about myself. I thought I was a great mother to Rani, nurturing, comforting, all the mummy things; but I look back and see I was holding onto her ankles. She needed to leave the nest but was afraid of leaving me. I should have pushed her out. I wanted us to be best friends instead of being the parent. It wasn't healthy and I blame myself for what's happened.'

'No. You can't do that. She was the one who was callous with a total disregard for what cutting off from you might do. She wasn't grown up about it at all.'

'I agree but then who prevented her emotional growth? Me. If she was desperate to break away, then maybe she couldn't handle it any other way. I get that now.' After a short pause, she added, 'I'm coming to terms with it.'

'So no more ISIS crisis? I did think you'd gone too far with that although with the way things are...'

'Adam reminded me about the identity crisis in the early twenties and a pulling away for independence. It's built into our psyche but I must have panicked. There was so much in the news about young women disappearing having been brainwashed online I guess it sunk into my subconscious.'

They followed Shap through the trees, walking briskly to fight off the cold wind. Shielding her eyes from the low lying sun, Sheila said, 'I hope you know where we are. I'm totally lost.'

Kendra pulled out a map and a compass. 'David wouldn't come on the Chase without these and ta da… a whistle for attracting attention.' They walked a bit further until Kendra stopped and knelt on the ground.

'This is the spot. He once planted some daffodil bulbs here and marked them on this map. Look.'

She unscrewed the lid of the urn holding David's ashes and scooped out a handful which she scattered around a fir tree. Sheila grabbed the dog's collar and pulled him back. 'Goodbye David,' was all she could say as she upturned the urn and shook out the rest of its contents. It felt surreal.

Sheila helped her onto her feet and handed her some wet wipes for her hands. 'You ok?'

'It's stupid isn't it? We say rest in peace and all that stuff to a pile of ash. He's gone. There is no David, just a memory of him.'

Slowly they walked back to the car, deep in their own thoughts.

'I'm sorry I've not been more supportive Kendy. I was frightened.'

'That my bad luck might rub off on you? That's not uncommon. Stuff happens. It's for me to deal with but I need my friend on side. You've been there for me. You and your forked tongue.' Kendra waggled two fingers on either side of her head, laughing as Sheila gave a playful slap to her arm.

Kendra adjusted the passenger seat so that there was more room in the foot well for Sheila's long legs. As she lifted the adjustment bar to release the seat, it slid backwards, revealing some damp pages torn from a notebook. Kendra twisted her body so she could pull them out.

'What's that?'

'I don't know yet. This looks like Ariana's handwriting.'

Sitting back in her seat she turned off the engine. Scanning the pages she could only make out part of a name, Dari… but the rest was too badly smudged.

'Is this a boyfriend?'

Kendra shook her head.

'She never mentioned him. But it looks as if they were an item at university. Look here. This bit.'

Sheila read it out. *I hate David. He threatened to spill the beans on D.* The rest was unintelligible. 'Kendy, it's best not read this stuff. It will only shock and upset you more. What the eye doesn't see… Besides what your kids get up to should stay between the pages of their diaries. You wrote that in your blog!'

'I agree but it might give me a clue.'

Sheila rolled her eyes and unwrapped a cough sweet. 'Leave it.'

'But don't you see? Dari is a Persian boy's name. She may have gone off with him. Got married or something and didn't dare tell me. And what's David got to do with it? It's the first lead I've had.'

'Kendra. Stop. Stop. You're getting worked up again and obsessing. I can always tell because your pupils dilate to the size of egg cups. Give me the papers. GIVE!'

Sheila had her hand out, her mouth set in a hard line.

'You've come so far, I won't let you slide back. If you don't hand them over, then I shall go and see Marco.'

Kendra's mouth fell open. She couldn't believe she was being bullied but she let the sheets drop into Sheila's lap before starting the car and driving home in silence.

When she rang Marco to tell him the story she finished by saying, 'I think she meant for me to find those papers at some point.'

'It's all speculation. I'd prefer to go with the most logical answer. They fell out of her notebook and she didn't realise.' Marco tugged at the collar of his shirt. Things were beginning to fall into place.

'That doesn't sound very likely to me.'

'So she's got or had a boyfriend. He has an Iranian name. Just like you.' The confession was burning his tongue but he'd made a promise to say nothing. 'Thing is Kendra, until you have certainty, your brain will be hypervigilant, looking for the tiniest last piece of the jig saw puzzle.'

'You should be the psychologist, not me.'

'I'm on the outside. I can be objective. Anyway, remember what you were telling me about an elastic band on the wrist? Flick it to stop the obsessing? I'm your elastic band. Now, I'm going to Symphony Hall tonight. It's "Sax in the City". It's just a casual, informal show for people going home from work and want a bit of relaxation first. You up for it?'

Kendra thought for a moment before agreeing.

'As long as I don't have to dress up.'

While they were out, Kendra felt on edge and kept turning round to see who was in the crowd. She felt eyes resting on her neck and following her around the Convention Centre where they stood at the bar soaking up the atmosphere. She put it down to self-consciousness as she'd not bothered to change. As the music started up, they made their way over to the front seats to get a good look at the band.

'After my wife died, I used to come to get out of the house. Believe it or not I was a tenor sax player when I was younger but I've not got the puff now. Andy Hamilton and The Blue Notes were my heroes.' Marco pointed into the band at a man in a striped jacket. 'That's Dutch Lewis. Always a treat to hear his solos.'

Marco took her hand and tapped his feet through every number. For Kendra the music, what bits she paid attention to, alternated between upbeat and catchy and melancholic. Jazz wasn't really her thing and at the interval she went out to get some fresh air.

'I won't be a minute.'

Marco followed her out. 'If you don't like the music we can go and eat or take a walk.'

Kendra gulped in some air and drank water from a plastic cup. 'It's not that.'

'Come on, let's have a stroll by the canal and you can tell me what's troubling you.'

He helped her down the steps onto the towpath and put his arm round her shoulders. They walked in silence, pausing to watch people in the nearby bars air kissing as they met friends or pulling out new purchases from designer bags to show them off. Normal Friday night life in the second city. Kendra suddenly wanted to go home. As they turned to take a short cut back to the station, she felt the colour drain from her face.

'Rani? Ariana?' Kendra began to run, leaving Marco to catch her up. 'Rani? Come back.'

A woman, the height of colouring of her daughter, turned to see where the voice was coming from.

'It's not her.' Kendra gripped the railing. 'I was sure…'

Guiding her towards an empty table at Canal 1, Marco ordered two glasses of brandy. Kendra couldn't stop shaking. Never in all his life had he felt such a total shit until that moment.

CHAPTER 39 ⌒—◯

𝓜arco was surprised to see Kendra push open the door of her spare bedroom bearing a tray of tea and toast. He was propped against a pile of pillows, a spy novel in his hand. Kendra sat on the edge of the bed, happy to be able to do some small thing for him. It had been a couple of weeks since her blackout in Brindley place. Marco had stayed with her most nights since then.

'Good morning,' he said, leaning up to kiss her cheek. 'Did you see these pictures of the solar eclipse? Magnificent. I have an astronomer friend who chases eclipses all round the world.'

Marco was scrolling through his tablet to find the images he'd bookmarked.

'Look. I read somewhere that when the moon blocks out the sun, it forces us to look for new opportunities. It can also mean something which has been hidden that comes to light after the eclipse. That's it in simple terms. I think it's a good omen.'

'I hope so. Tinks is doing a funny dance in the kitchen.'

'He needs to go out or there will be puddles. I forgot to take him for his walk last night.'

'Ok, don't get up. I'll take him now.'

As Kendra clipped the lead onto the dog's collar, pointing her finger in warning not to jump up, it felt strange having a man in the house that wasn't her husband. Marco was the perfect companion. Funny, supportive and undemanding. By the time they got back, he was cranking up the coffee machine. Tinks barked and ran round in circles at the sight of his bowl being filled then settled down to crunch.

'Come here,' he whispered in her hair as he pulled her close. 'There's so much I want to say.'

'Let's not spoil things. I'm in a good mood for once. Maybe it's that eclipse you were talking about. Hey, here's something funny. In the Sutton Gazette. *Suttonians stockpile food ready for war.*'

'Not funny but I know what you mean. That's what the preppers do in America. The survivalists. I don't think things are that bad yet.'

'What do you fancy doing today? Let's give Sutton Park a miss. I feel I've lived a life time walking round there. What about going to Wolverhampton or Dudley. For a change.'

They burst out laughing, stopping at the sound of the phone. Kendra scrambled to find her mobile amongst a pile of papers waiting to go into the recycling bin.

'Adam! Is everything ok?'

Her son could hardly speak. A whimpering in the background made Kendra hold her breath.

'Congratulations Grandma. That's Alice Shirin you can hear wanting food. She was six pounds and five ounces which is good considering Ally was so sick.'

Kendra shrieked.

'I'm so, so happy for you love. Alice Shirin Najafi. Shirin means sweet in Persian. I bet she is so, so sweet. How's Alison?'

'She's fine now. It was a bit tricky at the end. Alice was what they call a star gazer, face up presentation. They were going to use forceps but my brave girl did it all by herself.'

'Were you there?'

'Of course. The mystery and magic of birth never ceases to amaze me. I held her first while they were cleaning up.' Kendra heard her son's voice crack. 'It was wonderful Mum.'

Kendra thought back to when he and his sister were born. One easy and straightforward, the other, Rani, more challenging as if she didn't want to leave the comfort of her watery home.

'Ma, can you come down to Bristol today or tomorrow? I'll pick you up at Temple Meads and we'll drive down to Ally's parents in Devon. You've not seen them for ages. I've got a week's paternity leave but I can't take any more so we need your help and Ally is keen to move to our own place but it needs turning into a home. You're good at that. Let me know when you're coming. Must go.'

Marco and Kendra danced around the room, tripping over Tinks as he pushed his way through their legs.

'That's the best news ever.' Marco said, kissing her cheek.

'I think we should celebrate. I've got a small bottle of Verve Cliquot in the pantry. It was to be for Ariana's graduation but… we will have it now. With or without orange juice.'

Marco unwound the wire taking care to ease off the cork as Kendra covered her ears and backed away to the door. She'd found some Babycham glasses in a box and placed two on the table.

'These are so retro,' he commented. 'My mother had some just like them.'

As they sipped and reminisced, the bubbles went up Kendra's nose. She started to giggle. 'Life has changed so much in a year, it's hard to take it all in. I know David's gone but I had a feeling it was coming. If only Rani…'

'I know. Time and patience my love. Now I'm going to leave you to get on and pack. You've got a train to catch.'

'I thought I'd go down tomorrow.'

'No. I think you should go straight away. I have a feeling about these things too.'

'Thank you Marco, for everything.' They held each other for a long time in the hall, promising to keep in touch.

'Come on Tinks. Playtime's over. Give them my best wishes.'

Marco bent down to pick some rubbish that had blown onto the drive. Walking over to the bin, his attention was drawn to a black car, pulling up a few yards down the road. It looked like a taxi but on a closer look, Marco noted it was a Mercedes with partially blacked out windows. A man in a peaked cap got out of the car and went to open the boot. He removed some expensive looking luggage before helping the passenger out of the back seat.

Marco tugged on the dog's lead to pull him away from some interesting smells in the grass. He turned down a narrow alleyway between some houses and looked back towards the car. His stomach churned as he watched the scene unfold.

Through the triangular crook of his elbow, he saw a young woman in a smart black trouser suit and high heels. She spoke briefly with driver before checking for traffic. Her neat black hair swung in a sleek bob, giving her the air of chic Italian elegance.

He slipped further into the alleyway so he could watch her, his heart hammering in anticipation of where she might be going. He felt his antennae tuning in as she pulled her case along the pavement, carrying herself with a quiet confidence. She paused as she reached the entrance to Kendra's driveway. Marco bent down and picked up his dog, whispered something in his ear and giving him a squeeze, they made their way home.

Upstairs, Kendra was throwing things into a case, not worrying about things she might have forgotten. She could shop in Bristol. In the bathroom she sorted out some toiletries, stuffing them into a waterproof bag. An unsettled feeling that something was about to happen dogged her as she went through the upstairs doing her safety checks. She put it down to adrenaline. Little Alice had been delivered safely and that was all that mattered.

Downstairs she went through the house to make sure the doors and windows were locked. Since David's death, she'd become a bit obsessed with checking everything. Windows, check. Back door check. French windows check. Kettle, toaster off. Plugs out of sockets, check. Noticing the charger to her phone snaking under the chair, she pulled it out and stuffed it in her handbag, checking to make sure she had her keys and purse. Satisfied that the house was as secure as it could be, she slipped into her black coat, zipped up her ankle boots and rang for a cab.

'There's one close by. Two minutes?'

Kendra did a final check for missed calls and texts whilst waiting for the cab to pull up. Out of the living room window she saw it on the other side of the road. Fumbling for her keys, she was about to open the door when the bell rang. Turning round to have a final look at the house, she unlocked the mortice and turned the Yale. She couldn't understand why her nerves were jangling so much.

A young woman stood on the stone step in front of the door. Her olive skin glowed with a light tan, her green eyes over-bright. Kendra felt her legs turn to pulp and had to lean against the door jamb to stop herself from falling. Her world began to spin backwards as she absorbed the mirage in front of her. She was stunning. Kendra opened her mouth to say something but the words stuck to her tongue. She wanted to call out for David. The taxi was honking outside. Kendra clutched her chest fearing her heart was about to stop.

'Hello Mum.'

THE FUTURE CAN'T WAIT

THE FUTURE CAN'T WAIT

ACKNOWLEDGEMENTS

I would like to thank Matthew Smith at Urbane Publications for actively encouraging and supported my writing from the beginning. To all the Urbane authors that have tweeted my comments, blogs and flash fiction and sent me messages of support – a big thank you and a hug.

My two half Iranian daughters, Anousheh and Anisa provided the inspiration for this book. Paul, my man in the shed, who made endless cups of tea to keep me going.

Am I Kendra? Not quite, but I share similar experiences to her and learned a lot about motherhood whilst writing this book. We don't always get it right even if we are well intentioned.

I'd like to thank the bookshops and libraries who have hosted signings and talks for my debut novel. Without your support, I wouldn't have got his far. I hope our relationship can continue.

Finally I thank you, dear readers, for buying my books because it is you, who keep people like me, writing.

THE FUTURE CAN'T WAIT

BIOGRAPHY

Angelena has spent over thirty years training, coaching and counselling in the field of interpersonal conflict and communication using Eric Berne's model of Transactional Analysis. As a linguist, she has lived and worked overseas, travelled extensively and spent periods in Iran where she learned Farsi.

She is the author of three business books, published by Management Pocketbooks Ltd and is a freelance journalist.

A former resident and graduate of Birmingham, the setting for her debut novel, The Cruelty of Lambs, she is a passionate defender of a city she believes is misunderstood.

To find out more about Angelena, visit

www. angelenaboden.com

Email: **bodenangelena@gmail.com**

Twitter @angelenaboden,

Facebook: **bodenangelena**

ALSO BY ANGELENA BODEN

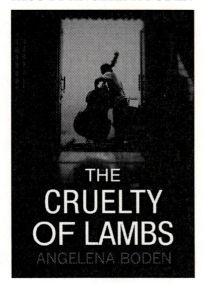

Only his music could reveal the truth ...

The career of acclaimed cellist, Iain Millar, is in tatters. Allegations of sexual harassment while teaching in a girl's school have left him unemployable, and he soon spirals into depression. Iain sees himself as a failure and falls into a dark place where his cello playing provides the only light.

When fresh revelations appear to implicate Iain in the abuse of his ambitious wife, Una Carrington, the world is quick to decide his guilt. Iain's precious antique cello then disappears, and even music is lost to him. Fergus O'Neal, a fellow string player, sets out to recover the missing instrument and Iain's only hope of redemption ...

Paperback: 320 pages
ISBN-13: 978-1911129660
Price: £8.99

Urbane Publications is dedicated to developing new author voices, and publishing fiction and non-fiction that challenges, thrills and fascinates.

From page-turning novels to innovative reference books, our goal is to publish what YOU want to read.

Find out more at
urbanepublications.com